THE GUILTY WIFE

BOOKS BY ALISON JAMES

Detective Rachel Prince series

Lola is Missing

Now She's Gone

Perfect Girls

The School Friend

The Man She Married

Her Sister's Child

ALISON JAMES

THE GUILTY WIFE

bookouture

Published by Bookouture in 2021

An imprint of Storyfire Ltd.
Carmelite House
50 Victoria Embankment
London EC4Y 0DZ

www.bookouture.com

ISBN: 978-1-80019-418-2
eBook ISBN: 978-1-80019-417-5

For everyone working on the NHS frontline, with grateful thanks.

PROLOGUE

'Welcome to paradise!'

The newlyweds are each handed a drink by a smiling member of the reception team: a brightly coloured glass of fruit punch, adorned with a flower. 'By choosing to stay with us, you have made the perfect choice for your honeymoon.'

This remark is addressed to another attractive, well-heeled couple who have also just arrived and been greeted with a drink. So they're not the only honeymoon couple staying at the resort. Which isn't surprising, given the place really is as close to paradise as you're likely to find. Swaying coconut palms, azure sea, shimmering white sand. Discreet villas with their own private gardens and pools. Perfect for an intimate, romantic holiday alone with your loved one. Perfect in every way, in fact, offering everything you could want.

Unless you wished your spouse was dead.

PART ONE

CHAPTER ONE

PIPPA

'Are these the flowers?'

Pippa Bryant frowns down at the bouquet, laid out reverentially on their bed of white tissue paper. She was expecting blooms in shades of cream and blush. These are garish yellows and golds. 'These aren't my flowers.' She turns to her cousin Lauren, who is acting as her maid of honour, colour rising in her cheeks. 'Christ's sake, Loz, I didn't order these! What are they playing at? They must have sent the wrong order.'

Lauren picks up the bouquet and examines it, as though the wrongness of the flowers is somehow in question. Pippa snatches them from her and tosses them back into the box. She feels panic rising through her body, surging from the soles of her feet to the top of her head, accompanied by an insistent ringing in her ears. The flowers are only a symptom of the problem. Of the feeling that something just isn't right between her and Alastair, and hasn't been for a while.

Sinking down onto the bed in the middle of the luxurious hotel suite, she fixes her gaze on her ivory lace wedding dress, spread out next to her. It's calf-length, rather than a long gown, but undeniably bridal, nonetheless. A pair of eye-wateringly expensive satin Jimmy Choos stand ready, next to the dressing table. Her chestnut hair has been swept up in an elegant chignon rather than her usual loose waves, and next to the dress is a diamante headband to top off the whole ensemble.

'I'm sure we can sort it out,' says Lauren, forcing a bright smile. She's a stolid, dependable sort, her blonde bob held in place with a diamond clip, and her curves already squeezed into her blush-pink bridesmaid's dress. 'I'll get on to the florist right away; get them to bike the right flowers over to us. Or something very similar if they've mislaid the originals.'

She goes to pick up her phone, but Pippa reaches out and grabs her wrist.

'It's not the flowers. Forget the bloody flowers.'

'Look, why don't you have a glass of this Prosecco?' Lauren pours some from the complimentary bottle provided by the hotel. 'You're just having an attack of nerves.'

Pippa shakes her head slowly. 'It's not nerves.'

'What then?'

'I don't want to do it. I don't want to get married.'

For weeks now she has been feeling a tension inside; not pre-wedding nerves but a sort of dread. The sensation has been one of watching her life from the outside; watching someone else prepare for her wedding. And as soon as the words are out of her mouth, that sets the seal on it. She knows what she needs to do.

Pippa starts rummaging through her open suitcase, searching for her normal clothes. She pulls out jeans and a sweatshirt and tugs them over her Myla bridal lingerie. 'I have to go and find Alastair.'

'D'you want me to come with you?' Lauren looks down doubtfully at her own long gown and high heels. 'I mean, we've come this far. Are you sure you want to—'

'I've got to. It's hard to explain, I've just got this feeling… you stay and hold the fort here.' Pippa laces her trainers. 'And if anyone asks, just tell them there's a slight delay because of the wrong flowers being delivered. Or whatever. Just stall them, okay?'

Out in the street, patches of pale blue sky are emerging from behind clouds after a squally April shower. Dodging the puddles, Pippa jumps into the middle of the road and hails a cab by almost falling onto its bonnet.

'Islington Register Office,' she tells the driver, before hiding behind her sunglasses. They are due to marry at two thirty, and it's already ten past two. Alastair, always punctual, will almost certainly be there already, probably most of the guests too.

Pippa spots him immediately, standing on the register office steps, wearing a well-cut navy suit and a dark pink silk tie. His skin is still tanned from their recent skiing trip, light brown hair swept back off his forehead. He's talking to a couple that Pippa vaguely recognises. One of his colleagues… Michael? and his girlfriend, Anna. No, Amy. She has met them a couple of times at the annual summer cricket match and barbecue held by Alastair's employers.

Michael – if that is his name – moves off, but Amy remains deep in conversation with Alastair. She's tiny, and he has to bend down to say something to her, making her laugh. As he does so, his lips almost touch her curtain of pale blonde hair.

Pippa is distracted from her mission for a second. Her fiancé is as handsome as ever. Her heart lurches in her chest as he looks up at her.

Her jeans and sweatshirt throw Alastair so completely that to begin with he doesn't recognise the woman he is there to marry. He is, after all, expecting a vision in cream lace. When he realises that this casually dressed woman with incongruous coiffed hair is his fiancée, he does a double take: startled at first, then concerned.

'Pips? What's up? Is there a problem?'

She puts a hand on his elbow and guides him away from the central steps – and the curious gaze of Amy and the other guests who have arrived early.

'Look, Al… look…'

She lowers her voice, because everyone is staring in their direction.

How on earth to explain it to him, when she doesn't really understand it herself? She could say that while she loves him, she's not *in* love with him, but that's such a cliché. She could suggest that without pressure from well-meaning friends, or their joint financial and domestic set-up, she suspects they would have parted ways before now. Confess that some tiny inner voice is telling her that he's not the man for her, but that she has no idea where this feeling comes from.

Anthony, Alastair's older brother and best man, starts to walk over to them, but Alastair waves him away impatiently, then turns back and glowers at Pippa. 'What the hell is this, Pips?'

'I don't think we should go through with it. This doesn't feel right. I don't think we're ready.'

'Not ready?' He gives a little laugh that comes out as a sneer. 'For God's sake, what sort of crap are you talking? We're not kids: we've been together six years.'

'I know, but—'

'Bloody hell, Pippa, this is so embarrassing.' He glances in the direction of the curious faces. 'I can't believe you'd do this now. In front of everyone we know.'

No mention that he loves me, or can't bear to lose me.

'I'm sorry,' she mutters.

'So, does this mean we're off? All of it?' He tugs his fingers up through his hair in an angry gesture, making it stand on end. 'Or are we just talking the wedding?'

'I don't know.' Tears suddenly prick the corner of Pippa's eyes, and she brushes them away impatiently with the back of her hand. Now is not the time to cry. Later perhaps, but not now.

Alastair is sweating. He reaches for his silk pocket square and dabs his forehead. Behind him the gaggle of guests are now whispering to one another. 'Fuck's sake, Pippa. What about the bloody honeymoon?'

So he's already moved on to the practicalities. Not heartbroken, then.

'Do you want it?'

He shakes his head angrily. 'No, I do not. Anyway, your parents paid for most of it. You can bloody well have it. Probably best if we're on different continents for a while, anyway.'

'Okay.' Pippa takes a step backwards, with Alastair still glowering at her. 'Look, please tell everyone I'm really sorry. But let them enjoy the reception. Drink champagne. Dance. Eat the cake. The cake is really good.'

She turns and runs back down the steps, rounding the corner to Laycock Street, where she asked the cab driver to wait for her. As it pulls away, she covers her eyes with her hands, so that she won't have to witness the chaotic scene she had just caused. The shock is making her shiver, but she knows it had to happen. It was the right thing.

Lauren is, as instructed, waiting in the hotel room. She has kicked off her shoes and is eating M&Ms from the minibar while she watches a re-run of *Come Dine With Me*.

'Do you have your car here?' Pippa demands, opening her suitcase and throwing her make-up bag and toiletries into it. She tugs the pins from her chignon and it falls in stiff, lacquered curls onto her neck.

'Yes. I left it in the hotel car park, down in the basement.'

'Great. I need you to drive me to Gatwick.'

Lauren sits up and forces her feet back into her silver shoes. 'Pip, you're not…?'

'Going on the honeymoon? You bet I am. It cost £6,000: I'm not going to let it go to waste.'

Lauren's eyes widen. 'Won't your fiancé have something to say about that?'

'He's my ex-fiancé now. And he said to take it. That's about all he did say, to be honest. He didn't exactly try hard to persuade me to go through with it.'

Pippa's voice breaks, and she reaches up and brushes tears from her eyes.

Concerned, Lauren places a hand on her cousin's arm. 'Christ. I thought everything between you two was fine, I mean I assumed…'

Pippa zips her case, and manages a strained smile. 'Let's just say things aren't always what they seem.'

Lauren raises an eyebrow, but gathers up her things and opens the door for Pippa as she wheels her suitcase into the corridor.

'If you say so. Honeymoon for one it is.'

CHAPTER TWO

DANIEL

Daniel Halligan opens his eyes a crack and squints upwards, using his hand to shade his eyes from the brilliant sun.

The sky above him is a vivid sapphire blue, with not even the suggestion of cloud. He sits up on the lounger and reaches for the beer that the butler has thoughtfully left beside him, in an ice bucket. The villa's private pool stretches away towards the ocean, surrounded by a garden of shady palm trees and purple bougainvillea. Apart from the occasional peal of laughter from the living area of the thatched villa, the only sound is the screech of parakeets, and the gentle sigh of the Indian Ocean.

Daniel is on his honeymoon, yet he is lying here alone. His bride, Tansy, is in the middle of a photoshoot, promoting the Excelsior Resort Mauritius to her three million Instagram followers.

'That's the deal, darl,' she explained in her Aussie drawl, with a faint lilt that betrays her Filipino origins. 'We get a fabulous honeymoon all paid for if I do a little spon-con while I'm there. Just a few piccies for the 'gram. No big deal.'

But it is a big deal. In order to satisfy her online following, Tansy has to post on social media every day. And it isn't just a question of a hastily taken selfie. These images are painstakingly curated, and often have to feature the brands who are sponsoring her. She has brought her 'glam squad' – as she terms them – on honeymoon, for

God's sake. There's Ljubica, Tansy's make-up artist, a sullen Croatian with watchful eyes; and Sebastian, her waspish hair stylist. The two of them are not staying in the newly-weds' villa, but they spend so much time fussing around Tansy that they might as well be.

Sebastian appears on the terrace now and flounces over to a frangipani tree, where he plucks a large creamy bloom.

'For her hair,' he says to no one in particular, pivoting on the balls of his bare feet before sashaying inside again. Daniel follows him, and stands in the open French window watching, as Sebastian tucks the flower into Tansy's glossy dark hair. She stands on tiptoes at an unnatural angle, stomach sucked in. Her skimpy turquoise bikini barely covers her buttocks, and a filmy white beach wrap billows behind her in the draught from an electric fan held by the devoted Ljubica, improvising a wind machine. As the breeze lifts her long hair, Tansy touches the fingers of her left hand to her face and smiles knowingly into the screen of the phone that Sebastian is wielding.

'That okay?' she asks, dropping the pose and marching over to view the results. She frowns. 'My thighs look fat. Let's go again. Oh, wait, hold on…'

She scurries off and comes back with a flask of vivid green liquid and a straw, which she proceeds to place provocatively against the tip of her tongue. 'Got to push the product in the content!'

It's only now, as she looks up from rearranging the white wrap, that she notices her husband.

'You okay, darl?' she demands, in a tone that suggests she does not care to know the answer.

'Not really,' replies Daniel, calmly. 'I didn't really plan on spending my honeymoon on my own.'

'Seriously, I won't be much longer.' Tansy waits while Ljubica touches up her make-up, then bunches her full lips into a duck-like pout, flask of green smoothie held at a provocative angle. 'Why don't you go to the bar? I'll join you when I'm done.'

'I don't want to go on my own. I won't know anyone.' He's aware he sounds petulant, like a child bored with waiting for a parent to finish some adult activity and pay him attention.

'Well, that's just too bad.' Tansy checks herself in a mirror, flicks her hair over her shoulder. 'Anyway, how about that Swedish guy we talked to the other night?' She's looking at the camera phone again, dipping her chin.

'Smize, darling!' coos Sebastian. 'Fabulous!'

'I suppose so,' Daniel sighs. 'If he's there.'

'I met his wife when I was in the spa yesterday,' Tansy goes on, as Sebastian shows her the latest shots. 'Seems like a nice chick. Well, I say chick – she's about your age. And they're on honeymoon too, just like us. Go find them.'

'I'll look out for them. But don't be too long. *Please*.'

'I won't. And if you see them, why not ask them to join us for dinner tonight.' Tansy waggles her fingertips at him without making eye contact, then goes back to choosing her favourite shot.

Having been dismissed, Daniel picks up his shirt from the lounger, slides his feet into his flip-flops and heads down the path towards the hotel's main building.

Ten minutes later, Daniel sits on a barstool under the shade of the thatched pergola, nursing a cold beer.

The bar is empty apart from one older couple, but gradually, as it draws nearer to lunchtime, more people wander in from the pool area. They seem to be mostly wealthy retirees or other honeymoon couples. The Swede the Halligans talked to at dinner walks in wearing swim shorts, drying his naked torso with a towel.

'Good afternoon,' he says to Daniel, a touch formally. 'I think we already met? Arne Lindgren.'

He's tall and lean, with an impressive suntan and wintry grey eyes that crease at the corners when he smiles. His hair, currently wet with pool water, is dark blond, greying at the temples.

'Daniel Halligan. Dan.' He extends a hand. 'Buy you a drink?'

'Thanks. I'll have a vodka soda.'

More because he's bored than because he wants to make a new friend, Daniel falls into making small talk with Arne. Daniel would be happy to stick to the weather and the hotel amenities, but with customary Nordic directness, Arne quizzes him about his job ('I'm in real estate' Daniel replies evasively), and talks at length about his own successful digital start-up providing online platforms and logistics to e-commerce subscription services. It sounds lucrative but incredibly dull.

'Are you here on your honeymoon?' Arne asks.

Daniel nods. 'You?'

'Also on honeymoon. My wife is coming to meet me here in a minute, actually.' Arne's English is fluent and barely accented. 'She is also British.'

'Ah,' says Daniel, redundantly.

'And your wife – she is the dark-haired lady we saw you with? She's Australian, I think?'

Daniel nods. 'She lives in Australia now – we both do – but her mother's from the Philippines. She was born there.'

'Aha. And what does she do? A model, yes?'

Daniel feels the heat rise up his neck, and presses his cold beer bottle to his cheek. 'She's… she's actually a social media influencer.'

Arne's left eyebrow lifts the faintest amount. 'Really? And she makes money from this?'

'Yes. Quite a lot of money, actually. She has a wellness business too, selling a health supplement. It's all about online promotion these days, right? Well, you'd know that, from your own line of work.'

He wonders if Arne would also be surprised to learn that one of his new wife's sponsorship deals was paying for their honeymoon at this very resort. Or 'comping it', to use Tansy's lingo. That, indeed, much of their very glamorous lifestyle is now funded this way. Not that he intends to confide in his fellow honeymooner. He still has some pride intact.

They make some more stilted small talk, until Arne's face lights up and he waves as his wife walks into the bar. 'Ah, good: Nikki's here.'

Daniel wonders which of them was more relieved at the arrival of a social lubricant in the form of a third person. Nikki Lindgren is a slim, attractive woman with dark brown hair cut in a short bob. It makes her look younger than her true age, which Daniel estimates to be around thirty-five. And she is a Londoner: she and Arne met when he was there on business.

'How about you, Dan?' she asks, sipping an ice-cold vodka and tonic through a straw. She wears a colourful printed cotton sarong knotted over her bikini. 'Are you from London?'

'I used to live there. From Surrey, originally.'

'Oh, wow! Me too. Well, until I left for uni, anyway.'

He nods. 'My wife and I are based in Sydney at the moment.'

'She's an Australian citizen,' Arne supplies, keen to get his wife up to speed. 'And guess what: they are on honeymoon too.'

Nikki is naming some of the places in Surrey she knows, but Daniel isn't really listening. Instead, he examines her face as she talks: the wide-spaced, doe-like eyes, the square-ish chin offset by a curving mouth. Not really his type, but an attractive woman nonetheless. And bright too. Probably not the sort of woman who would stoop to making a living plugging dubious health products on social media. He is about to ask her what she does for a job when Arne drains the last of his drink and stands up.

'I really need a shower and a siesta. Coming, darling?'

Nikki nods and slips off her bar stool.

'My wife thought we should all have dinner tonight,' Daniel says. 'You up for that?'

'Great idea.' Nikki smiles at him. 'See you later.'

As Daniel is walking back along the flower-lined paths, a text arrives from his bride.

Taking some shots down on the beach. See you later.

The glam squad has, naturally, accompanied her on this latest quest for content, so the villa is empty. Daniel sinks down on the edge of their huge, four-poster bed in relief. He will shower and change in a minute, but first he needs to talk to someone, to offload some of this churning unease and dysphoria.

He pulls up his younger brother's WhatsApp details and presses the phone icon.

'How's it going, dickhead?' Ben asks, cheerfully. He sounds as though he's in a wind tunnel. Probably still on the morning commute, given the UK is four hours behind.

'Oh, you know.' Daniel makes no effort to hide his glum tone.

'No, I don't know. Tell me.'

'I… er.' Daniel closes his eyes. 'Shit.'

'Shit, what? What's going on, bro?' Ben's tone is concerned now.

'I shouldn't have got married. It's a fucking disaster.'

'Well, now…' Ben is kindly, but there is a 'told you so' edge to his voice. 'I did try and warn you not to do it. She's not right for you, Dan, it's so fucking obvious. You said as much yourself, remember.'

Daniel lowers his head into his hands and rubs his forehead, mumbling into his phone. 'I know, I know. But given everything that happened, what choice did I have?'

CHAPTER THREE

PIPPA

The sign held by the limo driver reads *Mr and Mrs Whelan.*

'Just me,' Pippa says through clenched teeth when he remains fixed to the spot, waiting for the mislaid husband to emerge through the arrivals door at Mauritius International. After following him outside and being installed in the back of the car, she switches on her mobile.

It takes a few minutes to find service on the local network but, once connected, her phone vibrates incessantly in her hand as message after message downloads. Forty-eight WhatsApps, eleven missed calls and eight voicemails. She stares at the flashing screen.

Jesus. People aren't adopting a discreet silence, then. It would be naïve to expect that in the wake of the wedding-that-never-was. In the age of handheld web-based devices, that is no longer how the world works.

Most of the missed calls are from her mother. She has not, however, left a voicemail or texted, for which small mercy Pippa is grateful.

There's a four-word text from her younger brother, Jonathan.

What the actual fuck?

Just like him not to pussyfoot around the situation. The messages from her girlfriends are more sympathetic, keen to know if she's all right. There's only one text from Alastair, the last of the bunch to be sent. Pippa calculates from the time stamp that it must have been in the early hours UK time.

When you get back, there's stuff we need to talk about. A

That was Alastair: practical, sensible, unemotional. She sends him a brief reply saying she has arrived safely and that she will be in touch. Then she switches off her phone.

The Excelsior Resort sprawls around the curve of Turtle Bay, fringed by a pale gold beach and huge palms whispering in the light breeze. The sky is a clear, bright blue.

Pippa approaches the reception desk with a degree of self-consciousness. The staff are expecting a freshly married couple, and here she is alone; crumpled, sweaty and pale, in a place where everyone else is tanned and glamorous.

'I'm here by myself,' she tells the girl at the desk. As if that isn't obvious enough. 'My… fiancé was unable to travel.'

This news is greeted with a sympathetic smile and a glass of fruit punch. She drinks half of it, just to be polite, then a charming man called Kaleem drives her and her luggage to her room in a golf cart. She and Alastair weren't able to stretch to one of the villas with a private pool, but the thatched pavilion is still extremely comfortable, with a sunken marble bath and a terrace overlooking a fragrant tropical garden.

Pippa takes a shower and stretches out on the pristine bed in her complimentary bath robe, having first closed the shutters. She flew overnight and was awake for most of the flight, yet is still unable to sleep. A forest fire of emotions rages through her, ranging from relief to regret to fear. Alastair has been at the centre of her life for the past six years. Yes, the romance between them had faltered – or was it ever there at all? – but they share a home together, they have joint household accounts and bank accounts, they have the same friends. They became fully formed adults together, making a simultaneous transition from carefree, hedonistic twenty-somethings to established, mature thirty-somethings. What will her life look like without Alastair? Where will she live? How will she manage financially? Has she just made a horrible mistake? Hot tears scald the corners of her closed eyes and run down her neck as she gives way to a moment of self-pity.

Eventually the background hum of the air-conditioning unit soothes her to sleep. When she wakes up, it's growing dark. The bedside clock tells her that it's 8 p.m. local time. She switches on her mobile. More messages, plus a voicemail from her mother. She could listen to it, and read all the recriminatory texts and WhatsApp messages, or she could go in search of food. Her stomach rumbles loudly, making the decision for her.

Dinner it is.

When Pippa walks into the restaurant she is struck, just as she was when she arrived, by how groomed and sleek the Excelsior's clientele are.

She has styled her own hair to the best of her ability, and put on lipstick and a linen shift dress, but still she feels under-dressed and a touch scruffy. It's like walking onto the set of a movie. The air is thick with the scent of frangipani and jasmine. Glossy women in evening dresses and sparkling jewellery are up-lit by the banks of candles on the tables, and they all seem to have equally handsome cohorts. Nobody is eating alone.

Apart from one man.

He sits hunched over a corner table, holding a bottle of beer with one hand and scrolling through his phone with the other. Even though he's seated, it's clear he is much taller than average, and heavyset, so that the table looks too small for him. He's middle-aged, with a thick thatch of dark brown hair, streaked grey at the temples. Like Pippa, he's not part of a couple.

She hovers near his table, staring pointedly at the empty chair opposite him. Surely any second now he will glance in her direction and, recognising a fellow solo traveller, invite her to join him. But he does not. He keeps his eyes on his phone and ignores her. The maître d' appears and ushers her to an empty table for two on the far side of the restaurant.

'Here is perfect for you, madam, I think.'

You mean out of the way, so I don't make the place look untidy, thinks Pippa, but she smiles graciously and orders a glass of white wine, burying her face in the menu. She's next to a table of four: two couples. One couple look a little older than her; the other twosome is made up of a good-looking man she estimates to also be in his late thirties and a dark, exotic woman who is clearly much younger than him, probably no more than twenty-five. She waves her hands around, showing off a huge diamond solitaire and a flashy diamond wedding band. His wife then. Honeymooners, almost certainly, like her. Except that now she isn't. She's single.

As she waits for her order of grilled fish and salad to arrive, she amuses herself by watching the contrasting body language of the two couples. The man from the older couple is speaking English with a Scandinavian accent, and his wife has short, dark hair and an intelligent expression. They touch one another constantly but discreetly, and smile into one another's eyes when no one else is paying them attention. Each of them looks to their partner for affirmation when answering a question directed at them both.

The twenty-something bride, by contrast, pouts and blows air kisses in her handsome husband's direction when anyone is looking her way, but the second the attention is elsewhere she ignores him. Her shrill Australian twang quickly starts to aggravate Pippa's post-flight headache. Her husband, on the other hand, says little. He's arrestingly handsome, with the confidence and patrician bearing of the British public school system. He looks bored and – when his bride shrieks loudly and makes wild hand gestures – uncomfortable.

The two couples finish their meal before Pippa does and head off in the direction of the bar, but not before the young Australian girl has made them cluster together while she takes a selfie of the four of them. And then again, because apparently the composition of the first shot isn't perfect enough.

Once she has eaten, Pippa heads the same way, pausing to inhale great gusts of the tropical, flower-scented air as she crosses the garden courtyard.

The honeymoon couples are at a low table, and the burly man from the restaurant is on a bar stool, sipping a beer.

'Hi!' said Pippa brightly, as she approaches to make her order.

'Hi,' he returns. His smile is friendly enough, but again he makes no attempt to strike up a conversation. His eyes, she notices, are an arresting shade of blue.

'Here on holiday?' she persists.

He shakes his head, but offers nothing further.

At a loss, Pippa collects her daiquiri from the bartender and sits down, alone, at a table.

'Tansy, I *love* that dress,' the short-haired woman is saying to the Australian girl. She leans forward and touches the sleeve of a gauzy, expensive-looking pale lilac confection, studded with 3-D silk butterflies in shades of sherbet lemon, pale pink and turquoise. It sets off her glowing olive skin to perfection. 'It's exquisite.'

'It's by Iluka,' preens the girl, naming a top Australian resort wear designer. 'I've got a deal with them.'

'It's gorgeous,' sighs the older woman.

'Babe, you're welcome to it; I can't post pictures in the same outfit, anyway. We're about the same size, I reckon.'

'Are you sure?'

'No worries. I've got masses of Iluka stuff. I'll get housekeeping to clean it tomorrow and drop it round to you.'

The short-haired woman catches Pippa staring, making her flush and look away. But the woman only smiles at her and points at the dress again. 'Isn't it fabulous?'

'It is,' agrees Pippa, smiling shyly back. 'Really pretty.'

The Swede's wife looks as though she is about to invite Pippa into the conversation, but Tansy, the Australian, glances at her sharply, and any idea of extending a social lifeline is abandoned. The brief interaction only serves to make Pippa more self-conscious of her single state. She drains her daiquiri and stands up to leave. Enough of playing gooseberry: her bed beckons.

'That's very kind,' the Scandinavian is saying. 'Your wife is very generous, Daniel,' he adds to the other man.

Daniel smiles and says something Pippa doesn't quite catch as she walks away. She turns to look at the two couples now, both men with their attention focused on their respective brides. *This is what it's going to be like from now on*, she tells herself firmly. *The world is made up of couples and you're no longer one of them.*

Better get used to it.

CHAPTER FOUR

DANIEL

'How about that boat trip we talked about?'

Daniel strolls out onto the terrace of the villa, tugging on a polo shirt. It's nine in the morning and there is still a freshness to the morning air. He sits down and pours himself coffee from the cafetière on the table.

'Weather's going to be good, by all accounts. Not too hot and a bit of a breeze. It'll be perfect for getting out on the water.'

'Can't, babe,' drawls Tansy. She lights a cigarette and inhales on it deeply and with intent, before tipping her head right back and funnelling the smoke towards the dark blue sky. 'Chris wants me to do an Insta Live to tease the release of the new shake.'

Chris is Tansy's agent. Unlike the glam squad he isn't on their honeymoon in person, but as far as Daniel is concerned, he may as well be. He's still pulling the strings from a distance.

'How long is that going to take?' Daniel objects. 'Not more than half an hour, surely? You can bung your video up online after breakfast, and then come with me. There's a catamaran trip heading out to some of the small islands at ten thirty. They throw in lunch, and there are dolphin sightings. And turtles, probably. Sounds like fun.'

But Tansy is already shaking her head. 'Peak Instagram log-on time on a Monday is about 5 p.m. If I want to get the best audience back in Oz, Chris says I need to be live between eleven and twelve here.'

She sucks in an extravagantly long draught of cigarette smoke and sighs it out, her pointed, shocking-pink talons curling, extending like a cat's claws.

'Just as well your followers can't see you now,' Daniel says, sourly. 'What would they think of Miss Health Warrior then? Not exactly on-brand: hashtag nicotine addict.'

Tansy scowls at him. 'Nobody's perfect.'

'But you make your money from pretending to be.'

'At least I'm making money,' she snaps. 'Money that's paying for this honeymoon.'

'I thought this was a freebie.'

'You know what I mean. We wouldn't be in a position to get sponsored trips like this if it wasn't for *my* career.'

Daniel presses his hands to his forehead briefly. *Don't lose it, for God's sake. Keep things chilled.*

'I'm going to get things back on track. You know I will.'

Tansy stubs out her cigarette, flicking her glossy sable mane over her shoulder. 'We'll see. And, in the meantime, let's remember which side your bread's buttered, shall we, and try being a bit grateful?' She reaches in her bag and pulled out a fistful of Mauritian rupees, which she tosses onto the table. 'For your trip,' she announces, flatly. 'I assume you'll need some money.' Then she stands up, pirouettes on a bare, tanned foot and calls into the villa: 'Sebastian, do we have the new packaging prototype somewhere? We're going to need it for the content.'

'Got it!' comes Sebastian's sing-song voice. 'Time I got you shampooed, sweetness!'

Tansy flounces off without a backward glance at her new husband, to go and sell more of her 'miracle' shake, a product which Tansy's followers will happily buy by the bucketload if she tells them to. Because they buy into Tansy Dimaano, and everything she says or does.

After he has finished his breakfast – alone – Daniel thrusts the cash Tansy has left into the pocket of his shorts, gathers up his sunglasses and phone and heads across the hotel gardens to the beach.

A walk of a couple of hundred yards or so takes him to the jetty used by local commercial companies. There is a large white catamaran moored there, its deck shaded by an awning and flanked with cushioned benches. Arne and Nikki Lindgren are sitting on them, along with an elderly couple that Daniel hasn't seen before. Two of the crew, dressed in white polo shirts and shorts, are making safety checks on the boat while another stands on the dock welcoming the guests.

'Room for another?' Daniel asks.

'Of course, sir, welcome on board.' The man smiles broadly and ushers him onto the deck. He sits down next to the Lindgrens, lifting his hand in an awkward wave.

'No Tansy?' asks Nikki, leaning towards him with a smile.

'She's got to work, I'm afraid.'

'On her honeymoon?' Arne turns down the corners of his mouth, betraying what he feels about this.

Daniel ignores the implied disapproval. 'She sent that dress you liked to be cleaned,' he told Nikki, keen to change the subject. 'And then housekeeping will drop it over. I expect you'll get it later today.'

'Sweet of her,' Nikki smiles.

The steward who greeted them introduces himself as Imraan and hands around a tray of beers and colourful cocktails flavoured with grenadine. 'We'll be setting off shortly, folks, but for our manifest, we need to see some picture ID.'

The elderly couple, who turn out to be from Florida, hand over state identity cards, while Nikki Lindgren pulls out two European

Union passports from her bag: one British and one Swedish. Daniel fishes his own passport from the pocket of his shorts.

'I'll take these for now, and have them back to you later,' Imraan tells them. 'Meanwhile, please relax and enjoy. Our chef, Samuel, will be serving lunch in around an hour and a half.'

The catamaran pulls out of the dock, gliding over the still, turquoise waters towards the open sea. Sitting on the open deck with a beer in his hand, and a cooling breeze ruffling his hair, Daniel finally starts to relax. As the sun climbs, he feels the skin on the back of his neck starting to grow pink, and gratefully accepts Nikki's offer of sunscreen.

They moor off a tiny island for a lunch of barbecued seafood, salad and fresh fruit. Afterwards, snorkelling equipment is produced.

'I'm going to sit this one out,' Arne says, patting his abdomen ruefully. 'I ate too much lunch.'

'Me, too,' Daniel says quickly, when Nikki Lindgren looks hopefully in his direction. He does not want to get into the ocean. Being immersed in water is the last thing he wants.

'Oh, come on!' Nikki pleads. Daniel closes his eyes and pretends to be asleep. Eventually he hears two splashes as Nikki and one of the crew members jumps off the ladder on the side of the boat. Only then does he open his eyes and reach for another beer.

'You ever been snorkelling?' Arne asks.

'Yes, once.'

'And your wife didn't want to try it?'

'No.'

'I guess it's cool that you and your new bride are okay spending some of your time apart.' The Swede's tone betrays that he isn't convinced of this. 'That the two of you are… relaxed about things.'

'Well, yes.' Daniel looks away. 'Quite.'

After Nikki has snorkelled for forty-five minutes, she climbs back onto the boat and falls into Arne's waiting arms, laughing and exhilarated. He wraps her in a towel and kisses her playfully on the tip of her nose. Nikki wipes her face with the towel and kisses him back, full on the lips, while the older American couple exchange 'aren't they adorable' glances.

They're genuinely in love, Daniel thinks, as he watches them over the rim of his beer can. *Lucky sods*.

The crew raise the anchor and they cruise slowly back to Turtle Bay. Light-headed from the combination of several beers and a fiercely hot sun, Daniel falls into a doze on one of the loungers, only waking when the catamaran is docking back at the resort.

He yawns and rubs his hand over his face. His skin is tight with salt and his mouth tastes foul.

'Your passport, sir.' Imraan hands it over, and Daniel reaches to stuff it into his back pocket.

'Hold on, Dan.' Nikki appears at his side. 'I think they've mixed up the two UK passports. I've got yours.'

He pulls out the passport that Imraan has just given him and instinctively flips it open at the photo page. Other people's passport photos are always interesting.

'It's still in my maiden name,' Nikki is saying, her hand extended to take it from him. 'I haven't got round to changing it to Lindgren yet.'

Daniel glances at the photo of a younger Nikki, with longer hair. Despite the requisite serious expression, there's a spirited, intelligent expression in her eyes that makes her look pretty. He reads the name printed to the right of the photo.

Nicole Marie Simmons.

She's looking at him expectantly. He closes the passport abruptly and hands it back without a word.

CHAPTER FIVE

PIPPA

A honeymoon for one, Pippa is starting to realise, is not much fun.

She wishes she'd been able to arrange for Lauren to join her, or one of her girlfriends. Even her brother. Just to have someone to talk to over meals, or go on excursions with. It's only her second whole day at the resort and dining at her lonely table for one is starting to grate. And there is only so much pleasure you can derive from an exotic rum punch if there's no one to drink it with. Sitting alone on her terrace, she picks up her phone and instinctively goes to call Alastair, as she has thousands of times over the past six years. She cuts the call before it connects. It really isn't fair to him to use him as an emotional crutch; not after jilting him at the altar and calling time all together on their relationship.

They met at a work-related conference when Pippa was twenty-seven and Alastair twenty-nine. The event, held in a hotel in Harrogate, was titled 'Digital Innovation in Insurance', and was about as exciting as it sounded. Pippa gravitated towards Alastair at the evening social mixer because he had an open, friendly face and because he was the only other person under the age of forty. It turned out they had plenty in common, if 'in common' meant both joining large City insurance firms when they graduated from university, and both lacking the guts to move on from these first graduate jobs even though they were bored and marking time.

They sank a huge amount of lukewarm white wine and ended up having tipsy and unsatisfactory sex in Pippa's hotel room. Somewhat to her surprise, Alastair contacted her after their return to London, wanting to meet up again. Having been officially single for the previous three years (she didn't count a handful of flings that hadn't made it past the three-month mark), Pippa said yes, and before long they were dating. It proved agreeable to have one regular person to go out and about with, and the sex improved considerably after that first drunken encounter. In what seemed like no time at all, a year and a half had passed in this comfortable and unchallenging fashion. Alastair then suggested that it made no sense for them to continue to pay two lots of London rent, and so, a few months' shy of her twenty -ninth birthday, Pippa moved into his one-bedroom flat in Alexandra Palace.

Another year and a promotion later, and Alastair told her that now it made no sense for them to be wasting money on rent, so they started proactively saving for the deposit on a flat of their own. Pippa couldn't really argue with his fiscal logic, and if she and Alastair were not wildly happy, then they were certainly content. She'd never met anyone who'd tempted her to stray.

Dropping her phone into her bag, Pippa wraps a sarong over her bikini and slides on her flip-flops, pushing sunscreen and a bottle of water into her bag. A leaflet had been pushed under her door the night before about a private catamaran trip, and she decides she may as well fill some time aboard a boat as mooch around alone in her room.

As she emerges onto her terrace, her skin chills suddenly despite the heat. She has the strangest sense of being watched, observed. The undergrowth rustles faintly as she descends the steps. She jerks her head to her right. There is a Mauritian man standing right next to the wall of her bungalow, looking in her direction. He's short and slight, wearing tinted glasses with thick lenses and a shirt with the Excelsior logo. He jumps slightly when he realises she is looking in his direction, but extends a hand. 'Ashvin Babajee. General Manager. So lovely to make your acquaintance.'

His thin lips part to reveal a gold tooth. Pippa guesses him to be around fifty.

Pippa does not shake his hand. 'Can I help you?'

'Just checking the broadband cables. We are checking all the rooms… may I be of assistance to you on this beautiful morning?' His eyes roam over her bikini top.

She shakes her head and hurries off to the beach, but as she reaches the dock, she can see that the boat has just left. She is too late.

The next-best option to pass some time is to head to the resort's main pool and hope to find some congenial company. She positions herself on a lounger while the attentive staff bring her neatly rolled towels and a drinks menu. After stroking sunscreen onto her legs, she leans back as though being on her own in a luxury resort favoured by honeymooners is fine, really absolutely fine.

'Your drink, madam.'

After five minutes, the clinking of ice cubes alerts her to the arrival of her mai tai. Then, as she opens her eyes to take the drink from the pool boy's tray, she spots him: the large man who had been alone in the restaurant and the bar on her first evening. He sits hunched forward on the edge of a lounger, dressed in chinos and a shirt rather than swimming shorts, once again looking at his phone screen.

Emboldened by the slug of Bacardi she has just swallowed, she puts on her sunglasses, picks up her drink and strolls over to him. This time, she is determined, she isn't going to be fobbed off.

Hi!' She extends a hand. 'Pippa Bryant. And you are?'

Without really disguising his reluctance to chat, he puts down his phone and reaches out to shake the proffered hand. 'James Cardle. Jim.'

With the beginnings of a tan, and several days' worth of stubble, he is attractive in a craggy way. Pippa positions herself at the foot of a neighbouring lounger.

'Did you have someone at your pavilion checking your broadband earlier?' she asks him.

He shakes his head. 'Nope. Don't think so.'

'The manager, Babajee, was hanging around my room just now, and he said it was because all the rooms were being checked… he creeps me out, to be honest.'

Cardle merely grunts and reaches for a pack of cigarettes.

'How long have you been here?'

He has to think about this for a moment. 'About five days, I think.' His voice has a faint Northern twang.

'And you're on holiday?'

He shakes his head, blowing out smoke, but does not elaborate.

'So you're here for work?'

'Yes. In a manner of speaking.'

'Nice work if you can get it,' Pippa enthuses, her jollity sounding forced, even to her own ears. 'What is it you do?'

'How about you?' Cardle's change of subject is as unsubtle as they come. He reaches for the glass of beer on the table next to his lounger and takes a long gulp.

'I take it you *are* here on holiday?'

'On honeymoon, actually.'

'Really?' For the first time, there's a spark of genuine interest. 'Only I'm sure I saw you on your own in the restaurant and the bar.' He gestures towards her cocktail with his own drink. 'And you're on your own now, or you wouldn't be making conversation with random men by the pool. Is your husband ill or something?'

Pippa feels colour creeping up from her collarbone to the base of her neck. 'He's not here.'

'Funny kind of honeymoon that, leaving the husband behind.' He shrugs. 'But, hey, I'm divorced myself, so who am I to judge?

Maybe more people should try it – going on honeymoon without their spouse.'

'I'm… we're… we didn't go through with it. The getting married part. So I suppose technically I'm not on honeymoon, because I'm actually now single…' She's babbling, and the flush rises up her neck to her cheeks. 'But I came anyway, so as not to waste all this. Given it was non-refundable.' She gestures around them at the sparkling pool, the rustling palm fronds and the royal-blue sky.

She has his attention now, and he looks straight at her face, evaluating her. 'If you don't mind me asking, who jilted who?'

The colour in her cheeks deepens. 'It was me. Who called it off. But I'm not convinced he wanted to get married, either. Not deep down. There were… issues.'

Cardle gives a slight smile, shaking his head. 'Sounds like you both dodged a bullet, then.' He raises his glass in an ironic toast. 'Congratulations.'

Sitting on her terrace that evening, Pippa picks up her iPad and googles 'James Cardle'.

The first search result takes her straight to his website.

J. Cardle Private Investigations

As an experienced former police officer, I provide a discreet service which includes overt and covert surveillance, vehicle pursuit and tracking, missing person and asset tracing, bug sweeping, fraud prevention and matrimonial services.

Pippa feels a little frisson of excitement. He must be here to investigate somebody: probably one of her fellow holidaymakers. It was fairly obvious when they were by the pool that he didn't want to discuss what he was doing. That was all part of the 'discreet service'. Which is a shame, because she is bored, and could use some diverting intrigue. She's always been an avid reader of crime fiction and loves solving a mystery.

'Good evening, ma'am.'

One of the uniformed housekeeping staff walks by, turning to smile politely when she sees Pippa. She has her arms extended in front of her, and draped carefully over them is a polythene wrapped garment in a pale purple colour. Pippa instantly recognises it as the Iluka dress that Nikki Lindgren so admired. Tansy must have kept her promise and is now having it sent over to the Lindgrens' villa.

Pippa turns back to her search and pulls up some images of James Cardle. She finds one of a younger version with less grey hair, looking manly and serious in a dark suit and tie. But before she has the chance to fall even deeper down an internet search rabbit hole, she stops, reprimanding herself for being ridiculous. She's only taking an interest because she's at a loose end. She puts her iPad away and goes to take a shower, washing her hair and changing into an almond-green halter-necked dress.

On this occasion, she decides against eating alone in the restaurant. It's not a comfortable experience, and if Jim Cardle is in there, he could be forgiven for thinking she's stalking him. Instead, she pours herself a glass of wine from her fridge and orders room service.

She draws out the eating of her fried rice and prawns and a bowl of delicious mango sorbet for as long as she can, but soon the meal is finished and she's at a loose end again. She phones Lauren.

'Hey!' Lauren says, cheerfully. 'How's it going in paradise?'

'It's lovely…' Pippa sighs. 'Beautiful.'

'I sense a "but" coming…'

'At the risk of sounding like an entitled cow, I am a little bored. You know, being on my own all the time.'

'Surely there are people you can talk to. Haven't you met anyone?'

'They're all loved-up couples.'

'Come on, now.' Lauren is brisk. 'You can't be the only single person there. Aren't there even any hunky members of staff? A water-skiing instructor or something?'

Pippa hesitates a few seconds. 'There is this one guy…'

'Ooh, go on.'

So Pippa tells her about James Cardle, stressing that he hasn't been all that interested in chatting to her. 'And it's way too soon anyway. My head's a bit all over the place after the wedding not happening.'

'Yeah, but even so, Pips, he sounds like he could help pass some time. And how do you know he's not interested? Cracking-looking girl like you. Maybe he's just shy or intimidated or something?'

'He doesn't seem the type to be intimidated.'

'And you think he's there investigating someone? Exciting!'

'I assume so. He wasn't exactly forthcoming.'

'Why don't you try and find out more? Go and ask him for a drink. Do you know which is his room?'

'I think so. I saw him coming out of one of the little bungalow thingies just up the way from me. They call them pavilions here.'

'Well, there you are then. It's not too late there, is it?'

'It's about eight thirty.'

'So, not late at all. Knock on his door. Suggest a friendly drink. What's the worst that can happen?'

'He tells me to fuck off.'

'Exactly,' Lauren says, gleefully. 'But what will you have lost, really?'

'My pride?'

'Sod pride. It's overrated. Live a little.'

Lauren is right, Pippa decides. She needs to stop wallowing and act. She drapes a pashmina around her shoulders to keep off the evening breeze and touches up her make-up. *I ought to take something with me*, she thinks as she heads down the path. *It looks more neighbourly.*

Doubling back inside, she retrieves the half-bottle of champagne that was part of her honeymoon welcome basket. As she steps out again into the velvety, fragrant night air, something snags her peripheral vision. A gleam of a metal, a tiny flash of gold. There's someone standing on the path outside her pavilion. A slight figure, whose steel spectacle frames and gold tooth catch in the faint gleam from the porch light.

Ashvin Babajee.

Even though she recognises him, she startles. But before she can ask him what he's doing there he asks smoothly, 'Everything all right, madam?' with an obsequious little bow.

'Fine.' She glares over her shoulder, watching him, as she walks away. He heads off, with a strange scuttling gait, in the direction of the larger, more upscale villas nearer the beach.

A sudden fit of nerves makes her hesitate when she reaches the edge of Cardle's garden. Most of the lights in the pavilion are on, and there is the faint whiff of cigarette smoke in the air, implying he's smoking on the terrace. What if he's unwelcoming, or even downright rude?

'Hi!'

While she's dithering, he has spotted her. He stands up and waves his left hand. The lit tip of a cigarette glows in his right. He is very tall; well over six feet.

In for a penny, in for a pound... Holding the champagne aloft like a peace offering, she approaches the terrace.

'Poppy, is that right?'

'Close. Pippa.' She gestures with the bottle again. 'This was going to waste, so I thought you might like a glass.'

'Er, right, okay.' Cardle stubs out his cigarette in the ashtray. 'Come up and take a seat' – he waves to a small table and two chairs on the terrace next to him – 'and I'll go and get us some glasses. There must be some in here somewhere.'

He is just re-appearing with two champagne flutes in his hand when the sound of a woman's scream cuts through the pulsing sound of cicadas. It is followed by a second scream.

'What the…?' Cardle sets the glasses down on the table and cranes his neck in the direction of the noise. Pippa gets to her feet, following his gaze.

There are more voices now, raised and urgent, and the sound of running feet. Several uniformed staff hurtle past them down the pathway, followed by a couple of security guards.

Daniel Halligan appears in front of the pavilion, pale and sweating, his whole body trembling.

'What's up, mate?' Cardle demands. 'Do you know what's going on?'

The shaking man points behind him, back down the path in the direction of the beach. 'It's at our place… I was out taking a stroll, so I wasn't in, but the staff are saying… one of the maids… she found… oh, Christ!'

Pippa hurries towards him. 'Has someone been hurt?'

'Just come. Come with me, please. I can't face going in there on my own.'

Without further explanation, Daniel turns and starts running back in the direction of the commotion. Pippa glances at Cardle, who gives a helpless shrug and follows him, Pippa a few paces behind.

They end up three hundred yards away, at the Halligans' private villa. Daniel stops at the open terrace window, his hands pressed over his face. Several of the hotel staff are clustered around, talking in hushed voices, their expressions shocked. 'Apparently she's in there. But I can't—'

Cardle strides inside through the French window, with Pippa at his shoulder. They find themselves in a high-ceilinged reception room, lit with scented candles, ceiling fan swirling lazily. Next to the huge white sofa, recumbent against the coffee table, a woman lies on the tiled floor. There is a dark pool of congealed blood around her head and in her dark hair, and another huge smear of blood over the glass top and wrought iron legs of the coffee table. A clear liquid has spread in a pool over the floor, and there are shards of broken glass everywhere.

Cardle exhales loudly. 'Jesus bloody Christ!'

'The maid just came in and found her like that,' says Daniel, who is now standing in the open window. 'They're saying she's dead.'

Tansy's lilac gauze kaftan is splattered with red, the draught from the fan making the wings of the coloured silk butterflies flutter, as though alive. But it's not Tansy Halligan who lies there.

It's Nikki Lindgren.

CHAPTER SIX

PIPPA

'What I don't understand…' Cardle says the next morning, as he and Pippa sit having breakfast on one of the outdoor dining terraces, '…is what Nikki Lindgren would have been doing alone in the Halligans' villa.'

The two of them have gravitated towards each other in an unspoken mutual alliance after witnessing the previous night's horror together.

'It's obvious, surely?' says Pippa.

'Is it?'

'Well, yes. She'd been given Tansy's dress and wanted to go and thank her. And show her how she looked wearing it.'

'Why?' Cardle takes a gulp of his coffee and tears the corner off a large, buttery croissant. 'The point of that is?'

'Because it's what we women do.'

He sighs. 'I'll never understand you lot.'

'From what I overheard someone saying in reception, Tansy was at her hairdresser's villa getting herself ready for dinner. But Nikki wouldn't have known that.'

'No. Nor would the person who attacked her.' Cardle shakes his head, slowly.

'Are you suggesting…?'

‘That whoever bashed her head in saw a woman with dark hair, in Tansy Halligan’s villa, wearing Tansy Halligan’s dress.’ Cardle pauses.

‘So you think Tansy was the intended victim?’

‘Has to have been, surely?’

Pippa shakes her head slowly. ‘My God. If whoever it was got the wrong woman… Has anyone spoken to her husband? To Lindgren?’

‘He was too distraught to make much sense last night, apparently. The police will have to interview him, though. I expect they’ll be wanting statements from all of us.’

He goes back to eating his croissant, and Pippa sips her herbal tea. The silence is broken by peals of laughter from a group of diners who are clearly ignorant of the previous night’s tragedy. A flock of green echo parakeets swoop into a hibiscus tree, fluttering their brilliant wings against the coral-coloured blooms. Above them, the sky is a shimmering cobalt blue. The sensual, cornucopia feel of the place suddenly feels overwhelming, and Pippa drops her head, covering her face with her hands.

‘You all right?’ Cardle enquires.

She gives a heavy sigh. ‘Yes. It’s just… I suppose it’s some sort of delayed shock. Such a horrible thing to happen out of the blue, and on someone’s honeymoon. The last thing you expect.’

‘And your own honeymoon wasn’t exactly going to plan, anyway,’ Cardle observes drily. He takes another bite of his croissant and chews it, then adds in a more sympathetic tone, ‘Shall I ask them to bring you a brandy?’

‘No, it’s okay… I didn’t really sleep last night. Maybe I should try and get my head down.’ She pushes her chair back.

‘I expect I’ll see you later.’ He raises the remaining half of his croissant in a farewell salute, and beckons to the waiter to bring him more coffee.

Pippa walks slowly back to her pavilion and sinks down onto the edge of the bed. Pulling out her mobile, she hits Alastair's number, even though it's only 6 a.m. in the UK. He doesn't pick up. The shock of seeing Nikki Lindgren's battered body washes over her again, and she shivers, feels tears welling. She misses Alastair, misses him in a way she never has before. Was it a mistake to end things? Calling off the wedding had been sensible perhaps, given neither of them had really wanted it, but to throw away everything else they had built together… was their relationship really that bad? Surely they could have continued living together happily enough?

She tries Alastair's number again. No reply.

The Mauritius Police Force returns to the Excelsior Resort that morning and stays for almost three days. Uniformed officers, in blue shirts and caps reminiscent of the French police, comb the grounds. Scene of Crime personnel congregate at the Halligans' villa, and an inspector and a young sergeant from the homicide team take over one of the function rooms in the main building, turning it into a makeshift interview room.

'We are planning to speak to all the guests,' Inspector Ramsamy tells Pippa when it's her turn to give a statement. 'But obviously we are most eager to hear from the other British guests, the ones who knew the deceased.'

Pippa takes one of the bottles of water laid out on the table, swigs from it, then rests it on her lap, the ice-cold plastic soothing against the slightly sunburnt skin of her legs.

'I'm afraid I didn't really know Mrs Lindgren,' she says. The young sergeant is frantically scribbling in a notebook. Both officers seem out of their depth. 'I'm sorry. I've only been here a few days. I knew who she and her husband were by sight, but that was all.'

'So you didn't speak to her?'

'No – well, sort of. Just once. But it wasn't really a conversation as such, I just happened to be there when she was talking to Daniel Halligan's wife.' Pippa feels herself becoming flustered.

I'm sounding like a weirdo: they'll think there's something suspicious about me.

'She was admiring the dress Mrs Halligan was wearing. The same one she was wearing herself when she… when she was found.'

'And she spoke to you?'

'She saw me admiring the dress too, and she said, "Isn't it pretty?" Something along those lines. And I agreed. But then they all went off to drink at the bar, and that was the last I saw of her. Until…' Pippa hurriedly unscrews the cap from the water bottle, takes another mouthful. 'Until I saw her in the villa. The night she died.'

Inspector Ramsamy pushes horn-rimmed glasses up his nose. The sergeant's pen slides to and fro across the page, the sunlight catching it and making it glint. 'And why were you there? In the villa?'

'I was having a drink with another guest – Mr Cardle. James Cardle.'

The inspector consults his own notes. 'Ah, yes.'

'And then Daniel Halligan appeared, seeming distressed, and said something had happened at his villa—'

'Did he say what that was?'

'No, not really. He was flustered, upset. He said one of the maids had found something. He didn't want to go there alone, so we went with him.'

'And you went inside his villa with him?'

'Not at first. I went in with Mr Cardle. Daniel was standing there, looking in through the windows. He may have come inside after that, I don't remember. My first thought was that it was Daniel Halligan's wife, but when I got close it was clear that it wasn't her. The hair was too short, and her skin was too fair. I just stood there, frozen… I was in shock. There were more people arriving, crowding round her.'

'Did anyone try to help her? Help Mrs Lindgren?'

Pippa shakes her head. 'No. There was nothing to be done. It was obvious she was dead.'

'And you don't know Mr Lindgren?'

'No. I saw him around the place, at dinner and so on, but I've never spoken to him.'

Inspector Ramsamy nods at his sergeant, and the flashing pen stops. The notebook is closed. 'Thank you very much, Ms Bryant. That will be all.'

By the time the police have finished their investigation and cleared their resources from the resort, Pippa only has one day remaining of her week's stay. After her trip to the beach, she decides she will go and have lunch in the Excelsior's terrace restaurant. She showers and washes her hair, and changes into a striped T-shirt and white shorts that show off her now tanned legs.

Apart from the time Pippa spent being interviewed, she has either stayed in her pavilion and ordered room service or walked far enough along the beach to escape the bureaucratic invasion, choosing a waterside bar at the neighbouring hotel to buy drinks and snacks; an alternative location, where people's minds are not on a tragic death. Even so, she feels the strain of the change in atmosphere. An enquiry to the concierge confirms what she suspects: that she won't be able to change her flight and return to London sooner. She'll just have to stick it out.

Social contact with the other guests has been non-existent, but on the day that she was interviewed, as she returned to her room, she passed Daniel and Tansy Halligan on the terraced area outside reception. They were involved in an argument, their voices raised to a level that Pippa could easily overhear as she passed.

'You heard what they just said at the concierge desk,' Tansy was hissing at her husband. 'They can get us flights via Dubai, leaving in a couple of hours. We need to take them and just get the fuck out of this place.'

'And how's that going to look?' Daniel demanded. 'A woman dies in our suite in suspicious circumstances and we jump on a plane and piss off back to Australia!'

'The police already spent ages interviewing you, even though what happened has nothing to do with us! There's nothing more you and I can possibly tell them that will make a difference. But if we don't want it to wind up in the press and damage the brand, we need to get the hell out of here.'

'Ah, yes, the bloody brand!' Daniel was sneering now. 'You can't afford to have anything happen to that.'

'You mean *we* can't. Neither of us can. We're getting on that bloody plane.'

Pippa thinks back to the exchange as she walks onto the restaurant terrace now. It's quiet, and she wonders if other holidaymakers cut their losses and left, just as the Halligans did. Cardle is sitting at a table facing the beach, seemingly lost in thought. It's the first time she's seen him since they had breakfast together on the morning after Nikki Lindgren's death.

'How are you doing?' Cardle asks, when he sees Pippa. He doesn't stand up, but gestures to the other chair to indicate that she should join him at his table. It's only when she sits down that she notices a suitcase, small enough to be cabin luggage, propped next to the table, and a passport and some travel documents next to his plate.

'You're leaving?' she asks, pointlessly.

He nods, gesturing at his toasted sandwich and the ubiquitous fruit plate. 'Getting a taxi as soon as I've finished this lot. No point me hanging around. How about you?'

'I'm off tomorrow morning.' A waiter appears and she scans quickly through the menu, ordering a salad and a beer. Once he's gone, she turns to Cardle.

'Have you—?' She hesitates, wondering how to phrase her question. She wants to find out how much he knows about the police investigation, but isn't sure how to probe him without revealing that she knows that he himself is an investigator by profession. After all, he's never mentioned this to her; she discovered it via her online stalking. She doesn't want to come off as a nut job. She decides to play it safe, and extract as much information as she can without giving away that she's been googling him.

'Have you heard any more about Nikki Lindgren? Have the police said anything about what they think happened?'

'Yes, I have,' he says slowly, but does not elaborate. He sighs. 'I went to speak to her husband, offered whatever support I could.'

'But they haven't arrested anyone?'

Cardle shakes his head. 'I don't think they're going to. I had a long chat with young Sergeant Beeharry, off the record, and they're treating it as an accident. According to them, she was there to see Tansy Halligan, who was in the room of her make-up lady at the time Nikki called round. There was melted ice spilt on the floor, and Mrs Lindgren slipped on it, hitting the table and bashing her head on the marble surface.'

'Surely…' Pippa pours herself a glass of water from the jug on the table. 'I mean, there are security cameras dotted all around the place. I've noticed several. Surely the footage would help confirm what happened?'

Cardle puts down his fork. 'You'd have thought so. But according to your friend Mr Babajee, the cameras are all dummies. Or at least, they're not currently wired up to record anything.'

Pippa frowns. 'Really?'

'Apparently. Seems serious crime is normally so rare here, there's no need to have them operational on an ongoing basis. And the pathologist's findings on the deceased's injuries are consistent with the slipping and banging the head theory. There's no murder weapon, nothing's been stolen from the Halligans' villa, and there's absolutely no motive for anyone to kill Nikki Lindgren. Case closed.'

'And do you think they're right?'

He shrugs. 'What does it matter what I think?'

Pippa blushes. 'Look… I know what you do for a living, okay? I know that you're a PI. I looked you up online.'

He's looking straight at her now, his eyes the blue-grey of a stormy sea. 'Did you now?' To her relief he seems amused rather than annoyed. 'It's okay, I looked you up too. That's what we all do these days, isn't it? You graduated from Nottingham University in 2008 with a degree in Economics, and you work on the market analysis team at Portman Willis Insurance. Is that correct? Are you *that* Philippa Bryant?'

'You've got me bang to rights,' Pippa says, smiling back at him. 'So you… you're here on a job?'

The waiter puts Pippa's salad in front of her. 'Mr Cardle,' he says, turning to him. 'Your taxi is here.'

Cardle stands up. 'I was here on a job, yes.'

'Investigating someone staying here?'

'No one who's here now.'

'You mean—?'

'Can I trust you to keep it to yourself, Ms Bryant?' His tone is slightly mocking.

'Of course.'

'It was Tansy Halligan.' He gathers up his documents and grabs the handle of his case. 'And to my mind, it's perfectly plausible that someone could have mistaken Nikki Lindgren for Tansy and killed the wrong woman…'

Pippa sets down her knife and fork and stares up at him.

'…Because there are an awful lot of people who might have wanted Tansy Halligan dead.'

CHAPTER SEVEN

PIPPA

It only occurs to Pippa once she's checked in her luggage and picked up her boarding pass at Ramgoolam International that she doesn't know where she's going to be spending the night after she lands at Gatwick.

Of course she's thought about how her new circumstances will affect her living situation in the future. She thought about it frequently at the start of her 'honeymoon', but the death of Nikki Lindgren pushed her domestic problems from her mind. Now that she's wandering the duty-free area, waiting for her flight to be called, she's overcome with doubt. All her belongings are in the ground floor garden flat in Alexandra Palace, but only Alastair's name is on the lease. They hadn't quite got as far as acquiring the joint property they'd been saving for. They'd been perfectly content living in that flat together, and for all she knew they might have continued being so, if it hadn't been for Matt and Chloe.

It was New Year's Eve nearly a year and a half ago, and they agreed to go out for an over-priced meal in the West End with Alastair's oldest school friend, Matt, and his pregnant wife, Chloe.

Pippa would have much preferred to lounge on the sofa in her pyjamas with a bottle of cava and Jools Holland, but Matt and

Chloe were in town from the Midlands where they lived, staying in a fancy hotel for what they were referring to as their 'babymoon'. Alastair had been insistent. He didn't get to see Matt very often, and this was a special occasion for them.

Pippa had only met the couple at their wedding a year earlier, when she found Matt boorish and Chloe shrill but still, there they were in a bistro on the Charing Cross Road on New Year's Eve, having fought their way through the crowds, and facing an extortionate taxi ride home.

Chloe had squeezed her baby bump into a tight, sequinned dress and was making a big fuss over allowing herself half a glass of 'bubbly'. After a lot of fist bumping and back-slapping with Alastair, Matt only seemed to want to talk about their old school friends that he saw out and about on the golf links in Solihull.

Pippa twirled the stem of her wine glass in her fingers and watched the progress of their waiter as he took the orders of the other diners. The service was slow – probably a deliberate ploy to get the diners to order more drinks.

'So… you two.' Chloe twinkled at Pippa and Alastair. 'New Year's Eve, eh? What do we think? Do we think tonight might be the night? The night the Whelanator steps up to the plate.'

Pippa and Alastair exchanged blank looks. 'Might be what night?' asked Pippa, raising a hand to try and attract the waiter's attention. *For God's sake, let us just eat and get out of here…*

'The night Al proposes! Derr!' Chloe giggled as though she had drunk a bottle of Prosecco rather than one small glass.

'Yeah, come on, big guy,' said Matt. 'Isn't it time you made an honest woman of your lovely lady?'

Alastair's eyes registered dismay. Pippa felt her neck flush pink.

'Come on,' said Matt, giving his friend a playful shove. 'You've been together how long?'

'Four years. Nearly five.'

'Well, there you are then. Time to pop the question. I take it you *were* planning to pop the question, Whelan?'

'Um, well. Okay…' It was Alastair's turn to blush. Pippa had stared at him, unable to hide her discomfort.

'Hooray!' squealed Chloe. 'Congrats!' She waved her arm aggressively at the waiter who had been ignoring them. 'Bring us another bottle of bubbly! They've just got engaged!'

'I suppose we might as well,' Alastair said, when their taxi finally wove its way up Archway Road two hours later.

The crack and sparkle of fireworks lit up the sky with splashes of gold, crimson and purple. 'Get married, I mean.'

'I suppose so.' Pippa forced a smile.

'I mean, it makes sense.'

'Yes.' She watched a rocket explode into a fountain of blue stars.

'But not just yet, obviously. We need to carry on saving for our deposit.'

'Yes. Of course.'

And that was it. That was how they had decided to get married. They carried on putting money aside for their flat purchase for the rest of that year, and then Pippa – under pressure from friends and family, and desperate for them to escape the limbo of being an engaged couple – insisted they fix a date in the spring of the following year.

All because bloody Matt and Chloe had said they should.

The other issue with the flat – apart from it being in Alastair's name – is that there's only one bedroom.

When she and Lauren were texting while she was away, Lauren offered her own flat as a temporary haven, but Pippa knows it was out of cousinly duty rather than because it's an ideal solution.

Pippa would have to sleep on the sofa, and Lauren's flat mate, Ellie, is bossy and controlling, with an overbearing rugby player of a boyfriend. It would make for an awkward ménage.

When she's not in a light, unsatisfying doze, she spends the twelve-hour flight scrolling the contacts on her phone, wondering who might have a spare room she can borrow, and fearing she may end up back at her parents' house in Berkshire, commuting into London.

Once the flight has landed and she's cancelled the 'flight only' mode on her phone, it bleeps with a WhatsApp.

It's from Alastair.

You'll want to come back to the flat and sort out your stuff, so I'll arrange not to go back there after work. You can have the place to yourself for tonight at least.

Pippa replies as she waits for her suitcase at the baggage carousel.

Thanks, if you're sure you'll be okay?

I'll crash at Anthony's and come round to the flat tomorrow evening. We can talk about what we're going to do then.

Forcing her eyes to stay open long enough to get home, Pippa catches the Gatwick Express train, a Victoria line tube to Finsbury Park and finally a bus to the Alexandra Palace, where she and Alastair live in one of the pretty, tree-lined streets to the north of the palace grounds.

Her first thought on unlocking the door is that it's nice to be home. Even though it may not be her home for much longer. The second is that the place smells funny. But she's too tired to work out why.

Clean sheets, she thinks, as she sinks into the familiar bed. *And very unlike Al to get round to changing the bed linen for her arrival.*

This faint frisson of unease is her last and only thought before sleep overtakes her.

She wakes to one of those late April days that feel as chilly and sunless as November.

With her head pounding from a disorientating blend of dehydration and jet lag, she showers, dresses in the dark trousers and plain shirt she favours for work, and reaches into the back of the wardrobe to drag out her trench coat. Her hand brushes against something cool and smooth, and she realises it's the white PVC bag that was bought to cover her wedding dress. She pulls it out and inches the zip down just far enough to glimpse the ivory lace. On the floor of the wardrobe is the beige and gold box containing her Jimmy Choo bridal shoes. During the journey to Gatwick, Pippa and Lauren had agreed that Lauren would return to the hotel and remove the flowers and other wedding regalia. She must have arranged with Alastair to drop off the dress and shoes while Pippa was in Mauritius, though in the circumstances it would have been better if they'd wound up at the Bryant family home.

What am I going to do with them now? she wonders sadly, replacing the dress at the far end of the rail and setting off on her oh-so-familiar daily journey to the City. Her fellow commuters waiting for the 8.08 from Alexandra Palace to Moorgate look almost as miserable as she does, hunching their shoulders against the drizzle being sprayed against their faces by the unseasonably cold wind. Pippa feels as though she has drunk half a litre of vodka and worked her way through an entire pack of cigarettes, even though she had just one glass of wine on the flight and hasn't smoked since she was at university. She buys a flat white from the kiosk on the station platform, but it tastes sour and acrid and does nothing to relieve her headache. A text arrives on her phone, from an unknown number.

Better if u don't talk about Mauritius. Silence is golden bitch.

She stares at it for several seconds, a sensation of unease blending with her low mood. Was this from some resentful colleague, because she didn't invite any of them to her wedding? Or is it something else? Something to do with Nikki Lindgren?

The offices of Portman Willis are in a huge stone edifice on Gresham Street, halfway between Moorgate and Bank. She texted her parents and her brother to let them know she was safely back in the UK, but hasn't spoken to them. She hasn't updated her social media accounts either, so it occurs to her as she strides across the huge atrium towards the bank of lifts that everyone at work will think she's married; that she and Alastair have just flown back from Mauritius together, loved-up and sated by a week of conjugal bliss. She'll have to tell them that their assumption is wrong, but not yet. Not now. Not until she has seen Alastair and had a calm, rational discussion about their future. Because they could still have a future, even if it isn't the one they originally planned. There's still room for renegotiating a new, different kind of relationship.

'Wow, amazing tan!' squeals Heather, the administrative assistant to the team of analysts that Pippa works with. She's a well-meaning but not overly bright girl, with hair bleached a silver blonde and an intricate system of ear piercings. 'How was it? Was it amazing?'

'Yes, it was,' Pippa replies, forcing a smile as she drops her empty coffee cup into the bin. She doesn't elaborate, planning to keep her answers as vague as possible. Then it occurs to her that she doesn't have a wedding ring on her left hand. She and Alastair failed to exchange the platinum bands they had shopped for, what now feels like years ago. She's still wearing her engagement ring, though, so maybe no one will notice. She tugs her shirt sleeves down as far as they will go.

'You look a bit peaky,' observes Andy Moncrieff. He's an acerbic Scot who started in the same graduate intake as Pippa. Now that she has been promoted to a higher grade than him, he resents her furiously while pretending to be her mate. 'Got you knocked up already, has he?'

'Jet lag,' says Pippa. She avoids eye contact by reaching behind her computer terminal to switch it on. Her phone bleeps with a text.

See you this evening. A x

'Nice problem to have, eh?' Andy includes everyone in their open-plan area in this question. 'Case of jet lag after honeymooning at a five-star resort in the Indian Ocean while we all work our bollocks off. How the other half live!'

Pippa could point out that it's the first time she's taken time off since the previous September, and that she's entitled to use her annual leave how she likes. But she doesn't. She keeps her head down and pretends to be engrossed in the 187 emails waiting in her inbox. Any queries about the wedding are met with generic replies, and as the day wears on, so the novelty of her return wears off. Her colleagues have no way of knowing that mentions of Mauritius make her think not about her new husband, but about the bloodied body of Nikki Lindgren. And about Jim Cardle.

The day doesn't drag as much as Pippa feared it would, chiefly because she's very busy. Being busy gives her a good excuse to avoid demands for non-existent pictures of herself in her bridal finery, or her on the beach with Alastair. Now that everyone carries their photos on their phone, instant access to people's lives is expected at all times. She is happy to duck out of the office just before six, fully expecting the nuptial chatter to have died down the next day.

As she unlocks the front door to the flat, she receives another text from Alastair.

Sorry, got held up at the last minute. Will be back nearer eight.

Pippa drops her head into her hands. This is all she needs after a stressful day. She wants to patch things up with Alastair but has no idea how to go about it, and now he's not even here. Pulling herself together, she changes into jeans and one of her grottier sweaters, deciding now is as good a time as any to start packing up her stuff. Whatever happens, she will need to move out, at least for the time being. Perhaps their relationship might be saved. But if she and Alastair are to continue, it will have to be with a clean slate, and with some space. The problem was, she now realises, that they acted like an old married couple, even though they weren't married; they moved through all the predictable gears of a relationship without taking time to enjoy themselves. They need to return to their respective single states and see if they can recover some of the fun and spontaneity of their early days. Pippa quashes the thought that even when they were in their twenties, things between them were always steady rather than exciting. If they can live separately and start dating again – this time as a mature couple with decent incomes and some life experience – then who knows what could happen? But she needs some space to think it all through first.

Satisfied with this reasoning she has put together, Pippa interrupts the emptying of the wardrobe and goes into the kitchen to pour herself a glass of wine. There's an empty cardboard carton next to the recycling bin, and she sets it on the kitchen table, rummaging in the cupboards for the few pieces of crockery and cooking utensils she wants to take with her. She soon gets into a rhythm, punctuating each object successfully wrapped and stowed with a swig from her wine glass.

At seven forty-five, she finally hears Al's key in the front door.

'Through here!' she calls, reaching automatically into the cabinet for a second wine glass.

But it's not Alastair. It's a young, blonde woman, holding the door key to the flat in her hand.

She blushes slightly, then when she sees the half-filled box, nods encouragingly. 'Ah, you're packing.'

'Yes,' says Pippa, stiffly, still puzzled. 'And you are…?'

Then she realises. It's her: Amy. Amy, the girlfriend of Alastair's colleague. Amy, whose ear Alastair was whispering into when Pippa arrived at her own wedding. She's petite, with a doll-like prettiness; the hair slide, Peter Pan collar and Mary-Jane shoes combine to make her look no older than fifteen.

'Actually, I'm glad,' Amy says, with an awkward half-smile. 'You know, that he's finally got round to telling you.'

CHAPTER EIGHT

PIPPA

'I'm sorry. I *was* going to tell you…'

Pippa and Alastair are sitting at the kitchen table alone after his eventual return from work. Amy complied with Pippa's icy request that she leave thirty minutes earlier.

'…I planned to get home at seven and tell you then, but I was late leaving the office. So I texted Amy and told her not to come round, but by then she was on the tube and she didn't pick up the text til it was too late. She assumed you'd already be gone. She was mortified.'

'Awful for her.' Pippa splashes a generous amount of wine into her glass and gulps it aggressively.

'Pip, I am sorry. I really am. You shouldn't have had to find out about it like that.'

'Find out about what, exactly? That you've been having an affair?' She takes another large mouthful of wine and closes her eyes briefly as the cold liquid trickles down the back of her throat.

Alastair pauses a beat, which gives her the answer. 'We've been seeing each other, yes.'

'How long? And how long has she had a key to my home?'

'Not that long… since you went to Mauritius.'

'You've only been sleeping with her since I called off the wedding? That's something, I suppose.'

Alastair looks down at his hands. 'Well, not exactly. It started a while ago, but then I ended it. We tried not seeing each other, but then when you broke things off, we just couldn't—'

'Star-crossed lovers. Sweet.'

Pippa's heart is pounding with an uncomfortable blend of rage and shock. She crosses to the fridge and takes out another bottle of wine.

Alastair stands up and takes it from her, pouring himself a glass. 'Look, I need to tell you about it. We need to get it all out in the open, so we can all move on.'

'Go on.'

'It started after the work Christmas do, over a year ago. Just before we got engaged. Michael had to leave the party because of a family emergency. Amy stayed on alone and we danced, and ended up kissing.' Alastair catches the expression on Pippa's face and looks down at his glass. 'I dismissed it as typical office-party shenanigans.'

'But you didn't say anything to me.'

'I didn't think it was anything. Not worth mentioning. But she got in touch with me, and we ended up seeing each other.'

'You mean sleeping with each other.'

He colours. 'Yes. And by then you and I had decided to get married.'

'Technically it was Matt and Chloe who decided.'

Alastair manages the ghost of a smile. 'I suppose it was. And I will admit I did go on seeing Amy for a while after that. I was unsure about marriage and she was unhappy with Mike and wanted to break it off with him. As much as anything, we used one another as a shoulder to cry on…'

Pippa scowls as she tosses back more Pinot Grigio.

'But then when we had the date set for the wedding, I told her it was over. And we stopped seeing each other.' He catches Pippa's sceptical expression. 'We honestly did. The afternoon of the wedding was the first time I'd seen Amy in months, I swear.

But then you called it off, which let me know you didn't feel things were right, either. And that night, Amy ended things with Mike. Everything suddenly fell into place. And with you away and her unable to stay in the flat with Mike…'

'You moved her in here. Nice.'

'I should have told you sooner, Pip; I know that. Before you got back from Mauritius. I honestly just wanted you to have a nice time away – a proper break.'

'And if I hadn't called off the wedding?' Pippa asks, suddenly serious.

'I would have stayed away from Amy, obviously.'

Pippa stares at him for a few seconds. It doesn't seem obvious to her at all. But then nor is she surprised by what has happened. She was the first one to hold her hand up and say that something in their relationship was lacking. In the last six months they'd hardly had sex at all. Alastair, it seems, had dealt with the same feeling in a completely different way. She just feels foolish for not having realised what was happening under her nose. 'So, what now?'

'You stay here in the flat for a week or so – however long you need to sort something out. We'll divide up the savings account fifty-fifty, which will give you plenty to cover a deposit and rent on a new place.'

'Okay.' Pippa sighed. 'I suppose that's fair. I was going to move out, anyway, whatever happened. I just thought you and I might go on seeing one another…' She gives a bitter little laugh as she realises how foolish this sounds.

'I hope we still can. As friends.'

She gives a bleak little shrug. 'Maybe,' she says, without meaning it.

Finding a new rental in just a week is more or less impossible, Pippa discovers.

She makes appointments for viewings in the evening after work, only to be told that the properties have just gone under offer, or that they are grimy, dimly lit and over-priced. A day taken as annual leave and spent on viewings doesn't yield better results. Anywhere decent is either too expensive or already taken.

'What am I going to do?' she wails to Lauren on the phone. 'I'm going to wind up on a park bench.'

'Alastair can hardly just throw you out.'

'I know, but officially it's his flat. And he can't go on sofa surfing at Anthony's indefinitely.'

'There's always the sofa at mine,' Lauren says, though they both know it's not really an answer.

'I'll just have to keep on looking.'

At work, Pippa becomes increasingly tetchy and distracted, trying to follow up on viewings and field phone calls from estate agents keen to earn commission by offering her anywhere, suitable or not. She snaps at Heather, making her cry, and ends up having to buy flowers by way of apology.

At the end of the week, Lauren phones her while she's in the office. 'Just an idea, but I might have a suggestion for a place you could live. Meet me for a drink after work and I'll tell you about it.'

'Another personal call, Pippa?' Andy Moncrieff strolls past her desk, eyeing her mobile pointedly.

'Meaning what?'

'Just that there have been rather a lot of them lately. And we are supposed to be busting our asses completing the year-end asset management analysis. Shame you can't join in, now that you're back from your luxury holiday.'

'Are you trying to say that I'm not pulling my weight?' Pippa demands.

Andy raises an eyebrow suggestively. 'I'm not trying to say anything.' His tone is neutral, but clearly he is trying to say something. He's implying, as ever, that it was he who should have been promoted, not Pippa.

'Oh, just fuck off, Andy!' She's shouting suddenly, as a wave of rage courses through her. She stands up and hurls her mobile after him, catching him a glancing blow on his cheek.

'Ow!' He puts his hand up to where a dark red mark is forming. 'Seriously? You're assaulting me now?'

'Sorry,' Pippa mumbles, running off to the Ladies, where she sits for twenty minutes on the closed seat of a toilet, mopping up angry tears. When she emerges, Dawn Treadwell, her line manager, is waiting outside in the corridor.

'Pippa, I think we need to have a word.' Dawn's expression is stony. 'Come into my office, please.'

The door is closed firmly behind them, curious faces turned in their directions craning to hear.

'Andy Moncrieff claims you were just physically violent towards him.'

Pippa likes Dawn, who is a brisk but motherly woman in her late forties. There's a froideur about her now, and her normally ruddy face is a little pale.

'I chucked my phone in frustration.' Pippa's voice comes out as a croak. 'But I honestly didn't think it would hit him.'

'It's caused an injury. That counts as an assault.'

Pippa nods. She feels numb, as though this is happening to someone else.

'I know there are tensions between you two, but was there any reason for this… for something so completely out of character?'

'I've just found out that my fiancé's been having an affair. And I've got to find somewhere else to live.'

'Your fiancé? I thought you'd just got married.'

Pippa shakes her head. 'The wedding was called off. I went away, anyway.'

'I see.' Dawn thinks about this for a few seconds. 'I'm sorry to hear that.' Her tone softens a little. 'Look, Pippa, you have an immaculate conduct record. If you didn't, I'd have to let you go. You do realise that?'

She nods again, twisting a damp tissue between her hands.

'I'll have to clear this with HR, but I'm going to ask that you're signed off for a couple of months with stress. The alternative is a disciplinary hearing and probably termination of your contract. But it sounds as though there are some mitigating factors, and as long as Andy is prepared to go along with it – and I think he will be when he's calmed down – we can probably avoid that happening.'

'Thank you,' Pippa whispers.

'Obviously you'll need to get your stuff and go home now. And please do your best to avoid any further contact with Andy.' Dawn manages a weak smile. 'Someone will be in touch in a few days. And I hope you get things sorted out.'

Pippa doesn't go home. She doesn't really think of it as home, anyway. Instead, she takes the tube to Blackfriars, where Lauren works, and sits in a brasserie, dawdling over a hot chocolate.

Her cousin eventually joins her just after five.

'What's going on?' She knows instantly she sees Pippa's face that something is wrong. 'What's happened? Wait…' Lauren fishes for her purse and dumps her bag on her chair. 'This requires alcohol.'

She returns from the bar with a carafe of rose and a serving of fries. Pippa tells her everything, including Alastair's relationship with Amy and her assault on Andy Moncrieff.

'Bloody hell, Pips.' Lauren squeezes her hand, before popping several chips in her mouth. 'But, listen,' she continues, her mouth full of food, 'I have something that might cheer you up.'

'Go on.'

'Remember Granny's friend, Mrs Coombs?' Lauren and Pippa share a maternal grandmother, since their own mothers are sisters.

'Vaguely. Was she the one who always gave us Battenberg cake when we went round there for tea?'

'That's the one. Well, anyway, her younger sister – who's also pretty old, obviously – has a house in Clapham with a self-contained flat. She's looking for someone to live in it, for a nominal rent, in return for keeping an eye on the place and helping out occasionally with chores she can't manage.'

'Sounds interesting.'

'Cool. I'll phone Mrs Coombs and organise for you to meet the sister.'

The following afternoon, Pippa is standing on the doorstep of a large detached house on the north side of Clapham Common. Mrs Coombs' sister, Rosemary Vesey, was married to a wealthy captain of industry, and still lives in the house where she raised their four children.

'I rattle around in it,' she tells Pippa over leaf tea in porcelain cups, gesturing around the large formal drawing room. She's a small, sprightly woman in cashmere and pearls, with perfectly coiffed white hair. An ancient West Highland terrier – introduced as Gus – snuffles around their feet. 'People keep telling me I should "downsize"' – she says the word with distaste – 'but I can't bear to leave the place, unless it's in a wooden box. I do love my garden so much.'

The flat is over the garage, converted from what was the original carriage house. There's a bedroom with a tiny Victorian fireplace, a living room with a well-equipped kitchenette and a modest bathroom. The carpets and upholstery are shabby but of good quality, and although the décor dates back a couple of decades, Pippa feels sure she can make the place feel homely.

'I have a cleaner and a housekeeper,' Rosemary tells her. 'But they don't live in. It's just a question of having someone around at night in case I fall, or if there's something heavy I can't lift. And occasionally to give Gus a walk if I can't manage it.'

She proposes a ridiculously cheap £400 a month, which Pippa accepts gratefully before she can change her mind. Rosemary hands her a key and they arrange that moving in will take place over the weekend.

Pippa sends a text to Alastair as she heads back to the tube station.

I've found a place to move into. You and Amy can have the flat back from Sunday. P

CHAPTER NINE

PIPPA

The following week would have felt a little like a holiday, if only her life weren't falling apart.

Pippa spends it unpacking and making the flat above the carriage house feel more like home. The May weather is balmy, there are plenty of chic little shops and cafes to explore in nearby Northcote Road, and it should have been fun getting to know a completely new area of London. Pippa has only ever lived north of the river; first in a house share in Kilburn, and then in Alastair's flat in Alexandra Palace. But she's tense and jumpy, startling every time her phone bleeps, and at night seeing Nikki Lindgren's dead body every time she closes her eyes.

She keeps an eye on Rosemary, calling in to check on her and offering to help, but apart from keeping her company over a cup of tea or coffee and taking Gus for walks on the common, she is not required to do anything to earn her rent subsidy. The only contact from Alastair is the transfer of £23,000 to her account: half of the money they had saved as a deposit on their first home. A home they will now never buy.

On the Monday morning of her second week off, Pippa receives an email from Dawn Treadwell at Portman Willis.

Hi Pippa,

I know I said to take some time off, but I'm afraid I'm going to have to ask you to come back into the office as I need to speak to you about something. Can you do tomorrow at 11.30?

Dawn

Pippa replies that yes, of course, she can be there the following morning – she's still being paid her full salary, so can hardly refuse. She turns up at the offices in jeans and a hoodie, though, just to make a point.

Heather gives her a tentative 'Hi!' and a little wave, but everyone else just stares as she walks past her empty desk and into Dawn's office.

Dawn is wearing a shiny suit that doesn't fit her very well. Her face is pinched, and she arranges and rearranges the papers on her desk before saying, 'Pippa, you know I intended to try and… manage… your incident, but I'm afraid things have been taken out of my hands somewhat.' She picks up a pen and lays it down again at a slightly different angle.

'How so?'

'Andy isn't content to just let things lie. He's threatening to involve the police, and to give the story to the press. Obviously, Portman Willis can't afford such negative publicity: employees fighting in the office.'

Pippa looks back at Dawn for a long beat.

'When you say he's threatening, you mean…'

'I mean that he'll do so unless we formally terminate your contract.'

'Sack me, in other words.'

Dawn repositions the pen. 'Well—'

'And who will have my job when I'm gone? Let me take a wild guess… Andy Moncrieff.'

'That is yet to be determined,' Dawn says, stiffly. 'In any case, there is an official process to go through. You make a formal statement, then there has to be a hearing, where you will be interviewed by representatives from HR and senior staff not directly involved with this department, so that an unbiased—'

Pippa stands up. 'You know what? Don't bother. I resign. You can't sack me if I've already gone of my own accord.' She snatches the pen and some paper from Dawn's desk and scribbles a few lines on it, signing it with a flourish. 'There you are – my letter of resignation.' At the door, she turns on her heel and says more gently, 'I appreciate your efforts on my behalf, Dawn, I really do. But the fact is I've been wanting to leave for at least three years; I just didn't have the guts.'

She opens the door and adds loudly, so any lurking colleagues will hear: 'So please thank Andy for me. He's done me a favour.'

The first thing that Pippa does once she's back in her Clapham flat is to check her bank balance.

Most of her pay for April is still in her account. So with a month's salary and her share of the deposit money, she has something of a financial cushion. Her rent is only a few hundred a month, with heating, water and broadband all included. Rosemary's charming Polish housekeeper, Marysia, cooks far too much and frequently brings round the excess food: Tupperware loaded with hearty stew and dumplings, poppy seed rolls and gingerbread. In other words, she's well placed to live cheaply while out of work.

Not that she intends to remain unemployed for any longer than she has to. But she won't be able to find another position in insurance now that she's left Portman Willis under a cloud, and starting out in a completely new career is going to take time. As she walks Gus on the common that afternoon, letting him off the lead to scamper joyfully in the warm, late-spring sunshine, she is painfully aware that career inspiration is something she lacks. Why else would she have stayed at Portman Willis for so long when she didn't really enjoy it?

Back at the flat with a mug of tea, she makes a list of things she's good at. At school she was no academic star, but excelled at maths and economics. She's organised, methodical, good with numbers, comfortable in the digital world. Working for a large organisation doesn't appeal. The obvious answer would be to start some sort of business, something she could grow online with minimal outlay.

The mental image comes to her unbidden, as it does so frequently, of Nikki Lindgren's body lying on the floor, with the gauze butterflies on Tansy Halligan's dress appearing to flutter in the breeze. Tansy had said she had a sponsorship deal with the designer. Didn't she run some sort of e-commerce empire, and promote it through social media?

Intrigued suddenly, Pippa picks up her laptop and tries googling 'Tansy Halligan'. There are no results.

She tries 'Tansy Australia influencer' and the very first suggestion is 'Tansy Dimaano Instagram'. A search on Tansy Dimaano brings up 22,900 results, and image thumbnails that are instantly recognisable as Daniel Halligan's stunning bride.

Pippa goes to her Instagram account. She has 2.9 million followers and the bio reads:

Entrepreneur
Green Goddess
CEO @HirayaNutrition
Wifey

Pippa can't prevent an eye-roll at 'Wifey'. She is remembering how, when any attention was focused on them, she smiled and simpered at her husband, but failed to hide her contempt when she thought no one was watching her.

She scrolls through Tansy's pictures; glamorous, filtered shots which quickly become repetitive, blurring into one another. In most of them, Tansy is scantily clad in workout gear or swimwear, her olive skin glowing and her glossy, filler-enhanced lips puckered at the camera as she sucks green liquid through a straw. Occasionally she is dressed in designer evening wear and towering stilettos at a promotable Sydney bar or restaurant.

There are multiple posts from her bachelorette party and preparation for the wedding, and of course a lot of highly stylised shots of Tansy in an extravagant, jewel-encrusted wedding gown and flowing cathedral veil. Daniel, though, only appears in one of them, movie-star handsome in a tuxedo, with Tansy clinging to his arm and brandishing her bouquet like a weapon. '*We did it! #hubby #wifeyforlifey*' reads the caption. There are photos of Tansy in Mauritius, tagging the Excelsior Resort and acknowledging the content with #ad, but Daniel is absent from them. Pippa patiently scrolls back through the previous four months, then further; all the way back to the beginning of the previous year, but there are no posts featuring or mentioning Daniel Halligan. He's probably someone who disdains social media, Pippa concludes. Which seems to make him an unlikely spouse for Tansy Dimaano.

She goes to the website for Tansy's nutritional product. *Hiraya*, it explains, is an ancient Tagalog word meaning *fruit of one's hopes, dreams and aspirations*. The core product is Hiraya Green, a powdered shake, that claims to be full of antioxidants, vitamins and minerals. This grass-coloured gunk will, the site alleges, help you achieve optimal wellness, enhance energy and cure a whole range of ailments. Pippa scans down the long list of ingredients, which includes barley grass, dandelion leaf and mushroom extract. A new product has just been launched called 'Hiraya Golden'.

There's a photo of a smiling Tansy on a tropical beach, drinking the bright yellow shake. *Created from the Peruvian groundcherry, it will leave you with glowing, line-free skin and a whole new zest for life!*

So far so predictable, thinks Pippa. Yet another wellness guru exploiting consumer gullibility. There's a link entitled 'Hiraya Life', which brings up yet another photo of Tansy, this time performing an advanced yoga pose on a rooftop, a cityscape in the background.

> *If you would like to become a member of our vibrant, healthful community, then why not attend one of our fun, informal seminars at a location near you?*

There's a form to sign up for further information, and a list of dates and venues, not just in Sydney, Melbourne, Perth and Brisbane but further afield, in Bali, Djakarta and Auckland. So Tansy's empire is gaining global reach.

Pippa returns to the home page and clicks on the link for 'Tansy's story'.

> *Three years ago, I started to suffer from fatigue, stiff joints and strange rashes. After consulting several doctors, I was diagnosed with lupus, and told there was no cure. So I turned my back on conventional medicine and pursued holistic treatments. I stuck to a strict sugar-free, gluten-free diet (no alcohol or cigarettes!) and worked with a health food consultant to develop my own nutritional supplement. The result was Hiraya Green. Within weeks of starting to take it, my lupus symptoms disappeared, and I have been healthy ever since. Now it is my dearest hope that the fruit of my dreams, my Hiraya, can help other people like me.*

Pippa leans back against her chair, staring at her screen. So Tansy Dimaano is not just another Instagram gym bunny. She's a snake-oil saleswoman: a full-on fraud. And then she remembers Jim Cardle's words.

'There are an awful lot of people who might have wanted Tansy Halligan dead.'

CHAPTER TEN

PIPPA

Jim Cardle's business premises are in a modern, purpose-built office block just off Whitechapel Road.

Pippa stands in Greatorex Street for a few minutes, looking at the building and trying to work out what she's going to say. She tells herself that she might as well go and see him since she's so close by, having just dropped off her formal severance paperwork at Portman Willis. She's chosen to gloss over the fact that it's a twenty-minute walk between the two offices, and that she could have posted the paperwork rather than deliver it by hand. She takes a deep breath and presses the bell on the keypad marked '*J. Cardle Investigations*'.

There's no reply over the intercom, but the entrance buzzer is pressed. Pippa takes the lift to the top floor and taps gingerly on the door of Cardle's office. It's flung open, revealing a small, modern and rather soulless space with a small inner office containing a desk at one end, and an open-plan area with sofa, armchair and coffee table at the other. A doorway at the far end opens into what looks to be a kitchenette.

'Pippa.' Cardle's tall figure looms in the doorway, dressed in a white button-down shirt and jeans, the vestiges of his Mauritian tan still visible under several days of stubble. He sounds faintly irritated, and a little confused. 'Was I expecting you?'

'I was in the area, and I thought I'd drop in.' Since he already knows that she's googled him, there's no need to explain how she knows the location of his office. 'You know, just say "hi".'

'Well, hi.' He manages the suggestion of smile. 'Come in.'

The office is a shambles. There are box files and heaps of paper everywhere, including on top of a shiny new filing cabinet that doesn't look as though it's ever been opened. Pippa stares around her, taking it all in.

'Also, I wanted you to see this.'

She shows him the anonymous text she received. 'What do you think? Someone doesn't want us talking about Mauritius?'

'That's the logical conclusion, but fuck knows who could have sent it… shouldn't you be at work?' Cardle indicates the leggings, sweatshirt and trainers that she put on first thing to go for a run, with little Gus bouncing at her heels.

'I'm not at Portman Willis anymore. I resigned,' she adds, quickly. 'Three days ago.'

Cardle returns to his desk and sits down, scraping the back of his hand over the stubble. 'I see.'

'Also, Alastair and I really have broken up for good. Turns out he's been seeing someone else. So, I've moved to a new place, and I wanted a completely fresh start. To do something new. I've been wanting to leave my job for ages.'

'I see,' Cardle repeats.

She looks around her at the overt disorganisation. 'I could come and work for you, if you like? Get this lot filed and organised. You look like you could use some help with admin.'

Cardle raises his left eyebrow a fraction. 'Blimey, you don't waste any time, do you? No, thank you, it's a nice idea but I can't afford to take on more staff right now.'

'You wouldn't have to pay me. I'm okay for money at the moment.'

He looks around at the mess, his fingers combing the stubble. 'I don't know…'

'Why don't we talk about it over coffee?' Pippa goes into the kitchen, but all of the available mugs are in the sink, waiting to be washed. There's a musty, faintly rotting smell from the overflowing bin. 'I'll get takeout.'

Ignoring Cardle's faint murmur of objection, she returns ten minutes later with two steaming cups. She perches herself on the stained grey sofa, but Cardle remains stubbornly behind his desk.

'I'll be honest, another thing that prompted me to come round was reading about Tansy Halligan. Tansy Dimaano, I mean. That seems to be her preferred name.'

'Oh, yes?' The eyebrow goes up again. 'Why's that?'

'Nikki Lindgren's death. Us seeing her like that…' Pippa drops her gaze to her coffee cup. 'I think about it all the time. I dream about it sometimes too. It's a sort of PTSD, I think.'

'It was very shocking,' Cardle agrees. 'Hard to shake that image.'

'Are you still investigating Tansy?'

He nods, but does not elaborate.

'I went down quite the cyber rabbit hole researching her.' Pippa takes a tentative sip of the scalding liquid. 'She seems to be a… piece of work.'

'Aye, she is.'

'So why were you employed to investigate her? You never did say.'

'You know I can't break client confidentiality.'

'But that text means I'm kind of involved anyway: why else would I need to keep quiet about what happened in Mauritius? My safety's been threatened. And if I was to work here…' Pippa wheedles. 'I'd be allowed to know, surely? As an employee.'

'I haven't agreed to that, either.' Cardle tries to sound stern, but he's smiling slightly.

'Please. To be honest, having been there in Mauritius when someone attacked a woman they thought was her a few yards away from where you and I were sitting, I kind of feel as though I have a vested interest.'

'Okay, then.' He spreads his large hands on the edge of his desk, pushing himself back slightly. 'I'm not going to give any names, but a couple in Melbourne hired me. Their daughter worked for Tansy Dimaano, and she ended up committing suicide under... questionable circumstances.'

Pippa thinks about this for a few seconds, confused. 'This was in Australia?'

'That's right.'

'And the dead girl was Australian?'

'Yes.'

'But why would they hire an investigator from London?' Pippa frowns. 'That's hardly convenient. Surely they could have found someone nearer to home?'

'Maybe. But I've worked over there before, and I have a contact at the Australian Federal Police, who recommended me. Besides, Daniel Halligan is British and has family in London.'

Pippa takes another mouthful of coffee and sets the cup down on the coffee table, which needs a good clean.

'So you were working for these clients when you were in Mauritius?'

'I'd actually been in Australia first, meeting the family. I was all set to start my investigation when Tansy abruptly announced on social media that she had married Daniel Halligan and was honeymooning in Mauritius. My clients were so desperate for me to make a start that they paid to fly me out there. And then Nikki Lindgren was killed, in what is looking like a case of mistaken identity, and the Halligans fled the place as fast as they could.'

'So they went back to Australia?'

Cardle shrugs. 'As far as anyone can tell. Tansy's social media would suggest it, though I never believe something just because it's posted online. Anyway, I'm about to head back out there myself. I've made as much headway as I can from here, and I need to touch base with my clients before handing off to the Australian authorities.'

'Can I come with you?'

The words leave Pippa's mouth before she has had the chance to engage her brain. She colours slightly, as Cardle does an exaggerated double take.

'Sorry,' she mumbles. 'I don't know where that came from. Put it down to the novelty of being unemployed. I'll get going now, leave you to your work.'

He is smiling to himself and shaking his head.

'What?' she asks, throwing her coffee cup in the bin and gathering up bag and jacket.

'I was just remembering when another woman of my acquaintance asked exactly the same thing. If she could come to Australia with me, on what turned out to be a very complicated mission. And now here you are. Another trip down under, another sidekick.'

'And will this one be complicated?' Pippa reaches the door, and turns back to face him.

'I expect so.' He tosses his own cup into the wastepaper bin from a distance of at least ten feet, giving a brief smile of satisfaction at the successful shot before picking up his pen and one of the files in front of him. 'Ms Dimaano has a lot of resources at her disposal, and she's no dummy; her tracks are well covered. She's going to be quite a difficult one to nail down.'

Pippa nods slowly. 'I never really talked to Daniel Halligan except for that night when we… when he came to find us. But I'm starting to feel sorry for him.'

Cardle is shaking his head. 'Don't you go wasting your sympathy on him. I have a feeling Daniel Halligan is up to his neck in his wife's tangled web.'

PART TWO

CHAPTER ELEVEN

DANIEL

ONE YEAR EARLIER

Late on a Friday afternoon, the office of Cadogan International Realty is quiet. Potential clients are heading to beach or bar or even away for the weekend. Daniel Halligan looks up from his screen and glances around the room. A few of his colleagues are still at work, but they're either packing up their desks – Dean and Kris – or gossiping – Karen and Angelina. He slowly shuts down the windows on his browser, switches off his terminal and grabs the jacket of his linen suit. With a cursory, 'Good weekend, everyone', he heads out into Cross Street, in Sydney's Double Bay.

It's a clear autumn evening, with a pleasant warmth in the air, so he elects to walk the three blocks to the bar in Double Bay harbour where he has arranged to meet his girlfriend. Maxine is a high-flying commercial lawyer and will almost certainly not be finished at work yet, but he's happy to have a drink alone while he waits for her. He heads for the Double Decker, a hip cocktail bar on the boardwalk, and joins the throng of people queuing to buy drinks. There's a loud, and frankly annoying, group of twenty-somethings blocking the sea view through the picture windows. Their voices are grating, a cacophony of male braying and female shrieks.

Daniel orders a cold lager and watches them. In his mind's eye they are just adult children, the women in their puffed sleeves and crop tops, the men in cropped trousers that expose their ankles, bare feet in loafers. Conversation between them has little chance to develop because every thirty seconds or so, someone holds up a phone screen and demands that they all pose for photos, then busies themselves posting them directly to their social media feeds. The problem with social media, Daniel reflects, as he continues to observe, is that it makes ordinary people believe that they are extraordinary. And that their every decision or desire warrants sharing.

The worst offender among the girls acts like a ringleader, laughing the loudest, preening and pouting in the reflection of her own screen the most frequently. Daniel watches her with an appalled fascination. Her dark olive skin and shiny mahogany tresses suggest she might have some Asian heritage, but her build is more European, with long, smooth legs and an athlete's muscular shoulders and upper arms. She's wearing a tiny green satin dress that barely covers her voluptuous buttocks and clings to a pair of perky breasts. She catches Daniel looking in her direction and he turns away, embarrassed, but not before she's pressed the tip of her pink tongue against her glossy top lip in a provocative fashion.

Maxine texts him to let him know she'll be there in seven minutes. Not five, or ten, or even 'soon', but exactly seven. That's how Maxine's brain works: precise, focused and orderly. Daniel goes to the bar to fetch a second beer and a gin and tonic (with four ice cubes, as Maxine likes it), then moves table so that he can get a better view of the ocean. He's lucky, he tells himself, to live in this amazing city. Yes, selling high-end condos to wealthy overseas investors is unfulfilling, but he's only doing it as a temporary stopgap. He has his eyes on a much bigger prize.

The twenty-somethings are laughing again, although to Daniel's critical eye, their high spirits seem a little forced. When he was their age, knocking around in London with no idea what he wanted to do, he probably seemed equally vacuous. Certainly, it's taken him until now, at the age of thirty-seven, to become seriously ambitious. After a series of dead-end office jobs, at the age of twenty-five he joined the Grenadier Guards on an officer's commission. The forces life didn't suit him and after three years he resigned his commission, having reached the rank of captain. After another few years in the City, in financial sector jobs he enjoyed even less than the army, Daniel's widowed mother died and he inherited a sizeable sum of money. Instead of investing it in bricks and mortar – the sensible option – he bought a ticket to Australia.

After travelling the country for eighteen months he stopped in Sydney long enough to acquire a job in real estate. He found he was good at selling, and loved the outdoor lifestyle. He met Maxine Newcombe through a mutual friend, and was impressed by the confidence and capability of an older woman. Maxine was then thirty-nine, five years older than him. He was also impressed by her smart harbourside apartment in Elizabeth Bay, and moved in with her six months later, having ascertained first that she wasn't interested in getting married.

Daniel didn't want to marry, either: it was the last thing he wanted.

That was three years ago, and they are still happy together, up to a point. Daniel tells himself that whoever he ended up living with, it was never going to be rainbows and butterflies all the time. Okay, so Maxine's assertiveness now seems like bossiness, her love of order a bit controlling, her love of routine a trifle dull. But their life is peaceful, if predictable. They rub along well.

Maxine arrives six-and-a-half minutes later and sits down next to him, lifting her glass to the light to check the number of ice cubes. She runs precisely five kilometres at six o'clock every morning and is very fit, but her figure is what Daniel's mother would have called 'solid'. Her slightly coarse light brown hair is cut into a sensible jaw-length bob, and she wears the barest minimum of make-up.

'What time are you leaving tomorrow?' she asks, as she sips her drink.

'Not sure. Whenever.'

Maxine's brow creases. 'Only I'd like to know, so I can plan my schedule around it.'

'Sweetheart, it's Saturday tomorrow. It doesn't matter what you do. You could even do nothing.'

This suggestion merely elicits a further frown of disapproval, so Daniel changes the subject and asks about her day. Maxine gives concise answers while taking regular, measured sips of her drink, taking ten minutes to finish it as she always does.

The girl in the green dress is looking in Daniel's direction again. When she's sure she has his attention, she reaches forward to pick up her glass of champagne from the table, bending just far enough to give a glimpse of a black lace thong. He drains his glass and stands up. 'Shall we go pick up a takeaway on the way home?'

'I'm cooking sea bass,' Maxine says, smoothly. 'We discussed it this morning, remember? I told you I was going to slip out to the market in my lunch hour and pick up the fish and some veggies.'

'Fine,' says Daniel, deliberately keeping his eyes on Maxine's face and away from the group of millennial partiers. 'Let's grill it on the terrace.'

After they've cooked and eaten their meal, Maxine takes a shower and puts on scented body lotion, then spreads a clean towel out on top of the duvet. This is her way of telling Daniel that she wants sex, a ritual only ever performed on a Friday or Saturday evening. He obliges, closing his eyes and imagining that he's in bed with the exotic girl in the green dress.

The next morning sees him disembarking a plane at Gold Coast Airport into a fug of tropical humidity that makes his shirt stick to his back. He hires a car and drives inland for ten minutes through the suburban sprawl of Tweed Heads West until he reaches an area of winding inland creeks fringed with lush vegetation.

His heart leaps when he sees it. A hand-painted sign.

LOT FOR SALE: 105 acres

Premium development opportunity. Enquiries please phone 07 5561 4759

As promised, his contact is already waiting for him, clipboard in hand. He is a lot younger than Daniel is expecting, barely looking old enough to be out of school. He's wearing an open-necked shirt and ill-fitting suit trousers mismatched with trainers.

'Hi – Bryce Kelly. You Mr Halligan?'

Daniel shakes his hand. 'I think I must have been speaking to your father? Martin Kelly?'

'Actually, he's my grandpa.' He points to the pickup truck next to the side of the road. 'Why don't we hop in the ute? It'll take us too long to see the entire site on foot.'

Daniel climbs into the truck beside Bryce and they drive down a dusty track across flat, scrubby land that leads eventually down to the water's edge. The creek is so broad it resembles a lake, glinting deep turquoise in the unrelenting sun.

'Like it?' asks Bryce.

'It's magnificent,' agrees Daniel, shading his eyes as he watches a shimmering blue flycatcher dart across the water.

'Gramps inherited it from his grandfather. He was planning to build homes on it, and he got as far as drawing up plans, but he's had some health issues.'

'I'm sorry to hear that,' Daniel says, reflexively.

'Yeah, he had a heart attack. They patched him up, but he's still got a dodgy ticker.'

They complete a circuit of the property's boundaries before returning to the main road. 'So, d'you reckon you're interested?' Bryce asks as they climb out of the truck. 'Only we've had quite a few enquiries.'

'I certainly am.' Daniel smiles. 'I just need to look at the financial bottom line first.'

At the airport, waiting for his flight back to Sydney, he's fired up with excitement and desperate to talk to someone about it. A text arrives from Maxine, demanding to know his 'exact ETA'. He starts to answer it, then changes his mind. Instead, he phones his brother Ben, despite the fact that it's almost midnight in London.

'This place could be a gold mine,' he tells Ben, once he's given him an account of his morning. 'If I could get the upfront investment, there's a hell of a lot of money to be made.'

'So, what are you thinking?'

'I'll never get permission for high-rise. Not here. So I'm thinking a retirement village with a lot of small, single storey units. Clubhouse. Pool. Golf course. The over-fifties will pay a premium for that kind of thing if it's done well.'

'I say go for it. You can always bring in other investors. Offer a generous return and people will be falling over themselves. How much is the land?'

'They want nine hundred and fifty thousand dollars, but I reckon I can get them down a bit. With what's left of Mum's money and a bank loan, I can just about cover that myself. I'll still need to cover the construction and development costs.'

'Hold a seminar. Invite potential investors and give them a spiel. You're good at that kind of thing, and your job must expose you to plenty of the right sort of contacts.'

'By which you mean rich people.'

'Exactly, Dan. You need rich people.'

CHAPTER TWELVE

DANIEL

'I need you to help me.'

Daniel is in the office on Monday morning, staring intently at his computer screen, when a vaguely familiar voice interrupts his thoughts. He looks up, startled. There's a lag of a few seconds while his brain catches up with his vision, and confirms that yes, he is looking at *her*. The girl from the bar. The girl in the green dress. Except, this time, she's in full athleisure: leggings and a matching crop top that displays an expanse of smooth, tanned midriff. He coughs and clears his throat to try and disguise the fact that his body has visibly twitched.

'Sorry, hi.' he says, extending a hand. 'Daniel Halligan. How can I help you?'

'I'm interested in buying a condo.'

'Of course. Will you need help arranging finance? Only we have in-house mortgage consultants who can—'

'Cash,' she says, firmly.

Daniel tries not to stare at the strip of golden skin right in his eyeline. He takes out a notepad. 'And what sort of budget are you looking at?'

'I'd like to see the ones in the Belmont building.'

'The Belmont condos typically start at a minimum of three million.'

She shrugs, as though this is of no interest. She has large diamond studs in her ears, and more diamonds on her fingers. Or they could be zirconium; it's hard to tell these days.

Daniel's pen is poised. 'May I have your name?'

'You don't know who I am?' She gives an impatient little smile, one that suggests he must surely be joking.

'I'm sorry, I'm afraid I don't.'

'I'm Tansy Dimaano.'

This is said as though it means something. It registers nothing with Daniel, so he merely smiles. Tansy makes direct contact with her slanting, thick-lashed eyes. In that second he knows. He knows that she remembers him from the bar. And she knows that he remembers her too. Remembers the provocative tilt of her buttocks that he visualised during his humdrum thrusting into Maxine. A little jolt of electricity runs up his spine, and he feels warm blood surging up his neck and into his cheeks.

'You can look me up,' she says, her gaze boring into him. Her irises are a flecked golden-brown, like tortoiseshell. 'So, are you going to show me some condos?'

'When did you have in mind?'

'It has to be this evening.'

This evening Daniel and Maxine are having dinner with one of her lawyer colleagues and his wife at an upmarket restaurant in Rose Bay.

'Sure,' he says. 'I'll arrange some viewings and text you the details, but I'm afraid one of my colleagues will have to accompany—'

'No,' Tansy says, firmly. 'It has to be you.'

The first apartment is at the lower end of the price range that Cadogan typically markets. Showing Tansy Dimaano this is something of a test: to gauge her taste level, and the true limits of her bank account.

He has googled her, of course. A mere twenty seconds after she left the office. Her name appeared in the search box before he had got past 'Tansy D–', with over 20,000 hits. She owns a 'lifestyle brand' apparently; whatever that means. The image search results show her consuming some sort of health drink while striking a lot of barely clothed and provocative poses. He stopped on a lingerie shot, his mind making the automatic contrast between Tansy's gleaming curves and Maxine's rather boyish figure in her staid and practical flesh-coloured underwear. Then he quickly shut down the window.

'I don't think much of this one,' Tansy wrinkles her nose at the first property, a lower floor apartment in an older block. 'Too dark, too old-ladyish.'

She's dressed in a clinging black jersey dress, black tights (stockings actually, Daniel can't help noting as her hem rides up) and strappy five-inch black stilettos that bring her nearer his height. *Hooker shoes*, he thinks privately.

Tansy waves her hand impatiently around the living area, with its heavy, old-fashioned furniture and drapes. 'You could change all this, of course,' Daniel reminds her. 'An interior designer could work wonders.'

'Why would you bother, though?' she drawls. Her voice is pure Aussie, with a tinge of something more exotic.

'The bedroom's through there.' Daniel points.

'Aren't you coming in with me?' There's a suggestive tilt to her head.

'If you like.' He follows her.

She wrinkles her nose again, pushing her tongue out in a childlike expression of disgust. 'Eugh. I can't imagine fucking in that bed, can you?'

The tingle in his spine returns. 'Again, you wouldn't be getting the furniture—'

'Yeah, but the whole vibe is so depressing.'

Daniel's mobile vibrates with a call. He ignores it, knowing it will be Maxine. He hasn't explained where he is, just that he has been held up unexpectedly at work. Tansy clearly has excellent hearing, because she glances at the trouser pocket where his phone is. The glance strays over the rest of his groin.

'Your wife?'

'Girlfriend. But we… er, we live together.'

She raises an immaculately groomed eyebrow but makes no further comment, turning on her heel and stalking back to the front door. 'Okay, this one was shit. What's next?'

Next is a two-bedroom in a high-rise in Bathurst Street, modern and bright, with state-of-the-art appliances.

'It's a sub-penthouse,' Daniel explains. 'On at two million, seven hundred and fifty thousand.'

'It's better,' Tansy murmurs. 'But I don't know about the "sub" thing…' She catches his eye and touches her tongue to her top teeth. 'Unless it's in, like, a kinky way… you know: sub and dom.'

Daniel flushes. The phone buzzes in his pocket again.

'Oooh, that'll be wifey again. Wanting you.' The beam of the tortoiseshell eyes roams over his body.

'I told you; I'm not married.' Daniel is becoming annoyed. At least, that's the surface reaction. Below the surface something darker and more complex is brewing.

'Whatever.' Tansy flicks her hair. 'Let's see the bedroom. This is a little better,' she murmurs, as she runs her blood-coloured talons over the leather bed frame, then slides over the fitted wardrobes. 'But I'm not quite there yet. You'll know when I'm getting close.'

Daniel tries to ignore the coquettish smile, and the increased blood flow to his groin. 'Next, I've managed to find you something at the Belmont. Something rather special.'

'Good boy,' she purrs.

The final apartment is a full penthouse, at the top of what is currently Sydney's tallest residential tower. Floor-to-ceiling windows give spectacular views over Circular Quay, and the twilight sky is emblazoned with a light show of coral, indigo and gold.

Tansy whips out her phone and takes a selfie of herself against this glittering backdrop and then busies herself editing, filtering and hashtagging.

'Now *that's* a five-million-dollar view,' Daniel says, with a touch of smugness.

'Shall I tag you in?' she asks him.

'Tag me in?'

'On Insta.'

'I'm not on Instagram.' He gives what he knows must come across as a patronising smile. 'I'll leave that to the under thirty-fives.'

'You're over thirty-five? I wouldn't have guessed.' Tansy flicks an openly appreciative look over Daniel's head of thick, healthy hair and the defined pecs that are visible beneath his tailored shirt front. 'You work out?'

'I do.' He turns to avoid the appraising amber eyes, waving his hand around the interior space. 'There's oak parquet flooring throughout, and a marble kitchen which has Gaggenau appliances…'

'I don't cook.'

'The master suite has a large dressing room and his and hers bathrooms,' Daniel continues. 'And the floor-to-ceiling windows are continued through there too.'

'How much?'

'It's on at five million, nine hundred and ninety-five thousand.'

'Hmmm.' Tansy licks her lips. 'Let's see what the master bedroom's like.' She reaches out and grabs his wrist, her fingers curling round the bare skin below his shirt cuff. He feels a stirring of arousal that he's simultaneously ashamed of and powerless to resist.

'Now this is much better,' Tansy purrs, taking in the velvet-framed super-king bed, the huge chandelier and seductive lighting. 'Much more my speed.'

She spreads herself out on the pristine Egyptian cotton bedding with a little giggle, before reaching out and grabbing Daniel by the waistband of his trousers.

'Ms Dimaano—'

'Tansy.'

'Tansy, I can't—'

'Oh, but I think you can, *Mister* Halligan.' She drops her hand down to his unmistakeable erection. Before Daniel can respond, she's pulled him onto the bed beside her and is kissing him, her tongue a lithe little snake between his lips. The black dress is tugged off, leaving just the stilettos, stockings and some extremely skimpy black lace underwear. The only response he's capable of now is a low groan as he's manoeuvred on top of her.

It's not like it was in his daydream, though. That coupling was abandoned and animalistic and free. The production and deployment of a condom from Tansy's Chanel bag, brisk and business-like, makes his arousal level dwindle, as does the artful but oddly unsexy way she positions herself beneath him. As if she's posing for a camera again. The moans she emits at intervals seem contrived, and her facial expression when he glances down is one of faint boredom. It's perfunctory, and quickly over. Tansy checks her Instagram likes while Daniel attempts to make the bed look exactly as it did before they defiled it.

It's no big deal, Daniel tells himself as he heads home. It was just one of those random encounters that will never happen again. He's had a couple of one-night stands over the years while attending real estate conventions and they've never impacted on his life or his relationship with Maxine. As for Ms Tansy Dimaano – with any luck she'll buy the Belmont penthouse and he can hand off the paperwork to someone else in the office.

*

Maxine, it turns out, had been trying to call him to tell him she's rearranged their dinner with her colleague for another night, and that she's cooking supper for them at home. The door of the flat opens to the enticing smells of roast chicken and garlic bread. There are candles lit, jazz on the sound system. Maxine kisses him briskly but without recrimination and hands him a glass of wine. They chat about his plans for the land development deal over a delicious meal. He and Maxine have a pretty good life together, Daniel acknowledges. He's happy with her.

As she brings two cups of herbal tea into the bedroom and they settle down to do the crossword from that day's *Morning Herald*, he wonders what the hell he had been thinking to have sex with Tansy Dimaano. But that was exactly the problem: he hadn't been thinking at all.

CHAPTER THIRTEEN

DANIEL

'What we're offering at Horizon Lakes Village is not just a brand-new home. It's a whole new lifestyle, perfect for the active retiree. You'll be able to enjoy the superbly maintained one-hundred-acre grounds with the full-size Olympic pool, the barbecue area and walking track, without the hassle of ever having to mow the lawn. There's even a boating dock, for those of you who fancy a spot of fishing or a cruise on the water.'

Daniel pauses a second and looks around the conference room he has hired at a four-star hotel in the centre of the central business district. A rough count suggests about sixty heads in the audience, many of them with grey hair. Not a bad turnout. He sent out email invitations to the wealthiest clientele, whose details he had discreetly lifted from the Cadogan database, and took out a full-page ad in *Luxury Lifestyle* magazine. Now, several months later, the purchase of the Kellys' land has been completed, using $500,000 of his inheritance and a bank loan for the remaining $300,000 – he bargained hard over the price.

'In addition to being able to access the inland waterways that link the mountains and the sea' – an evocative slide of tropical rainforest appears on the screen behind him – 'you're no more than ten minutes from golden sandy beaches. A village bus will be available several times a day to drive you to the local shops and medical centre. Now, I know that for many of you, security is an important consideration in your later years, and at Horizon Lakes we'll be installing a 24-hour monitoring system, and on-site management will include overnight patrols, ensuring you can feel totally safe at any time of day.

'As for the homes themselves, you'll have a choice of two- and three-bedroom floorplans, all constructed and finished to the highest standard, with central air-conditioning in all units. The off-plan prices we're offering upfront make these a fantastic investment, but for those of you who are not yet ready to take this step in life, and let's face it, some of you aren't quite there yet…' – he looks round the room and grins at some of the younger audience members – '…Horizon Lakes Village represents a fantastic capital investment. So, please, stay and enjoy a glass of champagne, and I'll be sure to make the time to talk to everyone who's interested in this unique investment opportunity. Thank you all very much for coming.'

There's a polite ripple of applause. Daniel steps down from the podium as the lights go up and the servers start circulating with trays of sparkling wine and smoked salmon In one corner, Karen Fielding – a colleague from Cadogan – is manning a small table with a list of names, a laptop and a credit card reader. He's paid her $300 to help him out for the evening, taking names and banking details, and for those who are interested in purchasing a home, an initial holding deposit of $5,000.

'How did it go?' Maxine asks, when he finally returns home two hours later.

'Pretty well, I think,' he tells her with a satisfied smile. 'Plenty of people interested, both in the homes and in the investment side. More will come through once they've had a chance to think about it. Several of the people I talked to said they were going to give their friends the heads-up about the opportunity to get in on the ground floor.'

'Robbing a load of old folk of their hard-earned pension funds,' says Maxine, as she applies face cream, and Daniel can tell from her expression that she's not entirely joking.

'Something like that.'

In the office the next morning, Karen is showing Angelina pictures of the handbag she plans to buy with the proceeds of her evening's work for Daniel's newly named Roseland Investments. A forty-something single mother, with heavily bleached hair and an open and agreeable manner, she gets few opportunities to treat herself.

'Oh, wow, that's awesome,' Angelina says, encouragingly. 'Daniel, if you need anyone else to moonlight for you, I'm game too.'

'I'll bear that in mind.'

'Oh, and that client of yours phoned. Tansy Dimaano.'

Daniel's heart lurches in his chest. 'What did she want?' Having heard nothing more from Tansy for nearly a month, he assumed she had satisfied her property-buying lust elsewhere.

'She wants to see that three-bed on Macquarie Street. In the Astor building.'

'Can't Dean or Kris do it? Or Margot?' Margot Jeffers was the part-time agent who conducted weekend viewings when they were busy.

Angelina shakes her head. 'Nope, 'fraid not. She was insistent that it had to be you.'

Karen laughs. 'Yet another female client going all gooey over your movie-star looks, Danno.'

Daniel sighs. 'I guess I'll have to try and sort something out. Do we have an email address for her?' Email feels less personal, easier to hide behind.

'Nope. She wants you to call her back. The number's on your desk.'

He decides on texting rather than phoning.

Sorry, can't do viewing at the Astor today. Can arrange for someone else to meet you there if you're still interested in the property.

For eight minutes he pretends to be working, but his heart is pounding and he throws frequent looks in the direction of his phone screen. Eventually a reply arrives.

If ur too busy maybe I could ask yr girlfriend to stand in for you. She works at Lyle Fortis doesn't she

So, through some fairly basic online stalking – probably an old Facebook account that he hasn't used in years – Tansy has managed to work out Maxine's identity and where she works. The threat is very thinly veiled. Show the apartment or I'll tell your girlfriend what we did. He picks up his phone to type a reply.

I'll meet you at the Astor at 3 pm.

'I must admit, I'm surprised you wanted to see this place. I wouldn't have thought it was your style.'

Daniel meets Tansy outside the front of the historic Art Deco apartment building. She's wearing huge sunglasses, a gingham off-the-shoulder playsuit and high-heeled blue sandals.

'Why not?'

Because you're too much of an airhead to appreciate the historical value of the original lead-paned windows and mahogany flooring.

'I thought modern was more your thing. This was built in 1923. The rooms aren't particularly big.'

'As long as the bedroom's big enough, hey?' She pushes her sunglasses down her nose and scorches him with her flecked brown eyes. Despite himself, Daniel feels a faint stirring of excitement.

This time she doesn't wait until they're in the apartment itself, grabbing him in the lift and thrusting a hand down the front of his trousers, while flicking her tongue between his teeth. Nor does she feign interest in looking round the apartment, merely dragging him into the master bedroom, pushing him onto his back and mounting him.

The sex is no more satisfying than it was the first time. Unlike her smouldering, smiling online presence, the flesh and blood Tansy Dimaano is oddly lacking in warmth. During the ten minutes that they are lying in some stranger's bed at the Astor, he tries to draw her out on the subject of her business while she poses and adjusts her make-up in her phone's camera screen. She's not exactly forthcoming.

'I have a branded health drink. Called Hiraya. It's all there online.'

'And you can make decent money from this?'

'I make a shit ton of money.'

'By selling into retailers? Are you in supermarkets?'

'You can get it all over the place.' She appears to lose interest, fishing in her blue Birkin bag for a lipstick and painting her lips the colour of crushed cherries. He tries to persist with small talk, but now that she's been physically satisfied, she retreats behind a chilly demeanour. She displays no sense of humour, and no interest in anything other than herself.

Herself, and messing with Daniel's peace of mind, at least. When he returns to the office, there's a written notification from Tansy's attorney, making a full asking price offer for the Belmont penthouse. As he is obliged to, he passes on the offer to his delighted client, who accepts immediately. Then he texts Tansy.

Congratulations. You're now the owner of Apartment 1701, The Belmont.

She replies thirty minutes later.

Okay, cool.

Anger stirs inside him.

So why did you drag me over to the Astor to show you an apartment you had no intention of buying?

U didn't have to fuck me. Don't pretend u didn't enjoy it.

That's not the point, he starts texting, but deletes it. The more he shows he's affected by her behaviour, the worse it will be. She has a purchase underway now. So there'll be no more contact with Tansy Dimaano.

CHAPTER FOURTEEN

DANIEL

'Horizon Lakes sounds like a nice little earner, Danny. Or not so little.'

It's October, and Daniel is on the phone to his brother.

'The money's pouring in, if that's what you mean. We've sold twenty-three home sites, at an average of a million and a half each, plus the investment cash has netted another ten million or so.'

'But you have to pay them back. With interest.' There's a faint note of concern in Ben's voice. 'They're expecting big returns, presumably?'

'Sure,' says Dan, smoothly. 'Some of them next month, some next spring. But by then construction will be complete, and we'll have netted the final payments on the home purchases. There's still going to be a huge profit, even allowing for the fifteen per cent uplift on investment I'm going to have to repay.'

'So the architects and surveyors have done their bit?'

'The diggers are already up there, mate. The plans are drawn up and ready to go, the site prep and ground-breaking started about a week ago. Just waiting for the site layout survey report before we start flinging up walls.'

'Well.' Ben gives a little laugh. 'Sounds like it's all going to plan. I guess all I can say is good luck.'

He doesn't need luck, Daniel thinks as he turns back to his laptop and starts working out yet another costs spreadsheet. He's got this all worked out.

He now has a makeshift office in the spare room of Maxine's apartment, having left Cadogan to work for himself full time. And one of the best things about leaving Cadogan is that Tansy Dimaano no longer has his phone number. The one she used to contact him was for a dedicated work mobile supplied by his employers, but now he has a new phone with, more importantly, a new number.

He was summoned once, just before he resigned from Cadogan, to her newly purchased penthouse. Again, they had perfunctory, performative coitus, after which she had rapidly become distant.

'Why are you doing this?' he asked her. 'I don't get it.'

'What do you mean?' she asked sharply, as she adjusted the streaks of contour under her perfect cheekbones. 'Doing what?'

'Pursuing an affair that offers you so little. Using the threat of disclosure to persuade me to have sex with you… There must be hundreds of single men out there who would be happy to sleep with you.'

'I know,' she said, with a self-satisfied smirk. 'There are.'

'So you're seeing other people.'

'Of course.'

'So why me? Is it the forbidden fruit thing?'

She shrugged and turned her back to show that she was losing interest in the conversation. 'You've got a hot body. And the right sort of look.'

'The right sort of look for what?'

But she remained inscrutable, steely, and refused to be drawn further. After that encounter he had changed his number and Tansy had left Sydney for Bali and Kuala Lumpur, if her Instagram feed was to be believed. Daniel had been relieved that the whole tawdry business was done with.

The intercom buzzes. It's Des, the concierge and doorman of their building.

'There's someone here who wants to see you. I told her I never let people up to the apartment without checking with the resident first.'

Her. Surely not.

Daniel takes the lift down to the lobby but Des is there on his own. He points to the doors that lead to the street. Outside on the kerb, engine idling, is a gun-metal grey Bentley with blacked-out windows. The rear window slides down.

'Get in,' says Tansy, without smiling.

'And if I don't?'

'We could always go up to your apartment. Or is it Maxine Newcombe's apartment?

Daniel opens the door and slides into the Bentley next to Tansy. 'How did you find me?' he demands.

'It's easy enough if you have the right contacts…' She remains unmoved, looking down at her phone screen. 'Anyway, what am I supposed to do if you don't give me your phone number?'

'And why would I do that? You're no longer looking for an apartment, and I no longer work in real estate sales. Well, not as an employee, anyway.'

She gives him a sidelong glance and adjusts the plunging neckline of her top so that he gets a good view of her perky breasts.

'You know why, Daniel.'

But he doesn't know why, not really. Doesn't understand why she is so intent on pursuing a superficial attraction with someone she has nothing in common with. Is there pleasure in the manipulation? Maxine would probably say that she had a narcissistic personality disorder.

The car pulls up outside the Belmont building and the driver leaps out to open Tansy's door. She totters into the lobby on six-inch Louboutin heels, throwing Daniel a glance over her shoulder. 'Aren't you coming?'

'What happens if I don't?'

'I'm sure Wifey won't be very pleased.'

'She's not my fucking wife,' he corrects her yet again, but Tansy is already stepping through the open doors of the elevator.

This time he's so angry and on edge that even with a semi-naked Tansy twining herself around him, he fails to become aroused.

'Jesus,' she says, sourly. 'I thought you were at least good for a bit of playtime.'

'I've got a hell of a lot on my plate at the moment… Give me a couple of minutes, please.' Daniel untangles himself and walks into the living room, with its spectacular views. Tansy has filled it with ugly but expensive furniture in gilt and marble and crushed velvet. A marble table at the centre of the room has a huge planter filled with creamy white orchids. Why, he asks himself, has he allowed himself to get sucked into this again? But he knows the answer. It's because he can't afford to have Maxine finding out about the affair. He still needs Maxine's help and support to get his business off the ground.

He finds a drinks trolley loaded with bottles of spirits and pours himself a triple whisky, downing it in one go. The liquid burns through his body, warming him from the inside. He feels himself relax a little. Returning to the bedroom, he services Tansy in the way that she expects him to.

'That's better,' she murmurs, before pulling away from him and reaching, as always, for her phone.

'You never ask me about myself,' Daniel says, leaning back on the huge mound of pillows. 'You've not even asked me what I'm doing now I've left Cadogan.'

'I could find out about it if I wanted to.'

Ah, yes, the mysterious 'contacts'.

'How about your business then? Tell me about Hiraya. You never did say which retailers stock it.'

'I don't use retailers,' she says, flatly.

'How do you sell it then?'

'Through my Wellness Angels.'

'Your Angels?'

'My sales representatives. I've got around thirty thousand of them, worldwide.'

Daniel widens his eyes at this figure. 'That many? Are they salaried employees?'

'Of course not. They buy the product and if they sell it on to other people, they make a commission.'

'And if they don't?'

She gives a 'what do I care?' shrug before picking up a styling wand from her bedside table and tweaking the waves in her hair.

'So… it's a pyramid scheme.' He's out of bed now, pulling on his boxers and jeans.

'It's just direct sales, that's all. Perfectly above board, loads of companies sell that way. We're just selling a product, using independent consultants.'

Before he can stop her, she has reached into his jeans pocket for his mobile and used it to text his number to her own phone.

'So I can get in touch without having to drive over to your place.'

'Tansy, seriously, you don't need to get in touch.'

'Why would you say that?' She gives the pout of a disgruntled toddler.

'Because I'm not going to see you again.' He tugs his polo shirt over his head, fumbles for his shoes. 'This needs to end. In fact, it has ended, as far as I'm concerned.'

'We'll see.'

As she hands his phone back, it starts ringing. An unrecognised number with a Gold Coast area code. He thinks about rejecting the call, then remembers that the site surveyors were due to phone him with an initial report.

The man on the other end of the line introduces himself as Tucker Harvey.

'Listen… the Horizon Lakes Village development. I'm afraid we've got a massive problem.'

CHAPTER FIFTEEN

DANIEL

'You're going to have to halt construction.'

Daniel is back in Tweed Heads, having taken the earliest flight he could the following morning. He's sitting on the other side of Tucker Harvey's desk; Harvey is a brawny, thickset man with a buzz cut and florid face.

'How long for?'

'Indefinitely.'

A cold finger of fear traces its way down Daniel's spine. 'Surely not. Surely this can be fixed somehow?'

Harvey places his broad hands palms down on the desk, splaying his sausage-like fingers.

'You've got traces of PFOA in the soil and the groundwater. It's a fire-retardant chemical imported from the States and used by a lot of our Aussie firefighting services. There's been growing evidence for the past fifteen years or so that if it gets into drinking water or the food chain, it's associated with the incidence of certain cancers and autoimmune disorders, pregnancy problems, that kind of thing.'

Daniel drops his head into his hands and groans.

'It's commonly found near airports, where there's ongoing use of fire retardants. And you're right by the site of the old Coolangatta airport.'

'But contaminated land and water can be decontaminated, right? It's possible?'

'Up to a point. You'd have to get the environmental agencies involved, and on acreage that size it could be very, very expensive to fix. We're talking millions.'

'And how long before construction could go ahead?'

Harvey shrugs. 'Hard to say without doing more survey work and getting some boffins involved. I reckon you're looking at two years, maybe more.'

'Jesus.' Daniel exhales hard. The office is air-conditioned, but he can feel sweat trickling down his back.

'Let me get you a drink of water.' Harvey hauls himself out of his chair, pressing a huge paw on Daniel's shoulder as he passes. 'Look, I'm sorry, mate. It's a bloody nightmare – there's no point trying to dress it up as anything else.'

'Can I ask you something else,' says Daniel in a low voice, as he's handed a plastic cup of water.

'Shoot.'

'Did the Kellys know about this?'

'Now, *that* I can't speculate on—'

'Please.'

'I reckon they might've, yes.'

'What I don't understand,' Maxine says when Daniel returns to Sydney, looking tense and whey-faced, 'is why you didn't get this guy to do the environmental survey *before* you completed the purchase of the lot.'

She has been sympathetic, bringing Daniel cups of tea, running him a scented bath, but there's a slight edge to her voice. 'I mean, if I'd known that's what you were doing, I'd never have let you go through with it.'

'It was going to take too much time,' Daniel mutters. 'The Kellys were prepared to knock a hundred and fifty grand off the asking price provided I closed by the first of May.'

Maxine raises an eyebrow. 'And you didn't ask yourself why?'

He groans, walking over to the kitchen cabinet where they kept the liquor and pouring himself a whisky.

'That's not helpful, Max. What I need now is for you to get your lawyer's hat on and tell me what I should do.'

'Honestly? You really want to know?'

Daniel gulps the Scotch, the amber liquid scorching the back of his throat. 'Yes. Yes, I do.'

'Sell the land, pay back the investors and the purchasers. Wipe the slate clean and start over. Cut your losses.'

'Max, you know bloody well I can't do that.'

'Why not?'

'I won't be able to sell the land, for a start. Not now that the contamination is out in the open.'

'Someone will take it off your hands. It could be used for something non-residential. Or there might be an organisation out there big enough and rich enough to spend time and money fixing the problem.'

'Yes, but they're not going to pay eight hundred thousand for it, are they? It's now worth a fraction of that. I owe three hundred thousand dollars to the bank, and I can't refund all the investors and homebuyers because I've already ploughed a load of their money into upfront costs: building materials, construction labour.' He rakes his hand through his hair. 'So what do I do, Max?'

'You could sue the Kellys for misrepresentation and fraud.'

'But I'd have to prove that they knew about the contamination. What if I fail to prove it? Who knows, maybe they genuinely weren't aware. Then I'd owe the cost of litigation on top of everything else.'

'Go have that bath,' Maxine says, gently. She wraps her arms round his back and gives him a brief squeeze. 'We'll think of something. I'll ask someone at Lyle Fortis who specialises in land law. There may be something we can do.'

Alone in the bathroom, Daniel undresses and sinks into the scented bubbles, reaching for his phone to link a relaxing playlist to the Bluetooth speakers he persuaded Maxine to install.

There's a text on his phone, from an unknown sender.

Come over to my place tonight, I want u in my bed.

Tansy. In the shock of that day's events, he'd completely forgotten that she now had his mobile number. The very last thing he needs at this moment, with his new business sinking like a stone, is Tansy Dimaano. He taps in a hasty reply, before sinking back into the foam to the strains of Einaudi.

I won't be seeing you again. I'm blocking your number. D

'The problem you have,' Maxine's colleague, Warren Bishop, tells Daniel a few days later, 'is that Roseland Investments was founded with you as sole trader. In other words, you're unincorporated. If you'd created a limited company, that gives you certain protections in the event of your business failing.' He rearranges his pens on his desk. 'Provided, of course, you acted in good faith. As things stand, you're personally liable to repay your investors.'

Daniel looks across the desk, at the balding grey-suited man, with a backdrop of Sydney Harbour behind him.

'If you don't mind me saying, you've rushed this a bit. Normally the raising of capital would be a process that takes at least a year, and during that time you could have looked into incorporating the business. Why the hurry?'

'Because I couldn't wait to quit my job,' Daniel admits. 'And Roseland then became my only source of income. I had to get moving quickly.'

Bishop grimaces slightly. 'Well, I told Maxine I'd go through the paperwork and advise you. But aside from appealing to people's better natures and asking for more time to repay them, I'm not sure what can be done.'

'I have to repay the six-month maturities in a couple of weeks. Can I just take the money that's currently in the company account to do that?'

'You mean the money paid for the homes you haven't yet built?'

Daniel flushes slightly. 'Yes.'

'If you did that, you'd be paying existing investors with funds taken from newer investors. It could be seen as a Ponzi scheme. As such, it could be reported to the Australian Securities and Investments Commission. Who would have the authority to prosecute.' Bishop gives a thin smile. 'I couldn't in all conscience recommend that.'

'So what do I do?'

'Do you have a friend or family member with cash to spare who could step in and help you repay your investors? At least while you investigate getting the land decontaminated?'

Daniel shakes his head. 'I don't know anyone like that.'

After his meeting, Daniel wanders disconsolately around Circular Quay, delaying going home.

Maxine has been sympathetic up to a point, but can't hold back from thinly veiled recriminations. And now her expert colleague has failed to come up with anything other than 'find a rich friend'. He buys a lager at a quayside bar and sits outside, watching the ferries bustle back and forth to Manly, Taronga and Parramatta.

Eventually, after another two beers, he returns to the flat. Maxine has been trying to cheer him up by cooking his favourite meals, and he expects to smell supper cooking as he unlocks the front door, but there is nothing. It's almost eight o'clock. Normally she would have been home from work for at least an hour.

'Max?' he calls. 'Hun?'

She's sitting on the window seat, her knees drawn up to her chest, gazing out at the view. Her head doesn't turn in his direction, even as he approaches. 'What's going on?'

And then he sees, as she turns to face him, that she is furious. Silently, her hand shaking, she holds out her mobile.

It takes Daniel several seconds to register exactly what he's seeing. The image is dimly lit, and shot at an oblique angle. It's the bed he recognises first, the over-large, over-embellished frame made from pink crushed velvet. The bed in the master bedroom at the Belmont penthouse. Daniel is naked, on his back, his face clearly visible while Tansy straddles him, dressed in a complicated strappy piece of lingerie and six-inch heels. There must have been a hidden camera in or somewhere near the mirror on her vanity unit. It's such an obvious Tansy move, the only surprise is that he didn't think about the possibility before.

'How did you…? Where did this come from?'

'You're not denying it's you? Well, you can't really, can you? This arrived on my phone earlier today, from an unknown number.' She gives Daniel an icy glare. 'Unknown to me, anyway.'

'Look sweetheart, she's not… we're not—'

'You do recognise her then?'

He nods dumbly.

'So who is she? Where did you meet her?'

'I saw her at the Double Decker, the night we had a drink there.'

Maxine laughs bitterly. 'I thought she looked vaguely familiar. This is just unbelievable… I mean, you spotted her in a bar and what? Found out who she was so you could fuck her?'

'She was a client at Cadogan.'

'Oh, God, this gets better.' Maxine rolls her eyes. 'Of course she was. All those single women panting over Sydney's hottest real estate agent.'

'Well, she wasn't when we saw her in the bar. She became a client later.'

'Not just a client, clearly.'

'But Max, it's over.' Daniel approaches her, tries to wrap his arms around her, but she pushes him away. 'I swear to you… I don't know when this was taken, but it was months ago. She was… well, she was sort of stalking me.'

'Oh, yeah, of course she was. A gorgeous twenty-something woman is obsessed with you. Couldn't possibly have been the other way around.'

'But it wasn't, Max, you've got to believe me! She kept on demanding to see me, even though I made it clear I wasn't interested.'

Maxine snatches the phone back and holds the screen up to his face. 'Really making it clear to her, I'd say. Because that's the best way to do it, by screwing her.'

'I ended it. I'm not seeing her.' He closes his eyes and thinks about life without Maxine. Now, when he needs her support most, to help him unravel the mess his business life has become. He can't lose her. Not now.

'What's her name?'

He hesitates a second. 'Tansy. Tansy Dimaano.'

'Give me your phone.'

She takes his mobile and scrolls through the names in his Contacts. 'Go to Settings and look at the list of blocked contacts,' he urges her. 'I've blocked her number.'

After checking for herself, she drops the phone on the window seat, looking suddenly deflated. 'All right,' she says, quietly. 'So you promise it's over?'

'I swear it is,' he says, gripping her by her shoulders and turning her so that she's facing him. 'I swear on my life.'

CHAPTER SIXTEEN

DANIEL

The following week is taken up with further meetings, each feeling like an increasingly desperate grab at a straw.

Daniel sees a lawyer who is a specialist in environmental protection cases and charges fees to match. This woman, Nadya Melzer, uses a lot of very technical language and terms, and the only positive he can glean from her spiel is that apart from herself, Tucker Harvey, Maxine and her colleague, Warren Bishop, nobody yet knows about the problem at Horizon Lakes. The information is not yet in the public domain. If he can raise the requisite funds, then there is at least a small chance of remedying the problem.

Later that same day he has a meeting with a water systems engineer. Before this debacle he wasn't even aware that there was such a thing, but his sharp learning curve has taught him, among so many other lessons, that there is. The water engineer, a flashily handsome young Indian man called Ravi, is very upbeat.

'My advice to you is not to panic.' He smiles, showing immaculate white teeth. 'You're worried about contaminated water in the homes you're building, but PFOA and PFOS can be successfully removed from a water supply using a reverse osmosis system. We've supplied many, many such systems in residential commercial and industrial premises.'

Daniel smiles weakly. 'How much would that cost?'

'You can buy a residential filtration system for as little as two thousand dollars. But given the scale of the contamination on your land, I think you would need something a little more sophisticated. It would cost about eighteen thousand Australian dollars per unit. And, of course, there would be other benefits to the home owner. Cleaner, better-tasting water.'

Daniel performs the mental calculation. That would require a further half million dollars as an upfront expense. That was doable, surely? He could easily tweak the prices of the unsold units to absorb it. And if the units he was selling had guaranteed filtered, uncontaminated and pleasant-tasting water, then as Ravi just said, that could be a positive selling point. Active retirees were always interested in improving their health.

He thanks Ravi, assures him he will be in touch soon to discuss a quote, and returns home in a better frame of mind. Better, in fact, than he has experienced since that last fateful trip to the Gold Coast. His back straightens and his head lifts as he walks back along Park Street. Maybe, just maybe, he's not a total failure as a businessman. Maybe there's a chance of turning this whole thing around.

He texts Maxine and tells her he will pick up groceries and prepare supper for them. He's not as accomplished a cook as she is, but his expertise extends to grilled meat or fish cooked on the barbecue, and a salad.

She texts him back straightaway.

Thanks, darl. Back at 7.15 x

It's only when he gets back to the flat that he realises they are out of wine. No matter, he can use a delivery app to get the local grocery store to deliver some to the building. He and Max do it all the time. At 6.30, with the steaks brushed with oil ready to grill, and the salad chopped, the front doorbell rings.

'Delivery,' says a muffled voice from the other side of the door.

'Great, we'll be—'

His voice tails off as he wrenches it open. Tansy stands there, wearing a sheer organza trench coat and patent over-the-knee boots.

She holds out the brown paper bag containing the wine. 'I told the concierge I'd bring it up,' she says, with a pout. 'Funny thing – I didn't have any trouble persuading him I was invited to your party.'

'I'm not having a party.' The blood is ringing in Daniel's ears, making him stagger back slightly. This loss of balance allows Tansy to push past him and enter the apartment. 'And you can't be here.'

He holds out a hand to try and bar her way, but she's already in the living room.

'Hmmm…' She looks around her. 'Not a patch on my place, is it?'

'Fuck's sake, Tansy, I want you to leave.'

She waggles the bag containing the wine at him. 'What about this?'

'Give it to me.' He tries to snatch it, but she's too quick and whips it behind her back.

'Tell you what, I'll do you a deal. We have one glass of this together, and then I leave, okay?'

Daniel glances at the clock. Maxine is not due home for twenty-five minutes, but he's still reluctant. 'No,' he says, firmly. 'I'm not giving you a drink.'

'Suit yourself.' Tansy flicks her lustrous hair over her shoulder and gives the ghost of a smile. He marvels both at how beautiful she is and how that external beauty is wasted on a vapid, narcissistic interior. She sits herself down on the sofa and curls up her legs, exposing an expanse of naked golden thigh. The gauzy coat falls open, revealing that she's wearing nothing underneath except lingerie made of rose-gold satin.

'Okay, then.' Daniel sighs, reaching for one wine glass and a corkscrew. 'Five minutes.'

He pours a third of a glass of the lukewarm Chardonnay and hands it to her.

'You've got to have some too, or the deal's off.'

He pours himself some wine and stands a safe distance away, behind the kitchen island.

Tansy pats the sofa next to her. 'Come. Sit.'

He does so reluctantly, knowing that to refuse will only delay things further.

'So, how've you been? You left Cadogan to start your own property business, right? How's it going?'

Daniel is taken aback by the question. It's the first time she's ever showed any interest in his existence outside that of her reluctant gigolo. 'It's good. Going fine. A few hiccups along the way, but nothing that can't be sorted out.'

'And this is Queensland, yeah?'

'Yup. Well, just this side of the Queensland border, so officially in New South Wales. Just outside Tweed Heads.'

'Cool.'

She smiles a catlike smile and, quick as a knife, before Daniel can put down his wine glass, she's whipped off the trench coat and straddled his lap. Wine from his glass slops onto the sofa and trickles onto the floor.

'Tansy! Fuck's sake!'

Her hands are unbuttoning his shirt and she rocks her hips to and fro, thrusting her spectacular cleavage in his face. Despite himself, despite his anger, he feels himself becoming aroused. He tries to shift his weight to tip her off him but she's strong, and her naked thighs subject him to a python grip.

And then he hears it. The scrape of the front door key in the lock. Maxine.

*

Forty minutes later, Daniel finds himself on Ithaca Road holding his laptop bag and suitcase of hastily packed clothes.

He had tried, of course he tried, to explain, but he knew it was futile. Maxine saw a half-naked Tansy on his lap, two recently emptied glasses of wine, his shirt unbuttoned to his crotch. The story about Tansy happening to bring up a bottle of wine that he had ordered to be delivered sounded ludicrous, even though it happened to be true.

The only flicker of schadenfreude he had experienced was when Maxine marched across the room and grabbed Tansy by the back of her head, pulling out a weft of hair extensions. The shrill squeal and her look of shock was almost worth the end of a three-year relationship and being made homeless. Almost.

Maxine ejected Tansy from the flat first, but she was waiting outside in her Bentley when Daniel eventually left with his belongings.

'Come back to mine,' she said, through the car window. 'You can move in.'

'Fuck off, Tansy,' he replied, through gritted teeth. 'That's the last thing I would ever do.'

Unfazed and unemotional as ever, she just shrugged. 'Suit yourself. The offer's there if you change your mind.' The Bentley purred away from the kerb.

Instead, Daniel checks into the nearest three-star hotel. He will find a serviced apartment in the morning, he decides, after knocking back the scotch in the minibar. There's plenty of cash in his account, after all; there's probably some way to write it off as a legitimate business cost. He leans back on the bed and switches on the football, more to have some sound to distract himself than because he wants to watch it. He texts Maxine.

I can't tell you how sorry I am. I know you don't want to hear it, but honest to God she just turned up and jumped on me. None of it was my idea. Think about it: why would I have asked her round when I knew you were on your way home? D xxx

When he falls asleep three hours later, there is still no reply.

CHAPTER SEVENTEEN

DANIEL

Two days later, Daniel moves into a characterless serviced suite in a concrete high-rise in North Bondi.

His texts and calls to Maxine go unanswered, although eventually she sends a brief email granting him a time slot to come and collect the rest of his belongings; a time when she will not be there. Her hurt and anger seep through the stiff, formal tone of the email, leaving Daniel feeling horribly guilty. But the guilt does not stem from his betrayal of Maxine: he feels guilty because he doesn't love her, any more than he loves Tansy. He has never really loved her. Yes, he is extremely fond of her, and their life together was orderly, comfortable. But he knows he would have ended up leaving her eventually, one way or another. He just would have preferred it not to have happened like this.

He looks through Tansy's Instagram account occasionally when he is bored, marvelling as ever at the artful manipulation of her posts, at her instinct for selling, even if the product is herself. Somewhat to his surprise, she makes no attempt to contact him. Perhaps successfully splitting him from Maxine was all she wanted. Perhaps she's done with him now. Another surprise is finding that he notices this absence. The abrupt silence and apparent lack of interest makes him uneasy.

After further meetings at Eauzone, the water engineering company where he met Ravi, Daniel arranges for the appropriate filtration systems to be fitted at each of his properties, and hands over a substantial cheque. This is just a budget over-run, he tells himself. It happens all the time in property development. No big deal. He begins negotiations with a waste management conglomerate for a more detailed analysis of the soil at the Horizon Lakes site, and for them to come up with a proposal for an effective but affordable programme of soil remediation.

By the end of November he has repaid his original investors, emptying Roseland's coffers further. Since he now needs to sell the remaining building plots as a matter of urgency, he decides to target a fresh market. He decides on Canberra which, as a well-to-do inland city, has an endless supply of retirees longing to move to the coast. The other reason for choosing Canberra is that Cadogan International has a branch there, and he knows that his former colleague, Karen, has a friend who works in the office. After calling round to her house with a bouquet of flowers and a couple of hundred dollar bills, he receives in return an emailed copy of the Canberra branch's entire client database.

A week later, Daniel travels to a dry and dusty Canberra, where a golf club ballroom has been booked as an event space. His presentation goes well, with the inclusion of the latest water filtration technology in his homes attracting rather than discouraging business, just as Ravi had predicted. The evening ends with him garnering just enough sales to balance the books, assuming the buyers all go ahead and commit their money.

He celebrates by buying a drink for one of the hotel's event organisers in the bar, a pretty but uninteresting girl called Debra. The idea of inviting her up to his room has just crossed his mind when he catches sight of a familiar logo on the tote bag she's put on the floor next to her handbag.

Hiraya Nutrition

'You drink this stuff?' he asks her, pointing at the bag.

'Yeah. I love it,' she says, earnestly. 'Actually, I sell it. As a part-time thing.'

'So you're one of the "Wellness Angels"?' He makes air quotes.

'I am,' she smiles proudly.

'And… d'you mind me asking… have you made any money from it?'

Her rosy cheeks turn slightly more pink. 'Not yet, but I will, once I sell a bit more of the product. I'm getting there.'

'You have to buy the product up front yourself?'

'That's right.' She twirls the stem of her glass self-consciously. 'You invest money of your own, and you make a bonus when you get other people to become Angels, and when those people recruit and so on.'

'Sort of in a pyramid.'

Debra looks defensive. 'Yeah, but this stuff is awesome. Tansy Dimaano suffered from lupus and she cured herself.'

Now Daniel becomes self-conscious as he says, 'Actually, I know her.'

Debra's eyes widen, her mouth falls open. 'You've met her? Tansy? Oh, my God, I think she's *amazing*.' She draws out the middle syllable. 'What was she like?'

Daniel stands up and hands his credit card to the barman. 'Honestly, you don't want to know.'

As Daniel lands at Kingsford Smith airport the following morning, still congratulating himself on his financial high-wire act, he switches on his mobile to forty-seven missed calls. There's also an alert with a link to a breaking news story in *The Australian*.

Scandal of toxic land for planned retirement homes

Locals and retirees are alarmed at the plan by Sydney company Roseland Investments to build on a brown land site known to be contaminated with toxic firefighting chemicals. Research conducted as early as 2003 shows the substances PFOS and PFOA to be potentially extremely harmful to humans, yet Roseland – a one-man operation run by former real estate salesman and UK national Daniel Halligan – sold homes on the proposed Horizon Lakes development without due diligence or consultation with the relevant agencies. Attempts to reach Halligan for comment have so far been unsuccessful.

His phone rings in his hand while he is still reading, and carries on ringing constantly during his taxi ride back to the Bondi apartment. There are further alerts too, as the story is picked up by the *Melbourne Age*, the *Sydney Herald* and the *Brisbane Times*. Who has told them about it? Daniel wonders, as he pays the cab driver with shaking hands. Who would want to do this?

Someone he has aggrieved and slighted. Someone with a legitimate reason to punish him.

Once in the apartment, he slings his suitcase into the bedroom without opening it, and dials Maxine's number. This time she picks up.

'Did you do this?' His voice is barely a whisper. 'Did you go to the press about the land contamination?'

'No,' she says, coldly. 'I might be bloody angry with you, but I'd never stoop to doing something so shitty. I'm better than that, and you know it.'

'What the fuck do I do now?' he demands, though he's really addressing the universe in general rather than Maxine herself. 'The existing buyers are all going to pull out because now property values there will have crashed. And I'll never find new ones. I can't even sell the land, not until the soil and water clean-up is finished. And how the fuck am I going to pay for that now?'

'I don't know,' says Maxine, flatly. 'Karma sure is a bitch.'

And she hangs up.

By the end of the following week, every single one of the Horizon Lakes purchases has fallen through. Because Roseland failed to disclose the problem with the soil and the water supply upfront, the buyers' lawyers have no problem in getting their clients' contracts voided and demanding the return of their deposits. The investors are also getting nervous, sending threatening or litigious emails. The bank that mortgaged the land is also making noises about calling in the loan. It's a complete mess, and one that can only be solved with ready cash.

Daniel tries switching off his phone for a while, but that only leads to strangers showing up at the apartment day and night, pressing on the intercom bell or – worse – hammering on his door. After a succession of nights without sleep, he does the only thing he can think of.

He phones Tansy.

CHAPTER EIGHTEEN

DANIEL

'Well, this is interesting.'

Tansy is sitting on the terrace of her penthouse apartment, her bare legs emerging from a silk negligee the colour of sunflower petals. Her hair stylist, Sebastian, is removing rollers from her dark hair and teasing out the curls so that they fall down her back in a glossy mane. Daniel is about to speak, but she holds up a hand while her make-up is touched up by a sullen, heavy-browed woman who is introduced as Ljubica. Then Sebastian takes a handful of photos of Tansy drinking a tall glass of Hiraya Green through a straw.

Once the images are examined and pronounced satisfactory, she pushes the glass away with a shudder. 'Yuk! Disgusting stuff… you can post those now. With a caption saying, "Good morning!" – that sort of thing. Usual hashtags.'

Sebastian sashays back inside while a stony-faced Ljubica finishes clearing away her make-up kit and retreats.

'So,' says Tansy, turning back to face Daniel, and holding the flame of her Cartier lighter to the tip of a cigarette. 'You want me to lend you some money. Two million. That's a fuck of a lot of cash, Daniel.'

'I'm aware of that.'

'I mean, you're gorgeous, but I'm not sure you're *that* gorgeous. What's in it for me?'

'You'd get the money back, with interest. Just think of it as a business deal.'

Tansy pouts, pushing the Hiraya shake even further away and gripping the cigarette between her lips while she pours herself a cup of black coffee. 'I don't really need that kind of deal. I have enough investments already.'

'Tansy, please.' Daniel could not despise himself more for begging from this woman. For needing to beg. 'I'm completely on my own here. Normally I would be able to go to Maxine for help.'

Tansy puffs smoke from the corner of her mouth, trying to avoid her newly coiffed hair. 'She doesn't look like she has that kind of money.'

'Maybe not, but she could probably help me in some way. But I can't ask her now. You've put paid to that. Thanks to your antics, she doesn't want anything to do with me.'

'I'll tell you what.' She taps off ash with an elegant finger, narrows her amber eyes slightly. 'I'll give it to you if you marry me.'

Daniel feels a patch of cold sweat collecting at the base of his spine. *Not that. Anything but that.* 'No,' he says, heavily. 'I don't ever want to get married. I don't believe in it. Any anyway, why would *you* want to? You don't love me.' He gestures around at the extravagant apartment. 'And you certainly don't need a husband.'

She gives a little shrug. 'My commercial sponsorships are drying up. That tends to happen if you don't have anything new to bring in terms of content. But an engagement, a wedding, a pregnancy… that would generate loads of online interest. Followers of my story can't get enough of that sort of thing.'

'Your story. You mean you having lupus, and curing yourself?'

'My wellness journey, yes,' she says, impatiently, swirling a fuchsia nail around the rim of her coffee cup. 'I'm better now, obviously. No symptoms for ages. So… I need to do something new.'

'And you'd rescue me financially… but only if I married you.'

She nods.

'Does it have to be marriage? How about if we just start dating?' Daniel asks, desperately. The sweat patch is spreading over the back of his shirt. 'Wouldn't that get people interested? I could move in with you.'

How bad could it be? he asks himself, already knowing the answer to his own question. He still can't believe he's reduced to standing here pleading with this girl, someone he once spotted across a crowded bar in a group of entitled millennials. Someone he barely knows.

'It's not the same. It wouldn't generate nearly as much interest.' Tansy runs her gaze in a line from his groin to his face and back again. 'I'll tell you what, because we've had some fun times together, I'm going to try and help you. Come back here this afternoon, about four o'clock. There's someone I want you to meet.'

'This is Les Pella.'

Daniel has returned to the Belmont building that afternoon. What choice does he have? Every time he switches on his mobile, he's bombarded with demands for financial reimbursement. But whoever he was expecting to meet, it certainly wasn't this man. He's barely more than five feet tall but has the build of a boxer. The skin on his face is badly disfigured with the pock marks of severe acne, and the hair scraped back from his forehead is dyed blue-black.

Daniel extends his hand. The grip he meets in return is vigorous to the point of pain. *Take me seriously,* this handshake says, *I'm not someone to be underestimated.* 'Nice to meet you, Dan.'

'Daniel.'

The correction is ignored. 'I'm one of Ms Dimaano's advisers.' His voice is low, gravelly, at odds with his short stature.

'So you're a lawyer?'

This question is met with a slight head tilt. 'I understand you're having some legal difficulties of your own? Care to tell me about it?'

The uniformed housekeeper appears and ushers them to the dining table, where a tray of tea and sandwiches has been laid out. Tansy disappears to the bedroom to discuss outfits for another in her relentless round of photo shoots.

Daniel sets out his situation as concisely as he can, starting with his buying the plot of land in Tweed Heads.

'From what I can see, you're looking at this arse about face,' Pella says. 'You're being accused of misrepresentation in selling these homes, or at the least failing to do your due diligence. But what about these people who sold it to you?'

'The Kelly family.'

Pella grins, revealing a diamond stud in one of his canines 'Appropriate that they have the same surname as Australia's most notorious gangster, eh? What about *their* misrepresentation? You bought the land from them in good faith, and for a top price, compared to what it's worth now. Seems to me' – he picks up a china tea cup in one of his large paws and slurps his tea noisily – 'they owe you a refund on your purchase. A partial refund, at the very least.'

Daniel breaks off a piece of ginger biscuit and examines it, before putting it back on the plate. He has no appetite. 'Do you think I should be taking them to court?'

Pella shrugs. 'Or we could just speak to them.'

Tansy reappears at Daniel's elbow. 'I was thinking it would be fun to go up to Goldie. I haven't been up there for ages. We could take a PJ.'

Daniel frowns.

'Private jet.' Tansy eye-rolls at his ignorance. 'You could show me the resort.'

'You mean Horizon Lakes? There's not much to see at the moment, and at this rate there's not likely ever to be.'

Tansy gives one of her forced, humourless laughs. Over her shoulder Daniel can see that the housekeeper is lifting a set of Louis Vuitton luggage out of a cupboard. 'Don't be such a negative Nancy. We're all going to fly up there, and we're going to sort things. Right, Les?'

'That's right,' says Pella, with an expression that Daniel can't quite decipher. 'We're going to fix your little Kelly problem.'

CHAPTER NINETEEN

DANIEL

In the end, 'we' turns out to be no less than seven people on the private jet flying up to Coolangatta.

In addition to Daniel and Tansy there are the apparently indispensable Sebastian and Ljubica ('I need them to help me post content while I'm up there'), Les Pella and two other men whose role can't be anything other than to play the heavy. They dress like nightclub bouncers and act like hired muscle, chewing gum in inscrutable silence at the back of the plane.

As soon as they have boarded, Tansy sets about posting smiling selfies aimed to show off the cream leather interior and gold-plated fittings, the crystal glasses and chilled champagne waiting in an ice bucket. Tansy pours a glass each for herself and Daniel, then grabs him by the wrist and leads him to the far end of the plane, where there's a second cabin with a small, neat double bed.

'These curtains draw across,' she shows him. Her expression, as ever, is hard to read. 'To give us some privacy.' She pushes her lips into a pout and runs her hand up Daniel's inner thigh, although the gesture is mechanical rather than erotic.

Daniel pushes her hand away. 'Look, Tansy, I'm grateful to you for trying to help me, I really am, but I think in the circumstances it would be better if we kept things strictly professional.' He's aware that he sounds stiff and priggish. She would say he was 'being British'.

Her pout turns quickly to a scowl.

'Tansy, for God's sake.' Daniel rakes his hand through his hair, unable to contain his frustration. 'Why are you doing this? I mean, do you even like me? Because, to be honest, that's not the impression I get.'

Tansy shrugs. 'I told you, it's not about that. I need to have stuff going on, you know? I need—'

'Yes, I know.' Daniel sighs, tipping his head back and letting the ice-cold champagne cascade over the back of his throat. 'It's for your stories. For content. You explained that already. But, from my point of view, that's just not happening. It's not a direction I want to go in right now, okay?'

But he's speaking to her retreating back.

When they land in Tweed Heads, a limousine is waiting to drive them to a nearby four-star hotel. Tansy and Daniel are booked into the honeymoon suite, and since the place is full, there is little he can do about it.

But Tansy, with her usual capriciousness, shows no interest in dragging Daniel into the bedroom. She ignores him while Sebastian and Ljubica do her hair and make-up, then help her into a formal fitted dress and heels.

'You're going out?' Daniel asks.

'Yes,' she answers, shortly. 'I'm going to a Hiraya seminar up at the Paradise Island Resort. If I attend in person, the recruitment levels go through the roof.' She flicks her freshly teased waves over her shoulders and consults the Philippe Patek watch on her slim, tanned wrist. 'My car will be here any second.'

Five minutes after Tansy has left, there's a knock at the door and Les Pella is standing there with his dark-suited heavies. 'You ready, mate?' he drawls to Daniel. 'Time we went and had a little yarn with Martin Kelly.'

They drive in a rented car, heading due east from the Horizon Lakes property and down a long dusty track. They pass a plantation of pecan trees, grain silos and endless fields of maize, eventually arriving at a small white farmhouse with a low, pitched roof.

A tall, slightly stooped man appears on the wraparound veranda, shading his eyes with one hand as the car comes to a halt in a swirl of dust. He has thinning grey hair and the weather-beaten face of someone who has spent his working life outside.

'Martin Kelly?' Les asks, approaching the house.

'That's right,' the man says, warily. 'And you are?'

'I'm Les Pella, and this is my client, Daniel Halligan. Name should ring a bell. He dealt with your grandson, Bryce, but I reckon you should know who he is. He spent a fortune on your worthless piece of shit land down by the lake back there.'

He jerks his head in the direction they have just come. The hired muscle step forward menacingly, their hands clasped across the front of their bodies.

Martin Kelly steps back slightly, looking alarmed, and grabs the wooden pillar of the veranda. His breathing becomes laboured. 'I don't understand.'

'Let me spell it out for you.' Pella smiles. 'You sold a plot of land to my client here for eight hundred thousand dollars. He gave you that money in good faith. Trouble is, the land isn't worth anywhere near that, because the soil and water supply have been contaminated with fire retardants. Something you must have known.'

Kelly is shaking his head. 'I didn't. I swear I didn't. We've never done any development on the land, so I guess we never had any cause to find out. That's the buyer's responsibility. You know the old saying, *caveat emptor*. Buyer beware.'

'You what?' snarls Pella. The heavies take a step closer.

'Look, I'm sorry how things have turned out,' Kelly is addressing Daniel now. 'Really I am. But there's nothing I can do about it now.'

Daniel opens his mouth to speak, but Pella cuts across him. 'That's where you're wrong. There is something you can do. You're going to cut Mr Halligan here a banker's draft for half a million dollars, as compensation for selling him land that nobody will pay to bloody live on. We're staying at the Rainbow Bay Club, Coolangatta, and you've got til midday tomorrow to drop off the payment. Otherwise…' He looks meaningfully at his black-suited thugs. 'We may have to pop by for another little chat.'

'But I can't… I mean, I haven't got the money.' Kelly leans heavily on one of the pillars. 'It's tied up, you know. Invested.'

Les Pella shrugs, before turning back to the car. 'I guess we'll be seeing you, Mr Kelly. One way or another.'

Daniel is relieved to find the bridal suite empty when they return to the hotel. He goes for a run on Coolangatta Beach, then showers and orders room service.

When there's a knock on the door, he opens it, expecting to find a trolley bearing his Caesar salad and bottle of South Australian Riesling. Instead, Martin Kelly stands there, wearing the same dust-streaked trousers and shirt that he was wearing on the farm. His red face is beaded with sweat and he's wheezing slightly.

'You on your own?' he enquires, glancing around the room suspiciously.

'I am.'

'Good, I wanted to talk to you without your goons around.' He walks into the room, closing the door behind him, then reaches into the breast pocket of his shirt and pulls out a folded piece of paper.

'You've brought a cheque?' Daniel takes it from him and reads it. He frowns. 'Fifty thousand dollars? Are you kidding?'

'Straight up, that's all I can afford. I can't work these days because of my health issues, and the sale of the lake acreage was for my pension.'

Daniel scowls. 'But you've got a whole farm. That land must be worth a hell of lot. Sell some of it.'

'That's my kids' inheritance. And my grandkids'. I promised them that when I retired, I'd be handing over the whole place. Just like my grandfather did to me. It would kill them if they knew I'd handed over all my savings. I didn't dare even tell them I was seeing you. I just said I was going for a walk.'

'But things have changed, haven't they? And your family is just going to have to get used to it. We now know the land you sold me wasn't worth anywhere near what I paid: that's the reality now. Or maybe you knew that all along?'

'I didn't, I swear.' Kelly takes a handkerchief from his trouser pocket and mops his brow. 'We hooked up the utilities, but never got the analysis done. Maybe we should have; I don't know—'

'Of course you should!' Daniel shouts. 'I'm back to square one, only I can't even sell the plot and start again, because my name is now mud as a developer. I'm prepared to accept I should have done more due diligence but, even so, the least you could do is offer some realistic compensation. And I reckon that should be at least half what I paid.'

Kelly leans heavily on the back of the desk chair, his chest rising. 'Maybe I could raise a little more. If you give me a bit more time. I could possibly get you another fifty thousand.'

Daniel crosses the room so that he's only a couple of feet away from Kelly, raising his arms and letting them flap by his sides in a heavily ironic shrug. 'Oh, yes well, that's fine, then! We'll say no more about it and I'll walk away nearly three quarters of a million dollars down.'

'Look, mate, I'm really sorry.' Kelly puts up his hands, shrinking away from the younger man.

'Sorry won't cut it!' Daniel is shouting now, his spittle landing on Kelly's damp face. 'But if you like, you can tell the judge how sorry you are, because I will be seeing you in court. I'm happy to sue you for the money if I have to.' He gives Kelly's shoulder a rough shove, still looking directly at him. 'It's not like I have anything else to do right now.'

The older man staggers at the impact, stumbling backwards, his knees sagging slightly. Daniel's eyes widen at the sound of first spluttering, then choking. Martin Kelly is clutching at his throat, his eyes rolling wildly. His other hand waves redundantly in space and then he crashes to the floor, rolling onto his back. His eyes stare blankly. Daniel in turn stares back, frozen with shock.

A moment later, there's a tap on the door. 'Room service!'

Shit. Not now.

He opens the door a crack. 'I've changed my mind, I'm afraid. We're going to eat out. But I don't mind paying.' He snatches the bill folder from the waiter and scribbles his signature.

Once the trolley has been wheeled away and the door firmly shut, Daniel kneels down on the carpet next to Martin Kelly, feeling at his neck for a pulse. He can't find one. A cold ripple of fear curdles his stomach, followed by panic surging through his whole body. The hand on Kelly's neck is visibly shaking. He withdraws it, clenching it into a fist.

The key mechanism clicks and Daniel's heart leaps in his chest. Is it the in-room dining team again, or housekeeping? He doesn't have the Do Not Disturb sign hung on the door.

It's Tansy.

She drops her Birkin bag on the bed and raises both hands to her mouth. 'What. The fuck. Daniel?'

Daniel leans over Kelly, still trying to get a pulse. Some visceral instinct kicks in, and pressing one hand on top of the other he begins pumping hard on the older man's sternum. Even so, part of him remains completely detached, noticing the dandruff that dusts the shoulders of Kelly's shirt.

'Is he dead?' Tansy demands, shrilly. 'What did you do to him?'

'I… we were arguing, but I didn't touch him. Well, I did, I gave him a bit of a shove, but nothing much. Not hard.'

'Jesus, Daniel.'

He straightens up slightly. 'We should call for an ambulance.'

'Are you crazy?' Tansy hisses. 'The police will come too, and how will you prove this wasn't your fault? They could charge you with *murder*.'

Daniel looks down at the lifeless body, and then wildly at Tansy. 'So what the fuck do we do then? I think he's dead.'

This is not accurate. He knows Martin Kelly is dead. He's just not quite ready to accept it yet. He extends his arms briefly, wondering if he should restart CPR, then retracts them, hugging them across his chest. He can't remember what he's supposed to do. His mind is a dizzying blank.

Tansy has pulled her phone from the bag. 'We'll call Les. He'll know what to do.'

'Yes,' says Daniel, dully. 'Call Les.'

Pella appears three minutes later. He squats next to Kelly on short, thick haunches. His lack of neck makes his head disappear into his shoulders. He stands up again, shaking his head and wiping the back of his mottled red neck.

'Yep. He's gone. There wouldn't have been much point calling an ambulance.'

'Daniel was arguing with him,' Tansy says, in a childlike whine. 'He pushed him over.'

Pella glances up at Daniel. 'This true?'

'Well, yes, but—'

'Who else knows he's here?'

'No one, as far as I know. Not like I was expecting him. And he said he didn't dare tell his family he was coming to see me.'

'Good.' Pella nods. 'That's good.'

'What are we going to do?' Daniel can barely raise his voice above a whisper. 'We can hardly leave him here. And we can't exactly carry a dead body out of here either, can we?'

'I'll handle it,' says Pella, coldly. 'You just keep your mouth shut, okay?'

His handling of the situation inevitably involves the two heavies. They arrive in the suite an hour later dressed in the polo shirts and blue trousers the hotel domestic staff wear, and pushing a large laundry hamper. Kelly's body is loaded into it, covered with towels and sheets and wheeled away to the service lift.

Daniel goes into the bedroom, unable to witness this final act of indignity, but Tansy stands there and watches, cool as a cucumber, sipping a glass of sparkling wine.

CHAPTER TWENTY

DANIEL

Three days later, the local paper runs a short online obituary of Martin Kelly, whose body was found on his farmland after suffering a cardiac arrest while out for a walk.

'See,' Tansy says, when Daniel shows her the headline. 'Told you Les would handle it.'

They're back in Sydney, in Tansy's apartment. In theory, Daniel is sleeping in the spare bedroom, though he has been summoned into the master suite after dark for more emotionless coitus.

She pours them both coffee and pushes a mug towards Daniel, a glint in her eye. 'So, I was thinking a wedding in March, April, perhaps. And now it's the Christmas holidays, it would be the perfect time to do the reveal of the ring on Insta.'

'Tansy, I've told you. More than once. I don't ever want to get married. If I did, I'd already be married to Maxine.'

She wrinkles her nose. 'Don't know why you're being so stubborn about it. Easiest way to pay off your debts from the real estate deal. If you're my husband then obviously I'll cover all that. And we're already living together, anyway.'

'That's easily dealt with: I'll move out,' Daniel says, coldly. 'And I can still sue Kelly's estate for the cost of the land. That'll cover a lot of what I owe.'

'Ah, yes, but' – Tansy smiles sweetly and sinks her perfect white teeth into a slice of papaya – 'that will take a really long time, and there's no guarantee you'll win at the end of it.'

'I'll take the risk.'

'But surely, babe, there's an even bigger risk, just waiting round the corner.' She walks her fingers across the table and then brings them to a stop to illustrate her point.

Daniel narrows his eyes. 'What do you mean?'

'Well, if it came out in court that you had something to do with that guy Kelly's death… that wouldn't play out so well, would it?'

'I didn't have anything to do with his death. He had a pre-existing heart condition.'

Tansy laughs. 'Oh, come *on*, Daniel. Stop playing dumb. The guy dies in your hotel room, after you've had a fight with him. And instead of calling the authorities, you arrange to move his body to somewhere you know it will be found.'

'I didn't arrange it,' Daniel protests. 'You did.'

'*Call Les*,' Tansy smirks, imitating his voice. 'That's what you said. That amounts to you telling me to do it.'

They face off across the table. Daniel stares at her, at this beautiful, heartless, manipulative creature, for what feels like a long time. 'Let me get this straight…' His voice is barely above a whisper. 'You're saying that unless I marry you, you'll dob me in to the authorities about Martin Kelly's death. You're blackmailing me, in other words.'

'Come on, hun, that's such a shitty word.' Tansy pops a blueberry into her mouth. 'And why would it be so awful, anyway? Hiraya generated half a billion dollars in sales last year, for Christ's sake. You'd be a part of all that.'

Daniel swivels on his heel and walks back to the terrace doors.

'Was that a yes, I heard?' Tansy calls after him, her tone taunting.

'Okay,' Daniel mutters.

'Sorry, babe, didn't hear that.'

'I said okay.'

On New Year's Eve, while Tansy is out of the apartment, Daniel phones his brother Ben in London.

'Bloody hell, Dan, it's five in the morning here.'

'I know, sorry. But I've got some big news.'

'Which is?'

'I'm getting married.'

There's a long silence, then Ben emits a whistling sound. 'Blimey. I thought you said you never would. She must be quite something.'

Daniel does not reply.

'Dan? Mate? What's going on?'

And Daniel tells him. The whole sorry story, including the death of Martin Kelly and the cover-up afterwards. Because he has to talk to someone about it, or he'll go mad.

'Bro… I don't know what to say.' Ben's voice is faint with shock.

'Say it's a disaster. Because that's exactly what it is.'

'Don't do it, Danny, for Christ's sake. You don't need to do it. No one should ever enter into a marriage on that basis, let alone… look, I can help you out with the financial mess. I've still got most of Mum's money, tied up in bonds. I can lend it to you.'

'Thanks, but it's not just that, is it? If Tansy decides to blab, then I could be up on a homicide charge.'

'But from what you've just told me, you didn't actually kill anyone.'

'I know that. But I can't prove it. And I got involved in hiding the evidence—'

'You mean the body.'

'Yes, Ben, the body!' Daniel exhales hard. 'Exactly. Which is going to make me look guilty even if I'm not. I'm stuck.'

'There has to be a way out of it surely…'

The front door of the apartment slams. 'She's back, got to go.'

Daniel hangs up.

'Hey, guess what, hun?' Tansy drawls from the hallway. 'Where are you?'

Daniel emerges from the bedroom. 'What?'

'Comped us a honeymoon! The Excelsior Group is giving us a villa at their resort in Mauritius, in return for some social media promotion.' Tansy grins broadly, tossing her dark curls back from her face.

'But we agreed. We agreed no beach honeymoon. That's the last thing I'd ever want to do.'

'We agreed nothing, darl.' Tansy holds up the camera on her phone, using it as a mirror while she rubs some lipstick from her teeth. 'Okay, you said you didn't want to spend your honeymoon on a beach. But this is a freebie, normally worth thousands. It'll be fabulous, you'll see.'

Daniel's expression darkens.

'I've got some pictures of the place on my laptop… you can take a look at them. There'll be loads of other stuff for you to do, I'm sure. You don't have to be on the beach if you don't want to.'

She fetches her MacBook from the living room, enters the password then clicks on a link before handing it to Daniel.

'Take a look at these. I'm going to get in the shower.'

Daniel pours himself a glass of wine and sits down at the kitchen table to look at the photos. The resort on the edge of Turtle Bay does look very appealing: white sands, turquoise water, colourful flowers everywhere. And Tansy is right: there's a gym, a running track, tennis courts and several pools. He won't have to spend time on the beach if he doesn't want to.

From the master bathroom, he can hear the pulsing of water from the huge rainfall showerhead. Tansy is singing tunelessly to herself.

Daniel minimises the online brochure and clicks on the app that replicates the messages on Tansy's phone. He scrolls back through the messages, most of which seem to be sent to Sebastian and Ljubica. And then he finds a thread that has been sent to an unstored number. The date is 12th November.

> *There's an emergency in your flat: the water tank is leaking through the ceiling. You'd better come back as a matter of urgency.*

The recipient responds: 'Who is this?' and Tansy has typed, 'Building manager.'

Daniel takes out his own phone and checks the number of the message recipient against his list of contacts. It's Maxine's mobile. And the date is the day that the ever-punctual Maxine came home twenty minutes earlier than expected and caught him and Tansy together. He'd dismissed it as a coincidence, but it wasn't. Of course it wasn't. Tansy had orchestrated the whole thing. She must have taken Maxine's details from his phone when he wasn't looking.

Another thought occurs to him, one that sends a jolt of shock through him, like an electric current. He goes into Tansy's email account and opens the 'Sent' messages folder. There's very little in there and what is there is mostly monosyllabic replies to corporate queries.

Then he notices a saved page at the top of the browser's bookmarks bar. It's been labelled simply 'Email.' He clicks on it and is taken to an AOL inbox. The account doesn't reference Tansy but simply has the username 'Bondibasic93'.

And there it is. It wasn't difficult to find because there's only one message in the sent folder. The recipients are the press offices of the *Melbourne Age*, the *Sydney Herald*, the *Brisbane Times*, *The Australian* and half a dozen lesser-known publications. Daniel looks at the body of the email, even though he already knows exactly what it will say. It's a crude, ten-line summary of the land and water contamination problem at Horizon Lakes. It was Tansy who leaked the story. Tansy who betrayed him.

Tansy who, in a matter of weeks, is about to become his wife.

PART THREE

CHAPTER TWENTY-ONE

PIPPA

Pippa wipes down the table, arranges clean mugs on a tray and sets the newly acquired coffee machine to brew.

She looks around Jim Cardle's office with satisfaction. He has agreed to take her on for one week before he flies to Australia and already, after only three days, the place is looking quite different. Invoices and case paperwork are now in numbered files in the filing cabinet, the grey sofa has been treated with an upholstery cleaner and acquired some colourful cushions. Pot plants on available surfaces lend a splash of greenery. She even has her own, somewhat makeshift, desk in one corner.

Her mobile rings with a withheld number. She accepts the call. Silence.

'Hello?'

Nothing, just the faint static that indicates someone is on the other end of the line.

'Hello? This is Pippa Bryant. Can I help you?'

Silence. The call is cut.

As she stares at the screen, her heart beating rapidly, the landline rings, making her startle so much she drops her mobile. Cardle comes out of his office, where he has been writing up surveillance notes, and looks askance at her. He snatches up the receiver.

'Cardle.'

He listens for a few minutes, merely interjecting with the occasional 'Oh' and 'I see'.

'Well, that was interesting,' he says, when he hangs up. 'And not necessarily what I was expecting.'

'Who was it?'

'Arne Lindgren.'

'Nikki Lindgren's husband?'

'The very same. Says he wants to drop by and talk to me. About Daniel Halligan. Are you okay?'

Pippa puts down the pile of mail she was about to open and looks at Cardle. 'I just had a weird call. Someone who didn't say anything, then hung up.'

Cardle frowns. 'For the time being, I suggest you only take calls from numbers you recognise.'

Pippa nods, switching her mobile to silent and shoving it into her bag. 'Was Lindgren implying that he thinks Daniel had something to do with Nikki's death?'

Cardle shrugs. 'I guess we're about to find out.'

Pippa turns a letter to and fro in her hands. 'Only, I've been thinking about that. I've thought about it over and over. When I was in the restaurant with the four of them at the resort… Nikki and Arne were obviously so in love and Tansy wanted everyone to believe she and Daniel were too. But as I was leaving, I turned and looked back over my shoulder and I saw Daniel watching Tansy when he thought he wasn't being observed.'

Cardle stops scribbling on his notepad and sets down his pen. 'Go on.'

'He was glowering at her with a face like thunder. Pure hatred. It sent a shiver through me.'

'So, let me get this straight.' Cardle shifts in his chair so that he's looking at Pippa directly. 'You're saying that of all the people who might have wanted Tansy Halligan dead and could have mistaken Nikki for her that night, you think her own husband was top of the list?'

'Yes.' Pippa nods. 'I suppose I am. Because that was the exact thought that went through my mind when I saw him looking at her. I thought: *If looks could kill.*'

Arne Lindgren arrives at the office later that afternoon.

Pippa remembers him as a vital, muscular man with sun-bleached blond hair and an impressive tan. Now he appears shrunken, grey, washed out. Despite the warm weather, his face is pale and his hair is lank and in need of a cut.

'Mr Cardle.' He shakes Cardle's hand, then catches sight of Pippa. 'I'm sorry, have we met?'

'This is my associate, Pippa Bryant,' Cardle says quickly. 'She was also holidaying in Turtle Bay, when…' His voice tails off.

'Ah. I thought I recognised you.' Lindgren gives the merest smile before turning back to Cardle. 'Should we go out somewhere? I have my driver outside.'

'It's all right, whatever you need to say you can say in front of Pippa. I trust her one hundred per cent.'

Pippa feels a warm glow of recognition flood through her and wants to grin with delight at this accolade, but manages to keep her demeanour professional. 'Can I get you anything, Mr Lindgren? Tea? Coffee?'

'Just some water, please.'

Cardle indicates that Lindgren should sit down on the sofa and lowers himself into the chair opposite.

'When we were in Mauritius' – Lindgren's voice cracks and he closes his eyes, lost for a moment in the memory – 'you very kindly came to speak to me, to ask if there was anything you could do. I kept the business card you gave me, and ever since then I've been wanting the chance to speak to you. You see, I simply don't accept the findings of the Mauritian police. They don't have a coroner there, but police findings are passed to the court, and the presiding judge declared Nikki's death an accident. But I think she was killed deliberately, or at least as the result of an argument that went badly wrong.'

'I see,' says Cardle, slowly.

'They told me there were glasses out and water spilt on the floor, but there's no reason for her to have been drinking in someone else's villa. We know she wasn't alone, because there was more than one glass. And slipping and hitting her head…Nikki wasn't like that. She was very… together.'

Cardle exchanges a look with Pippa, who is sitting behind her corner desk. 'We did wonder whether the argument in question could have been between Daniel Halligan and his wife. In other words, that Daniel thought Nikki was his wife. Because she was wearing Tansy's Iluka dress. They were both petite, dark-haired – in a dim light, perhaps—'

'Yes,' says Lindgren, in little more than a whisper. 'That is something I have thought about also. In fact, it's been hard to think about anything else. He had the means and the opportunity, although his motive seems… well, it seems unlikely, that he would intend to harm his wife. They were also on honeymoon, after all.'

This elicits a raised eyebrow from Cardle. 'Trust me, in my extensive experience of marital disharmony, a fight with one's spouse is still possible. Even on honeymoon.'

'I expect you're right,' Lindgren says bitterly, taking a sip of water. 'Though my own experience was very different.'

'And you didn't know the Halligans? You hadn't met them before your joint honeymoons?'

Lindgren shakes his head. 'No, we met for the first time at the resort.' He shrugs, his lips pressed in a tight line. 'And Halligan seemed like a decent enough man, was always perfectly pleasant to Nikki and me. But still, in my mind, he has many questions to answer. It was his villa, he was in the vicinity, and he left the place as soon as he was able, without even speaking to me.'

Cardle rests his elbows on his knees, momentarily lost in thought.

'So, Mr Cardle, will you look into this for me? I need answers. I can't go on living my life like this, without knowing.' Lindgren's body collapses in on itself, and he closes his eyes for a few seconds. 'It's torture. Sheer torture.'

'I'd like to help, Mr Lindgren, but I'm about to go on a business trip to Australia—'

'Well, that's perfect timing then, surely? Since the Halligans live in Australia.'

'That doesn't mean they're there now.'

'It still seems the logical place to start. Let me pay for your flight—'

'That's covered already, but the point is this: my services have already been engaged by someone else, and given what you've been through, I wouldn't want to be offering your case less than my full attention.'

Lindgren gestures towards Pippa. 'But if you had someone assisting you, then surely? I'll pay for Ms Bryant's flight, and she can help you with any additional enquiries. Would that be all right with you, Miss Bryant?'

'Pippa, please.' She nods, avoiding looking in Cardle's direction. 'Yes, that's absolutely fine with me.'

'I'll cover all expenses. Any expenses. I'll double your usual fee, but please just help me get to the bottom of this.'

After Cardle has shaken Lindgren's hand and shown him out of the building he returns to his desk, picking up the file for the recently divorced man he has had under surveillance for several weeks. Their client, his ex-wife, is convinced he disposed of financial assets just prior to divorce papers being filed.

Pippa glances across at him surreptitiously, waiting for him to speak. For quite a long time he remains silent, flicking through his surveillance notes and uploading photos from his phone to the hard drive. Eventually, when Pippa crosses the room to switch on the kettle, he raises his head.

'So, tell me, is this what usually happens to you?'

She feels herself redden slightly as she reaches down mugs from the shelf. 'What d'you mean?'

'I mean, do things usually work out just the way you want them to? Only you were dead keen to come to Australia with me, and I said no, and yet here we are with your ticket paid for by my client.'

Pippa pours tea from the pot into a mug and carries it over to his desk. 'Okay, you tell *me* something… is it really such an awful prospect, me coming with you?'

Their eyes meet for a long moment, and Pippa feels a little prickle of heat at the base of her spine.

'I've no doubt you'll be useful,' he says, drily, averting the discomfiting gaze of his blue-grey eyes. 'But I do have a hard and fast rule.'

'What's that?' Pippa asks, though she has a good idea.

'Keep things strictly to business. Never get involved with work colleagues.' He keeps his eyes down and his voice steady as he adds, almost inaudibly: 'However attractive they might be.'

CHAPTER TWENTY-TWO

PIPPA

As a consequence of having a flight booked through Arne Lindgren's office, Pippa receives a free upgrade to first class; Cardle, on the other hand, is in premium economy for the twenty-hour trip to Melbourne.

'We could swap,' Pippa suggests, feeling faintly embarrassed. 'For at least part of the journey. I'm sure the cabin crew wouldn't mind.'

'Not a problem,' Cardle says, gruffly, patting the pocket of his bomber jacket. 'I've got a couple of Diazepam in here, which I'm going to be washing down with several glasses of red. I'll be out for the count until we touch down. All the scented hand towels and vintage champagne would be wasted on me. You enjoy it.'

As ever, Pippa barely manages to sleep once airborne. For years, she has never travelled anywhere without Alastair, and now she is taking her second long-haul trip without him in only a month. She thought she had adjusted to life without him, but the emotional lability brought on by being at 30,000 feet makes her feel suddenly weepy. What is she doing, she demands of herself, flying to the literal end of the earth with a man she barely knows? Why did she want this?

Because she has dozed for a total of around four hours, the jet lag hits her like a speeding truck as soon as they have disembarked the plane in Melbourne.

'You look surprisingly rough for someone who's travelled in first,' Cardle observes, as they ride into the city centre in a cab. The late autumn day is cloudy and cool, and to Pippa's jaded eye the suburbs that slip past the taxi window could be somewhere in the Home Counties. It's not what she was expecting and she can't quite suppress a frisson of disappointment.

'I know you're supposed to try and power through the time difference, but I need to get my head down,' she tells Cardle, once they've checked in. 'At least for a few hours.' It's only 8 a.m., but feels like midnight.

'Set an alarm for one,' Cardle tells her. 'Then we'll go and get some lunch together, find somewhere nice.'

Pippa looks directly into his deep-set eyes. 'I thought you kept things strictly business,' she says, trying to sound brisk and business-like herself, despite a level of exhaustion that is making her knees sag.

'Of course.' He smiles. 'I only meant that since Arne Lindgren's bankrolling any and all expenses, we can find somewhere that serves decent food.'

To Pippa's delight, when she wakes up a few hours later, the grey skies have cleared.

The sun is shining on vibrant autumn foliage in shades of cinnamon, amber and gold, and the Victorian architecture makes the city feel a lot more European than she had anticipated. They go to an Italian restaurant in Carlton, a couple of blocks from the University of Melbourne, and sit under large windows in a white-painted lapboard booth. Cardle orders rigatoni with vodka sauce and Pippa chooses the Skull Island prawns with capellini, both of them refusing the offer of a glass of wine and sticking to mineral water.

'Feeling better?' he asks, watching Pippa load up her fork with the pasta.

'A little,' she concedes. 'I could still sleep for twelve hours if given the chance.'

'Well, while you're still awake, we'd better discuss the plan of action…' He tears off a chunk of rustic bread and dips it in the scarlet sauce left on his plate. 'So. We have two jobs, and two clients, and conveniently they happen to be linked, in so far as the subject of the first is married to the subject of the second. Like a game of Happy Families, featuring Mr Ponzi and Ms Pyramid.'

Pippa raises an eyebrow.

'I'll come on to that. However, we're not going to try and work the two cases simultaneously, despite Lindgren effectively providing me with a full-time assistant.' He lowers his head to his plate and mutters, 'Whether I wanted one or not.'

'We're not?'

Cardle shakes his head. 'No. We're going to deal with Tansy Halligan first, which is why we're in Melbourne, and then we'll move on to trying to answer some of Lindgren's questions about Daniel Halligan.'

Pippa frowns. 'But Tansy doesn't live here. In Melbourne.'

'She doesn't. But my clients do. Dr and Mrs Webber. They're the couple I mentioned to you. He's a radiologist at the Royal Melbourne Hospital, she works in education. They have a daughter called Meredith.' He sighs heavily. '*Had* a daughter called Meredith. She killed herself at the end of last year.'

'You told me it had something to do with Tansy Halligan?'

'Tansy Dimaano, as she prefers to be known, yes. With her business, at least.'

'The health drinks that cured her of lupus.'

'Exactly,' says Cardle, heavily. He waves the waitress over and orders a double espresso. 'Hiraya is a multi-level marketing company. It's effectively a pyramid scheme, though they've jumped through the necessary legal loopholes to prevent it being classified as such.'

'Because pyramid schemes are illegal.'

'They are. But from what the Webbers ascertained after their daughter's death, Hiraya is operating what's known as a closed system, meaning the products they sell aren't really reaching the open retail market. They're simply selling the stuff within the ranks of the distributors they recruit. In order to sell this gunk for them and try and make a profit, you have to invest your own cash in buying it upfront. But at what's effectively a retail price, rather than wholesale. In other words, if the stuff costs a dollar to manufacture and would sell in a health food store for five dollars, it's at somewhere nearer five dollars that these so-called "Wellness Angels" are purchasing it from Hiraya.'

Cardle's coffee arrives and Pippa orders a mint tea. Despite her heavy eyelids, she doesn't want caffeine keeping her awake later.

'And Meredith Webber was a Wellness Angel?'

'That's right. She suffered from lupus herself, and was all too happy to buy into the myth that this was a life-changing product. She spent all her money on Dimaano's snake oil, and more money besides, money she didn't have. She couldn't shift enough of the stuff, got heavily into debt, couldn't find a way out of her financial problems, and ended up hanging herself in the garage.'

'Oh, Christ. Poor girl. Her poor parents.'

'To be honest, I wasn't sure how much I could do to help them, but as you can imagine, I badly wanted to try.'

Pippa nods slowly, feeling tears prick her eyes.

'So I agreed to at least attempt to find a way of nailing Tansy Dimaano. Of getting her toxic empire shut down. I've been round and round the houses with the legalities and the red tape, and I've come up with something that might just work.'

'Which is?'

'I'll tell you about it tomorrow. I need you to catch up on your sleep first.' He gives Pippa a long look. 'How's life working out without that fiancé of yours?'

She's caught momentarily off guard. 'And this is keeping things professional… how, exactly?'

'Call it a staff welfare check.' He grins.

'I think' – she avoids meeting Cardle's eye – 'I miss the idea of him rather than Alastair himself.'

'You make him sound like a bad habit you've kicked.'

'I guess in a way he was. We'd been a couple for so long, I'd become used to operating as one half of a pair. It feels weird being on my own suddenly. He was a sort of human security blanket.'

Cardle laughs. 'Doesn't sound very sexy.'

Pippa smiles ruefully. 'No, I suppose not. How about you? You said you were divorced, right? But you're not living with anyone now?'

He shakes his head. 'Nope. Not at the moment.'

'Kids?'

'Two. One of each. I see them as much as I can, but it's not the same as living with them.' He sighs.

'Any significant other?' Pippa can't help feeling curious. 'A girlfriend?'

'Let's get the bill,' he says, abruptly. 'And then we'll have a walk in Carlton Gardens. I can have a fag, and you can get some fresh air.'

'Not if you're smoking.' She gives him a sidelong glance.

'Fair enough. But I need you to try and stay awake at least until it's dark.'

'So, are you—'

But he's already striding towards the till. 'Long day tomorrow.'

CHAPTER TWENTY-THREE

PIPPA

'You up for a bit of play-acting?'

The next morning, Cardle and Pippa are taking advantage of the breakfast buffet included in their hotel deal. After sleeping as heavily as she can remember for twelve hours straight, Pippa feels marginally less jet-lagged, but is still grateful for the unlimited top-ups of strong coffee.

'You want me to act?' she asks, incredulously, spooning yoghurt onto the bowl of berries in front of her.

'In a manner of speaking,' Cardle replies, briskly. He's wearing a washed-out grey T-shirt and faded black jeans. His hair is still damp from the shower and a faint whiff of old-fashioned shaving soap reaches Pippa from across the table.

'Here's the thing…' He drains a glass of papaya juice and starts attacking a slice of toast with the butter knife. 'Tansy's got her multi-level marketing set-up locked down. It's privately owned and the investment of these so-called "Wellness Angels" is kept sufficiently low that it doesn't come under the umbrella of a franchise. That would expose it to further regulation.'

Pippa nods, taking a mouthful of the excellent scalding coffee.

'However, it is considered fraudulent to make false claims about your product. To claim that it can help cure cancer, or rheumatoid arthritis or…'

'Or lupus,' supplies Pippa.

'Exactly. Or lupus. Now, obviously, there are problems with proving or disproving such a claim. If you suffer from a particular health condition and you drink the Hiraya shakes, and your symptoms get better… well, then it's not necessarily misleading to attribute it to that product. Unless—'

'Unless you didn't have the condition to start with.'

The look Cardle gives Pippa is one of approval, tinged with surprise.

'Well, that's the first thing I thought of when I read her bio on the website,' Pippa continues. 'Where's the evidence that she actually suffers from lupus? She's never presented herself as anything other than fit as the proverbial flea.'

He nods. 'But if we could prove that she was lying about it, then that opens her up to investigation by both the Therapeutic Goods Administration, which is part of Australia's Department of Health, and the Competition and Consumer Commission, which is the equivalent of the FTC in the States.' He beckons a waitress over to refill their coffee cups. 'The FTC has successfully brought legal action against some prominent pyramid schemes over there.'

'So, how do my acting skills come into it?' asks Pippa, intrigued.

'We need to access Tansy's health records. And, fortunately for us, she uses a network of private GP practices called Fleur de Lys Health. I know this because she's paid to promote them on her social media accounts, and she frequently tags them when she visits their Sydney clinic. Mostly for cosmetic treatments, obviously; she's hardly likely to advertise the fact she's going there for a pap smear.'

Pippa raises her eyebrows. 'Oh, I don't know… that strikes me as exactly the sort of thing she *would* do. It's very on-brand for her wellness warrior shtick.'

Cardle laughs. 'Good point. But the thing is, she's registered with them for all her health needs and, as far as I can see, she has been for several years. It's a countrywide resource… there are three Fleur de Lys clinics here in Melbourne, and patients like Tansy who travel a lot can access a doctor at any time. Which suggests their digital records have to be centralised and available in all their clinics.'

'We're going to go to one of the clinics here and… what?' Pippa asks. 'Am I going to pass myself off as Tansy?'

Cardle throws down his napkin and pushes back his chair. 'You'll see. Come on, we need to get going.'

The Fleur de Lys clinic is in an anonymous modern building on the broad thoroughfare of Canterbury Road, between the central business district and the foreshore.

'We'll get them to create a patient file for you,' Cardle tells Pippa. 'That way the receptionist will have to open the patient records software.'

'Am I going to have to see a doctor?' She scrunches up her nose. 'Only there's absolutely nothing wrong with me, and I'm not sure I could fake being ill.'

He shakes his head a little impatiently. 'They have cosmetic and holistic treatments, as well as a GP service. Let's stick to something relatively cheap and cheerful. And I'll be waiting for you in the clinic, because I'm your husband.'

Pippa holds up her bare left hand, the third finger now devoid of an engagement ring.

'All right then, your boyfriend… what?' he demands, his tone chippy. 'Is that really so far-fetched?'

No, it's not, Pippa thinks. *Who wouldn't want to date this burly, good-looking ex-cop with the distinct air of macho about him?*

'I expect we can convince them,' she says, lightly.

'Good. While you're in the treatment area, I need you to create a diversion.'

'What kind of diversion?'

'Anything dramatic enough to get the receptionist away from her desk for a couple of minutes. You'll think of something.'

Her heart is pounding as they approach the front reception desk in the thickly carpeted first-floor suite of rooms. Instinctively, she finds herself reaching for Cardle's arm and clinging to it as the receptionist smiles up at them. Only to lend authenticity to their story, she tells herself firmly. Not because it feels good.

'Hi, can I help you?' The girl is wearing a name badge which says 'Jolie'.

With the hand not clutching Cardle, Pippa reaches up and touches her neck, grimacing. 'We're over here on holiday, and I've cricked my neck somehow… it's really becoming a problem. Do you have someone free who could give me a massage, try and loosen it up a bit?'

'Let's see now… are you registered with us already?'

Pippa shakes her head.

'I'll need to go ahead and do that quickly, then I've got…' Jolie checks a schedule on her monitor. 'I've got Ruby free, for a Swedish deep-tissue massage. That would be a hundred and fifty dollars.'

'Fine.' Pippa reaches automatically for her credit cards, but Cardle whips out his wallet and pulls out a handful of notes. 'We'll pay cash,' he says, quickly.

An invented name, date of birth and address are given and duly noted on Jolie's computer terminal, then a petite white-coated Asian girl appears and beckons Pippa to a treatment room at the end of a carpeted corridor. Pippa glances over her shoulder at Cardle, who gives a smile of encouragement before sitting down with a magazine.

The room is lit with a bank of tea lights, and there's a diffuser giving off a strong, slightly sickly scent. Whale song is playing softly. Ruby briskly covers the treatment bed with fresh paper, then hands Pippa a pile of fluffy pink towels.

'Strip off to your undies, then pop yourself on the bed with a towel over you. I'll be back in a couple of minutes.'

Once she's gone, Pippa looks around the room desperately, wondering what she can do. Candles. Live flames. It has to be that, surely? Her mind suddenly dredges up a memory of being in a GCSE physics lesson at school, and some of the more disruptive boys lighting a fire in a wastepaper basket at the back of the classroom.

She takes a corner of the paper couch roll and holds it to one of the tea lights. It smoulders at first, then eventually begins to burn vigorously. Dropping the ball of fire into a bin in the corner, Pippa thrusts it high above her head so that the acrid fumes reach the smoke alarm on the ceiling. Within seconds the alarm is issuing a deafening screaming sound.

'Fire!' Pippa shouts, flinging the door of the treatment room open. 'The room's on fire!'

There's a sound of scurrying feet as first Ruby, then Jolie, appear.

'What the hell happened?' Ruby demands curtly. 'I only left her for a second,' she says to the receptionist. 'I don't know what—'

'Quick, for God's sake, keep that door closed!' Jolie snaps. 'We don't want it spreading…' She glances into the treatment room. 'It's okay, it's only in the bin… do you know where Martina keeps the fire extinguisher?'

But it's too late. The smoke wafting into the corridor has reached the sprinkler system, and the carpets are being drenched with water droplets, with a second alarm sound adding to the mayhem. As Ruby and Jolie head off in search of the sprinkler controls, swearing loudly, Pippa slips through the fire exit door and runs down the stairs to street level.

'Excellent work,' Cardle says, when they eventually meet up on the street corner.

'So my "girlfriend"' – he makes air quotes – 'is a little fire-starter. Who'd have thought it?'

Pippa experiences a frisson of pleasure at having proved useful to the investigation. 'Did you get enough time?' she asks, leaning forward with her hands on her thighs to steady herself. She's out of breath, and the adrenaline is still thundering through her body, making her feel slightly high.

'Worked like a charm. I pulled up Tansy's record, which dates back to 2014 and seems pretty comprehensive. Can you remember when she claimed to have lupus?'

They walk briskly along Canterbury Road, away from the Fleur de Lys clinic, and Cardle holds up his arm to hail a cab.

'It was a couple of years ago, I think,' Pippa says. 'I'd have to check her website.'

'I didn't get long enough to read through the entries, obviously, but I took screenshots.'

A taxi pulls up, and once they're seated in the back, Cardle starts going through the images on his phone's camera roll. 'It's pretty standard stuff… mostly gynae related… contraceptive implants and so on… an inhaler for her seasonal allergies… a urinary tract infection, for which she was prescribed an antibiotic.'

'Does it say which one?' Pippa hangs onto the door handle as the taxi takes a sharp bend, then glances over at Cardle's phone.

'Says here – Bactrim. Why?'

'Hold on a second…' Pippa pulls out her own phone and looks on her internet browser. 'According to several sources, Bactrim should not be prescribed to anyone who's suffering with or has suffered from lupus.'

'Interesting…' Cardle turns and grins at her, before looking back at the photographed record. 'The box for contra-indications has been left blank by the GP, as has the place where you would fill in any pre-existing conditions. Their record-keeping seems pretty meticulous, but there's no mention at all of what constitutes a pretty serious illness. Funny that.'

'It is.' Pippa can hardly suppress her own smile as the taxi pulls up at their hotel. 'It's almost as if Tansy Dimaano never had lupus at all.'

CHAPTER TWENTY-FOUR

PIPPA

'Nice place,' says Cardle, as they approach the Webbers' home. It's a detached red-brick Federation villa, with ornate iron fretwork edging the veranda and a pretty garden, in the well-heeled south-eastern suburb of Malvern.

Pippa nods agreement, trying to avoid her gaze straying to the separate garage block. They're welcomed inside by Nigel Webber, a distinguished-looking, softly spoken man whose dark hair is streaked iron grey.

'Catherine's in the kitchen,' he says, once Pippa has been introduced. 'Come through.'

Catherine Webber is thin and blonde, with the faded looks of someone who must once have been pretty. Pippa judges her to be about forty-five, but she appears older. On the sideboard next to the kitchen table there is a large framed photo of a smiling girl with a mane of light gold hair.

'Is that Meredith?' Pippa asks straightaway, anxious to banish the unavoidable elephant in the room.

'Yes, that's Merry,' says Nigel Webber, with a sad smile. His wife, who has turned away to boil the kettle, hangs her head briefly. 'I know that you know some of what happened, Mr Cardle, but for the sake of Miss Bryant here—'

'Pippa, please.'

'Pippa.' He nods. 'Of course... I'll go through it again, for your benefit.'

'If you don't mind—?'

'It's actually nice to talk about her.' He looks at his wife, who's placing a tray of coffee on the table. 'Isn't it, Catherine?'

'It is,' she sighs. 'Most people feel they need to avoid the topic.'

'Was she your only child?' Pippa asks.

'We've got a son, Barnaby. He's away at uni in Western Australia.' Catherine Webber pours them coffee and sits down. 'This has been so hard for him too. He's doing pretty well now, but it always used to be Meredith who was the academic star. She was always such a high flyer. A great athlete, and on a gifted and talented programme at school. Then, shortly after she'd done her Highers, she started having some health issues. Headaches, rashes, joint pain, mouth ulcers. Her hair started falling out...' Catherine Webber glances at the photo and her eyes sparkle with tears.

'She was diagnosed with lupus,' Nigel Webber takes up the narrative. 'As you probably know, it's a very difficult condition for the medical profession to treat effectively. Merry was desperate to do all she could to optimise her health, and as part of her online research, she found this company Hiraya, which claimed its drinks could get rid of symptoms of lupus.'

'She was at that very impressionable age,' Catherine Webber says, dabbing the corner of her eyes with a tissue. 'You know how girls these days are so influenced by stuff they read online, and by so-called celebrities they read about.'

'That's why they're called "influencers",' Nigel Webber chips in drily.

'Merry became obsessed with Tansy Dimaano, because she was beautiful and glamorous and she'd managed to overcome lupus. So when she read about a Hiraya event taking place as part of a wellness conference in Melbourne, she was desperate to go. We weren't sure, were we, Nigel?'

He shakes his head.

'But she was so enthused about it, and we thought well, it's only a vitamin supplement at the end of the day, how much harm can it do?' Catherine can't keep the bitterness from her voice. 'She was a little secretive about it at first, but we found out several weeks later, when boxes of stuff started being delivered to the house, that she'd signed up to be one of their sales representatives.'

'Their "Angels",' says Pippa, with a grimace.

'Quite. Only she had to put all this money up front. She had to purchase a starter kit which was two thousand dollars, then there was a monthly website fee, a membership fee, business cards, promotional leaflets, shipping… it just got ridiculous. They had these layers within the hierarchy—'

'The pyramid,' Webber interjects again, not even attempting to keep the contempt from his voice.

'You started as a Baby Angel, then you graduated to a Winged Angel, and eventually a Boss Angel. Meredith was told that she would do better and make more commission as a Winged Angel, but to do that she had to invest more. And she was given these quotas she had to reach, like recruiting thirty people in thirty days, and ordering at least four thousand dollars' worth of product every month. It turned into a nightmare for her. She was bright and outgoing, but she was still so young, and she just didn't have the ruthless streak you needed to rope people into buying the stuff. And Hiraya doesn't care if you sell the product on to a consumer, as long as you order the stuff. So to make her quotas she was ordering boxes of shakes and just having it shipped to herself, where it sat unsold in…' Her voice falters. 'In the garage.'

'It's an economic phenomenon known as "honouring sunk costs",' Webber says, repressively. 'Or, in the vernacular, throwing good money after bad.' He offers the coffee pot to first Pippa, then Cardle but they both decline. 'She took out another credit card without us knowing, and started charging the wretched stuff to that. The interest rate was sky high, and it wasn't long before she was struggling to make the repayments. She wasn't really selling anything. Hassling people for money just wasn't her style. Her "upline" – that's what they call the distributor immediately above her in the pyramid – told her she needed to host events, and to post promotional content on Facebook at least six times a day. Then they started pressuring her to claim that Hiraya's green shake had helped her with her lupus symptoms.'

'Which of course it hadn't,' murmurs Catherine, dabbing her eyes again and shoving her tissue into her pocket. 'She was still suffering on and off.'

'As with all autoimmune issues, stress exacerbates the illness,' sighs her husband. 'And on top of that, she was being hassled by the "Boss Angels" – he grimaces as he makes air quotes again – 'who told her that if she was failing to recruit enough people then that was her fault for not having the right attitude. And she was being pursued by the credit card company after failing to make payments. She had a couple of letters threatening legal action. And that was when…' His voice shakes and he closes his eyes for a few seconds. 'When she decided she couldn't go on.'

'Of course we had no idea about this until afterwards,' Catherine says fiercely, defensively. 'We'd have helped her of course, if we'd known. Paid off her debts, helped her get out of Hiraya's clutches. But by the time we found out any of it, it was too late.'

'We just want it stopped,' Webber says, firmly. 'We don't want any other girls winding up in Merry's position. We need to try and find a way to shut Hiraya down. That's why we contacted you, Jim. A cousin of mine who works in the International branch of the Federal Police mentioned having come across you on a murder case. Our family lawyer told us Hiraya is operating within the bounds of commercial law, but we're sure there has to be something we can find on Dimaano.'

Cardle leans forward in his chair and clasps his hands. 'As it happens, I think there is.'

He tells the Webbers about finding evidence that Tansy has never suffered from lupus herself, thereby opening herself and her company to legal action for fraud.

'Of course, it could result in nothing more than an official warning not to make unfounded claims that have no basis in science,' he warns. 'But the publicity and the exposure of her lies will be very damaging to her brand. We're also, coincidentally, looking into her husband, Daniel Halligan, but that's a separate issue, and I don't want you to worry about that for now. I'm going to prepare a report of my findings for the Department of Health and the Consumer Commission and, for the time being at least, the ball will be in their court.'

Webber drops his head. 'Thank you,' he says, simply. 'I want to thank you, most sincerely, from both of us.' Catherine Webber places her hand over his and squeezes it. Instinctively they both look in the direction of the photo of their golden-haired daughter. 'And from Meredith.'

'Wow, that was heavy.' Pippa exhales as they walk down the drive to wait for their Uber.

Cardle merely grunts, hands in his jeans pockets, his expression grim.

'Are the authorities you mentioned here, or…'

'In Canberra.'

'Are we going there next?'

He shakes his head. 'Not yet. I can email stuff over to them to get the ball rolling.'

'But we're not staying here in Melbourne.'

He holds up his arm as a Prius coasts to a stop next to them. 'Nope. We're off to Sydney.'

CHAPTER TWENTY-FIVE

PIPPA

'We really ought to thank Tansy Dimaano,' Cardle says, with only the merest twinkle in his eyes betraying irony. 'Her inability to stop posting about herself online has made my job a whole lot easier.'

He and Pippa took a commuter flight from Melbourne to Sydney first thing that morning, and by eleven o'clock they are on a street in the city centre outside the looming steel and glass tower of the Belmont apartment block. The weather is warm and balmy after Melbourne, and both of them have abandoned wearing a jacket.

'Saves us thumbing through the electoral roll or address-finding software,' Cardle continues, pointing to the top of the building, 'when she brags on Instagram about living in the penthouse at one of Sydney's most prestigious addresses.'

They are intercepted, inevitably, by a uniformed concierge.

'We're here to see Daniel and Tansy Halligan,' Cardle tells him. 'It's the seventeenth floor, isn't it?' He turns towards the bank of lifts.

'One moment please. Let me just phone and see if it's all right for you to go up…'

The concierge holds up a hand to try and stop them, but Cardle has already grabbed Pippa by the hand and pulled her towards the lift that has just pinged to signal its arrival on the ground floor.

The doors are opening to let out a delivery man in a branded shirt and cap.

'Oi!' the concierge shouts angrily. 'You can't just—'

The lift doors cut him off and Pippa jabs at the button marked 'P'. Only then does Cardle seem to realise that he's still holding Pippa by the hand.

'Sorry,' he mumbles, and the skin beneath his dark stubble turns a shade darker.

'That's quite all right.' Pippa smiles. 'There was no time for social niceties.'

A woman in a grey dress and white apron opens the door of the penthouse. Behind her, visible through floor-to-ceiling windows, is the spectacular backdrop of Circular Quay.

'Are Mr and Mrs Halligan in?' Cardle holds up one of his business cards.

'Not here right now,' the woman says, her English heavily accented. 'Away. Out of town.'

'Both of them?' he demands.

'Yes. Both away.'

He's at least twelve inches taller than her, and takes advantage of being able to look over the housekeeper's head and past her into the vestibule. 'Are you sure?'

But before he can put a foot over the threshold, the door is slammed firmly in their faces.

'Bugger,' Cardle mutters, trudging back to the lift. 'Coffee?'

Outside, they find a coffee shop a few hundred yards away and sit at a pavement table with an umbrella. He smokes a cigarette while they wait for their order to arrive.

'I wonder where she's gone,' Pippa says. 'Maybe to visit one of her sales networks in Asia.'

'Nope.' He is shaking his head. 'She's there all right, we're just being lied to.'

'How d'you know?'

'That delivery man who conveniently left the lift as we got in… he was from a florist and had just brought a big arrangement of flowers. I spotted it on the kitchen counter when the housekeeper opened the door. You don't get fancy flowers costing hundreds of dollars delivered when you're not currently at home. Also, the housekeeper was in the middle of setting up a tray of breakfast, and I'm guessing it wasn't for herself. And a shower was running somewhere; I could hear it. Again, I'm guessing it wasn't a member of her staff.'

'Wow,' says Pippa. 'I'm impressed.'

Cardle shrugs. 'Anyone would think I did this for a living.' A smile flickers briefly across his face. 'What does her social media say she's up to?'

Pippa takes out her phone and swipes through Tansy Dimaano's Instagram page, sipping her coffee.

'She put up one of her bullshit inspirational posts yesterday, which basically features her staring at the horizon after an expensive blowout… The day before… something similar, only she's looking into a huge gilt mirror.'

'Literal smoke and mirrors then,' he observes drily, helping himself to a croissant.

Pippa continues to scroll. 'There's been nothing with the location tagged for a while. And no mention at all of Daniel since the start of the honeymoon. They got married in the middle of April; it was mentioned on several gossip sites.'

'Interesting. And he's not on social media himself, is he?'

She shakes her head. 'So what happens now?'

'We're going to get ourselves a rental car.'

'Where are we going?'

'Nowhere.' Cardle grins. 'But I'm afraid it's time to do some good old-fashioned surveillance, and that's best done in a car. For a start, it's not physically possible to stand out on the street for hours at a time. Apart from the discomfort, you're way too obvious. A car allows you to sit down, and also gives you some cover, makes you a bit more anonymous. You can just park up and observe.'

'I've never done surveillance before,' says Pippa, feeling a rush of excitement. 'I mean, obviously I haven't.'

'Watch and learn, Grasshopper, watch and learn.'

They pick up a mid-range silver saloon car from the Avis premises on Pitt Street and park as close as legally possible to the front of the Belmont building, angled so that they can see who is leaving the building.

It's midday when they take up their post, and by the afternoon Pippa's legs are cramping, there's an unpleasant taste in her mouth and the two of them have run out of small talk.

She's just about to ask Cardle if she can get out and stretch her legs when a Bentley with blacked-out windows pulls up at the front door of the Belmont and stays there with its engine idling.

'Hold on.' Pippa pulls her legs down from the dashboard and leans forward. A familiar figure emerges from the Belmont, long sable mane glinting in the sunshine. She's wearing tight jeans, a black blazer and black ankle boots with ridiculously high heels.

'Quick, she's getting in her car!'

But Cardle is already on the pavement, intercepting Tansy as she leans forward to climb through the door the driver is holding open for her. His bulk blocks her path, and he towers over her.

'We need a word, Tansy,' he says, not unpleasantly.

She frowns, clearly recognising both Cardle and Pippa but unsure from where.

'Actually, it's Daniel we need to speak to. Is he in the apartment?'

'Excuse me,' the driver remonstrates, 'you can't just…' He tails off, intimidated by Cardle's size.

'No, he's not,' Tansy says coldly, her amber eyes flashing. 'We're not together any longer.'

'So where is he?'

She pulls her plump lips into a grimace. 'I really don't know.' She glances up at Cardle. 'Honestly, I don't. That's the truth.'

The truth, Tansy, Pippa thinks sceptically. *Not a concept you're familiar with.* Suddenly she's seeing Meredith Webber's face and feels an overwhelming surge of anger. But Cardle is remaining polite, calm, professional. She knows she has to follow suit.

'You've no idea where he might be? Is he in Australia?'

'Like I said, I have no idea. In fact, if you find him, I'd quite like to speak to him.' She ducks her head under Cardle's armpit and climbs into the back seat of the limousine. The driver slams her door shut, clambers into the front seat and drives off, accelerating sharply.

'You didn't say anything to Tansy about not having lupus,' Pippa points out, as they drive back to their hotel on Philip Street.

'Don't want her freaking out and hiding evidence,' Cardle explains. 'Or finding a way to falsify her medical records.'

They take the lift up to the floor where both their rooms are. 'I'm going to write up my report for the Therapeutic Goods Administration and the Competition and Consumer Commission now; get them sent off to Canberra,' Cardle says when they reach his door. 'So I guess I'll see you tomorrow.'

Pippa hesitates.

'Was there something else?' Their eyes meet.

I liked it when you held my hand.

That's what Pippa wants to say, but she doesn't. 'Just… thank you for today. For teaching me about surveillance. And… well, for letting me come with you on this trip.'

He looks at her for a long beat. 'No problem.'

CHAPTER TWENTY-SIX

PIPPA

'I thought you enjoyed the thrill of the stake-out,' Cardle says to Pippa early the next morning, as she's twisting and fidgeting in the front seat of the hire car.

They're still watching Tansy Dimaano's apartment. The obvious possibility – that she might not be telling them the truth about her husband's absence – remains.

'How long will we be here?' Pippa asks, picking at her fingernails and deciding she really needs a manicure.

'As long as it takes.' Cardle is solid, monolithic, gazing straight ahead through the windscreen. He hasn't shaved and there are dark circles under his eyes, but he doesn't struggle with sitting still the way Pippa does. She drank a large latte just before they set off and is now regretting it, her bladder uncomfortably full.

'Tell you what,' Cardle says, without taking his eyes off the entrance to the Belmont building. 'This doesn't really need both of us. It's not like we're cops who are going to pursue and arrest Halligan if we spot him. I take it you packed your laptop when we left London?'

'Of course.'

'In that case, why don't you head back to the hotel and start doing some more digging on Daniel Halligan. Try and find anything that might tell us where he's gone, and why.'

Relieved, Pippa climbs out of the car and walks back to the hotel. After a shower, a change of clothes and a coffee from room service, she's descended happily into an online research rabbit hole. She bookmarks web pages, scribbles notes on the pad of paper on the desk, and eventually wanders down to the hotel's business centre to print off the information she wants to share with Cardle. She's just returning to her room, when her phone buzzes with a call.

It's Alastair.

'Hi, sorry to ring so late—'

'Actually, it's early. I'm in Australia.'

There's a stunned silence for a second or two.

'Australia? Bloody hell, Pips, that's a hell of a long way to go for a holiday.'

'I'm not on holiday. I'm working.'

'Working? What… not permanently, surely?'

'No, I'll be back in a week or so. Is everything okay?'

She knows Alastair, and that he wouldn't just be ringing for a chat.

'Yes, but there's something I need to tell you. Before anyone else finds out.'

Pippa's heart sinks. She knows instinctively what's coming.

'Amy and I are engaged.'

She makes a small sound: half-gulp, half-cough.

'Pippa, are you okay?'

'Yes, fine… Congratulations.'

She sees herself at the register office, her wedding dress hanging unworn in the hotel room and Amy reaching up to whisper something in Alastair's ear. Amy, who was there as a guest but who will now be the bride; Amy, who will become Mrs Whelan: a title she never attained herself.

'We wanted to make sure you heard it from me, before anyone else had the chance to break the news to you. Only the announcement's going in *The Times* tomorrow.'

'That's great…' Pippa says, weakly. 'Like I said, congratulations. To both of you.'

Before Alastair can thank her, she cuts the call. As she does so, her phone buzzes with a text. Unknown sender. Her whole body turns cold.

You were told to keep quiet. You didn't listen.

Cardle returns from his stint of surveillance at ten that evening, and Pippa meets him in the hotel brasserie.

'How do you know Daniel hasn't slipped out of the apartment the second you left?' she asks. She's ordered a glass of white wine, and Cardle is tucking into a burger, fries and a large beer.

'I don't,' he says, through a mouthful of burger. 'But nobody can be on watch twenty-four hours a day. We could take shifts, if you fancy heading back out there?' He dips one of the fries in mayonnaise and raises one eyebrow at her.

'No… well, yes, if you want me to, of course.'

'It's okay, I was kidding. But I will be back out there early doors tomorrow.'

'For how long?'

'Another day or two. I'll try and get up to the apartment and check in person again, probably while Tansy's out. But unless she's got him imprisoned up there, which doesn't seem her style, I don't think he's there.'

Pippa just nods, and sips her beer.

'How did you get on?'

'Pretty well…' Pippa pulls out the sheaf of printed pages from her bag. 'According to the Australian Securities and Investments Commission, Daniel Halligan was the CEO and sole proprietor of a company called Roseland Investments, but the paperwork was filed to deregister it back in April, just before Daniel and Tansy were married.'

He raises an eyebrow. 'Go on.'

'When I tried to find out more about Roseland, I came across this…'

She pulls out a copy of a newspaper article and puts it down on the table between them. Cardle reads it aloud, still munching on fries.

Scandal of toxic land for planned retirement homes

> *Locals and retirees are alarmed at the plan by Sydney company Roseland Investments to build on a brown land site known to be contaminated with toxic firefighting chemicals…*

He reads to the end of the article, then looks up at her. 'Excellent work. My hunch was correct: like his wife, he's embroiled in dodgy business dealings. There's nothing to suggest Tansy was an investor or co-owner?'

'Not that I could find, no.'

Pippa sips her wine in silence.

'You okay?' Cardle looks at her through narrowed eyes, taking in the line of tension around her jaw. 'Only you've been very quiet this evening.'

She shows him the second, threatening text. He raises an eyebrow but remains unperturbed. 'Just as well you've got me to keep an eye on you.'

'What should I do?'

'Let's have a look.' She hands her phone to him and he clicks the information icon, before shaking his head and handing it back. 'Keep it. We should be able to trace the number, but for now, ignore.' He notices her expression, still withdrawn. 'Anything else bothering you?'

Pippa tells him about her phone call from Alastair.

'Sorry to hear that,' Cardle says, but his tone is brisk. 'You didn't want to marry him yourself, so I suppose it was only a matter of time before someone else did.'

'Thanks for the sympathy,' she says, coldly.

'Come on now, Pip.' He smiles, and she can't help a faint rush of pleasure at the use of a pet name. 'You deserve better than him. A lot better.'

*

After another day's stint watching the Belmont with no further sign of Daniel Halligan, Cardle tells Pippa that he's drawing a line under surveillance.

'I've checked with Transport for New South Wales, and the only vehicle registered to Halligan is a black Audi Q7. And that's parked in one of the penthouse parking bays underneath the Belmont.' He pulls up a photo on his phone and shows it to Pippa. 'Meanwhile, Tansy's going about her business as usual, and I think by now we can be pretty sure her husband's not there.' The two of them are back in the hotel brasserie, Pippa with another glass of wine and Cardle tucking into a second lager. 'We can drop the hire car off at the airport in the morning.'

'The airport?'

'Yup.' Cardle runs a huge paw over his stubbled chin. 'We're going to go up to the Queensland border and take a look at Halligan's dodgy building plot. See if we can find out more by talking to the locals.'

'About that…' Pippa twirls the stem of her glass. 'I checked with the New South Wales Land Registry, and Daniel bought the tract of land from a man called Martin Kelly. Prior to that, it belonged to the Kelly family for decades. Since the turn of the last century.'

He gives her a long look. 'You're getting pretty good at this stuff,' he says, keeping his tone light. 'I'll have to look to my laurels.' Before Pippa can reply, he drains his glass. 'Come on, we've got an early start in the morning. Flight's at eight thirty.'

Pippa is relieved when Cardle texts her later and tells her they're not checking out of the Sydney hotel, but to bring an overnight bag with her just in case.

Pippa is bleary-eyed and monosyllabic at the airport, only perking up a little when they disembark the plane at Coolangatta, to be met by a blast of tropical sunshine.

Tweed Heads reminds her a little of Florida, all palm trees and tanned retirees in golf carts. They pick up a car and drive the short distance inland to the Horizon Lakes Village site. A faded billboard is still in place, promising '*The perfect way of life for active seniors.*' It features photos of tanned, smiling faces next to a gleaming blue swimming pool and vivid green golf course. In contrast to these images, the land itself is swampy and barren, with a Portacabin office, a handful of home sites at the foundation stage, and a couple of land-moving excavators abandoned next to half-dug holes.

'Not exactly living the retirement dream, is it?' Cardle asks drily, as they get out of the car and look around. He shades his eyes and squints into the middle distance, reaching into his shirt pocket for his shades. On the horizon, as the name promises, the turquoise water of the lake is just visible.

'I suppose it could have been a nice place to live,' Pippa says, though she's not entirely convinced, 'if it had been finished.'

The door of the Portacabin swings open and a man emerges wearing a hard hat and high visibility vest over a sleeveless T-shirt. He does a double take when he sees the car and its two occupants in city clothes.

'G'day… can I help you?'

'We were hoping to speak to Martin Kelly. I don't suppose you happen to know where we'd find him?'

The man pushes his hard hat back and scratches his forehead. 'Well now, I do and I don't… You'll find him at the cemetery. He died six months ago.'

CHAPTER TWENTY-SEVEN

PIPPA

The Kelly homestead is at the end of an interminable dirt track, surrounded by a vast acreage of orchards and crops.

The white farmhouse with its wraparound veranda looks to Pippa's eye like every movie and TV show she has ever watched about the Australian outback. When a male figure emerges on the porch, alerted by the sound of tyres on gravel, she expects him to be wearing a wide-brimmed hat with corks dangling from it. Instead they're greeted by an attractive man in his forties, with a broad smile and deep lines around his eyes.

'Hi,' he says, extending a hand even though he was not expecting them. 'Tom Kelly.'

By way of explanation, Cardle hands over one of his business cards. 'We were hoping to talk to Martin Kelly. But I understand he's—'

'My dad. Yeah, I'm afraid he passed away just before Christmas. What was it you wanted to talk to him about?' He narrows his eyes slightly. 'Though let me take a wild guess… Horizon Lakes, right?'

'That's right,' says Cardle, with a rueful smile. 'What happened to your father? Do you mind me asking?'

Tom beckons them onto the porch. 'Come in out of the sun for a bit… can I get you folks a cold drink?'

He returns with cold cans of soda and the three of them sit down at a weather-beaten table made from the local timber. 'Dad had a heart attack,' he tells them. 'His second one. Went out for a walk on the farm, something he often did in the evening and… well, it must have been pretty sudden. We found him the next morning.'

'I'm sorry,' offers Pippa. 'That must have been a shock.'

'Yeah…' Tom opens a can of 7 Up with a loud crack, and tips his head back to drink it. 'Yeah, it was. Of course all the hassle over the Horizon Lakes deal didn't help. He got very stressed when things turned nasty.'

Cardle and Pippa exchange a glance. 'What kind of hassle?' asks Cardle.

'Well, the sale went through fine at the outset. Sweet as a nut. My son, Bryce, handled the viewings, showed it to this guy Halligan, who was extremely keen to move on it. Wanted to rush things through and get building – didn't do his due diligence, you know? And, yeah, Bryce is young and green… someone more experienced might have mentioned the need to get an environmental survey…' He pours another long draught of lemonade into his mouth, slamming down the can. 'Anyway, Halligan discovers all these problems with contamination down the line and, all of a sudden, it's our fault, and he threatens to sue Dad for half the cost of the land. So it's no big stretch of the imagination to think that the stress contributed to the heart attack.'

'And did he?' Cardle asks, swigging from his own can and swatting at the flies swarming around it, attracted by the sugary liquid. 'Did Halligan sue?'

'No, that's the weird thing.' Tom shrugs. 'He suddenly dropped it, never followed through. Not that we weren't glad, you understand. I can only suppose that Dad's death pricked his conscience. He'd seemed desperate for the money; claimed he was unable to pay back the buyers who'd handed over deposit money and then wanted to back out. But that was a crock because I know people he paid back in full.'

Cardle taps his fingers on the side of the can. 'You know someone who was buying one of the homes?'

'Yeah. My wife's second cousin and her husband. They were planning to retire down here. From Brisbane.'

'I don't suppose you could put us in touch with them?'

'No worries.' Tom stands up. 'Wait here a second and I'll fetch their address.'

Tom Kelly's cousin, Joyce Aherne, lives in a detached brick bungalow in the Brisbane suburb of Rochedale South, just over an hour's drive from Tweed Heads.

Tom has contacted her to explain the purpose of Pippa and Cardle's impromptu visit, and she's there to greet them at the front door with the mixture of anxiety and excitement normally reserved for special guests.

'Come in, come in,' she says, ushering them into a spacious open-plan lounge where ceiling fans are whirring lazily. She's a plump woman in her mid-sixties, with hair dyed a rather harsh shade of copper. 'I've made you some sandwiches.'

'That's very kind,' murmurs Pippa, as Joyce bustles around fetching cutlery, paper napkins and a huge platter of open-faced sandwiches. She pours them all glasses of iced tea, and sits down, beaming at them.

'I'm sorry Wilf couldn't be here. My husband. But he's out on the golf course, I'm afraid. He's always at that wretched golf course.' She rolls her eyes in a *men – what can you do?* gesture. 'Of course, the on-site golf course was one of the reasons Wilf was keen to buy the house at Horizon Lakes,' she goes on, helping Cardle to a prawn mayonnaise sandwich. 'I understand from Tom that you had some questions about that?'

'That's right,' Cardle says, through a mouthful of prawns, licking mayonnaise from his fingers. 'I wondered if you could tell us about what happened when you discovered that there was a problem with the land the houses were being built on?'

'Well,' says Joyce, smoothing her napkin over her lap. She proffers the platter in Pippa's direction. 'Another sandwich, dear? Though I don't suppose you want to spoil your lovely figure with too much bread... We knew nothing about it until one of Wilf's pals at the golf club read something about it in the *Brisbane Times*. We went straight to our lawyer, who said we shouldn't touch the place with a barge pole. He contacted Roseland to demand our deposit back. Well, they wouldn't pay at first. Said there was a long line of creditors ahead of us, and the funds weren't available. And we were really worried, because a hundred and fifty thousand dollars is a lot of money to us. We couldn't afford to lose it. We'd accepted an offer on this place, and we had to pull out of the sale, which was a shame.'

'Did you have any dealings with Daniel Halligan directly?' Cardle asks.

Joyce shakes her head. 'No, I don't think so. His name may have been on some of the paperwork we got, but I certainly never spoke to him. I know other people who met him at the sales launch...' She offers the plate to her guests again.

'But you got your money back?' Pippa holds up a hand to indicate she's had enough sandwiches.

'Well, that was the funny thing, we were getting nowhere, and our lawyer was talking about having no choice but to go through the courts, and then all of a sudden a cheque arrived, for the full amount of the deposit. No explanation, just a banker's draft from Roseland Investments. So we were back to square one with the house hunting but, as Wilf says, at least we weren't out of pocket.'

'And when was this exactly?' Pippa asks, sipping iced tea so sweet it makes her fillings jangle.

Joyce thinks for a moment. 'It must have been some time in January. Because I remember we'd not long been back from Tweed Heads when we got the cheque. We'd been down for Martin's funeral.'

'And he died... when, exactly?'

'It was in December,' says Joyce, her naturally buoyant air temporarily deflated. 'They had to delay the funeral until after the New Year, though. Such a shame. He was a lovely man.'

'And you say you know of other people who bought plots at Horizon Lakes Village?' Cardle's running his fingers over his stubble, a gesture Pippa now knows means his brain is working overtime.

'A couple of them, yes. Someone Wilf plays golf with... Stan somebody or other... he and his wife bought one. And one of our neighbours – her sister went to a marketing event in Canberra and signed up to buy one. And she went because somebody she worked with had already invested in the development.'

Cardle and Pippa exchange glances. 'And what happened to their deposit money, do you know?'

'Well now, that's the funny thing... hold on a minute and I'll tell you.' Joyce disappears into the kitchen and returns with a plate of coconut-covered Lamington cakes. 'Kettle's on: tea or coffee, either of you?'

'Coffee, please.' Cardle helps himself to one of the cakes, adding quickly before Joyce can disappear again, 'You were saying? About the money?'

'Yes, the funny thing is that from what we've heard, exactly the same thing happened to the other buyers, but not to the lady who'd put money in as an investment. They were all making legal threats and getting nowhere and then all of a sudden, boom...' Joyce fans her fingers to indicate an explosion. 'The people wanting to buy a plot abruptly get all their money back just like we did, no explanation.'

'But not the investor?'

Joyce shakes her head. 'No, apparently not. She put in quite a bit more cash than we did, and, last I heard, she was still trying to get her investment back. Whether it's the luck of the draw as to who they repaid and who they didn't, I couldn't say. As I say, at least Wilf and I aren't out of pocket.'

'Would you be able to put us in touch with this lady?' asks Cardle, pulling out a business card. 'My email address is on here.'

'Now then, not off the top of my head,' says Joyce, regretfully, 'No. To be honest, I can't recall her name. I'd have to ask around and check her details.'

'Well, drop me a line if you manage to find out.' Cardle takes a second Lamington before standing up.

'Your coffee…' Joyce looks disappointed. 'I was just about to—'

'Don't worry about it, we've already eaten like royalty.' He extends a large hand. 'You've been extremely helpful.'

'So, what do you think?' Cardle turns to look at Pippa as they drive back down the M1 to the Gold Coast. 'Daniel Halligan and his magic money tree.'

'It certainly sounds dodgy,' agrees Pippa. 'But we need to know more.'

'We know enough, surely? He's threatening to sue poor Martin Kelly for a huge sum because he can't afford to pay his creditors, Kelly literally drops dead, and yet without taking his estate to court, Halligan can suddenly afford to repay everyone, no questions asked.'

Pippa stares out of the window at the endless groves of eucalyptus and gum trees that fringe the Pacific coastal plain. 'What are you implying?'

'Look at the timing. He's suddenly flush with money at the start of this year. What else happened to him earlier this year?'

'Ohhh…' says Pippa, her eyes widening.

'Exactly. He acquired a wealthy wife.'

CHAPTER TWENTY-EIGHT

PIPPA

'So how do we go about locating Halligan now? What would you normally do?'

Pippa and Cardle are sitting outside a bar in Dawes Point, watching the sun go down over the harbour. As the sky fades to pink and violet, a light breeze ruffles Pippa's hair, tingeing her tawny locks with gold. She pushes it away from her face self-consciously, aware that he's watching her.

'Normally, back in the UK, I have my tame sources. And investigative databases that the likes of you can't access. But it's harder here; I'm working blind, to an extent. He's not driving a car… not his own car, anyway… he doesn't own property, and his utility bills are in Tansy's name.'

'What about his mobile?' asks Pippa, taking an appreciative sip of her vodka and soda and leaning back in her chair. Their flight back from Coolangatta only touched down an hour earlier, after what proved to be a very long day.

'Again, if we were in the UK, I could approach my contacts with the network providers, but I don't have the same access here.'

'It looks like he had a commission in the British army for a few years, but after that the trail goes cold. And he's a complete social media refusenik.' Pippa sighs. 'He doesn't use Facebook or Instagram, or even LinkedIn. Although…'

She sits up in her chair, remembering something. 'I did come across a mention when I was doing my internet trawl on him. He worked in real estate in Sydney before he set up Roseland. Where was it?' She clicks through a series of links on an internet search engine. 'Yes… between 2017 and the end of last year he worked as a sales negotiator for Cadogan International.'

She shows Cardle a corporate profile picture, with Halligan looking photogenic and handsome in his suit and tie.

'Hmm,' he grunts, squinting at it. 'I suppose there's nothing to be lost by talking to them. That's tomorrow's agenda.'

'Oh, my goodness, you want Danno!' the woman with bleached-blonde hair exclaims when they visit the Cross Street office of Cadogan International the next morning. According to her name badge, she is called Karen Fielding. 'Of course I know him. Haven't seen him in months, though.'

'And you don't know where he is now?'

Karen's grin fades a little. 'Oh, Christ, he's not in trouble, is he? You're not the cops?'

Cardle shakes his head. 'We just need to have a chat with him.'

'Were you friends?' Pippa asks.

Karen looks coy. 'I guess you could say we were mates, yes. I mean, of course I fancied the guy; every woman I knew did. Our female clients used to go ga-ga over him. After he stopped working here, I helped him out a bit, setting up his new venture.'

'And do you know his wife?' Cardle asks.

'His wife?' Karen's eyebrows shoot up. 'Dan wasn't married – said he'd never do it either. He had a girlfriend—'

'Tansy Dimaano?' Pippa probes.

'Nah, she was called Maxine. A lawyer. They lived together. She seemed decent enough; bit straight-laced, though. No, hang on a minute…'

She turns to the terminal on her desk and starts clicking through the records on her screen. 'Tansy Dimaano… I knew that rang a bell. She was a client. She bought a six-million-dollar apartment and Dan handled the sale…' She looks up again at Cardle and Pippa, her eyes wide. 'Are you saying he married *her*?'

Pippa nods. 'Yes. In April.'

'Wow! Never saw that coming… I mean, it was fairly obvious that she was after him, but Dan was always dead against tying the knot. Used to say he didn't believe in it. Laughed at people who thought it would make them happy.'

Pippa shrugs. 'Well, he did it.'

'Can't you just ask his wife where he is, then?' Karen looks confused.

'She doesn't know,' says Cardle, flatly. 'Do you have a phone number for him?'

'Yeah, sure…' Karen reaches in her bag for her phone. 'I've still got his mobile number in my contacts.'

She hands her phone to Pippa, who makes a note of the number. 'Thanks, Karen.' Pippa smiles and gives the phone back. 'You've been incredibly helpful.'

Only Karen Fielding's input turns out not to be so helpful after all.

'Bloody phone's switched off,' Cardle growls, after trying it several times as they walk back to the hotel. 'Straight to voicemail… "The person you're calling is unavailable." No big surprise there.' He reaches for his cigarettes and lights up.

Pippa, reluctant to add to his exasperation by asking what he intends to do, says nothing.

'You said he was in the army back home?' he asks.

'Yes. Until eight or nine years ago.'

'And, at some point after that, he washes up here in Sydney. Presumably after developing itchy feet, or having a mid-life crisis.

And from what Karen told us, he met someone here and moved in with her. Had a taste of settling down for a while.'

'That's about as much as we know.'

They've reached the hotel now, and the doorman is greeting them with a slight tip of his hat. Cardle ignores him, grinding out his cigarette stub underfoot.

'What are you thinking?' Pippa asks, lengthening her stride to keep up with him as he marches towards the lifts.

'I'm thinking that when the shit hits the fan and his property deal goes tits up, the obvious move is for him to go back to the UK. That's where he was born and grew up… do we know about his family?'

Pippa shakes her head.

They've reached the door of Cardle's room now. He says, 'I might as well get on with running a search on that—'

'—using the special databases that aren't for the likes of me?' Pippa teases.

'Something like that.'

He phones her half an hour later, as she is about to get in the shower.

'Couple of things…'

'Go on.'

'I've had an email from the woman who invested in Roseland, the one Joyce Aherne mentioned. Lady called Pamela Darby. Retired civil servant.'

'And?' Pippa asks.

'Turns out she has been repaid after all.'

'So Joyce was wrong?'

'No, that's the thing, Joyce was right. Pamela wasn't repaid in the first wave of refunds. She'd been told she would get her money back, but she'd have to wait another twelve months. And then out of the blue she received an online transfer for the full amount. She said it was only around a couple of weeks ago.'

Pippa thinks for a moment. 'So, the first lot were repaid a couple of months before the Halligans were married, and at least one other after they got back from their honeymoon. Do you think that's significant?'

'Don't know. Could be.' She can hear Cardle flick his cigarette lighter.

'And the other thing?'

'Halligan's parents are both dead, but he has a brother. And as far as I can tell, that brother is living in London.'

'Don't tell me…' Pippa is already reaching into the top of the wardrobe and lifting down her suitcase.

'We're going to fly back to London. My gut is telling me that if he's left Australia, then that's where he's gone.'

Pippa doesn't think the jet lag could be any worse than it was when they arrived in Melbourne, but her assumption proves false.

Cardle tells her to take Monday off before returning to the office, and she spends most of it asleep. She's happy to be back in her little annexe above Rosemary's carriage house in Clapham, to be reunited with Gus and to enjoy the basket of homemade bread that Marysia has left for her. It feels as though she has been away a lot longer than ten days.

When she returns to the office on Tuesday morning, Cardle is busy talking to a new client, a man who fears his business partner is swindling him. She busies herself with restocking the fridge, answering emails and dealing with the post that has arrived while they were away on the trip, but the mundanity of the tasks frustrates her. She feels both exhausted and wired, and can't quite shake a feeling that Cardle is ignoring her, unsure how to treat her.

Eventually he comes and stands by her desk, pulling on his jacket.

'I'm off to Islington, to speak to Ben Halligan. Daniel's brother.'

Pippa reaches instinctively for her bag, but he shakes his head. 'It's okay, it doesn't need two of us. You stay here and cover the phones.'

And with that he is gone.

Probably for the best, Pippa tells herself. *I'm still really tired; what better excuse to go home and have a bath and an early night?* But beneath the self-administered pep talk she's smarting. When they were in Australia, Cardle seemed happy to have her as his sidekick. To teach her the tricks of the trade. To benefit from her aptitude for online research. Now that they're back in the office, she's been relegated to the role of filing clerk once more.

'How did it go?' she asks Cardle the next morning, deliberately keeping her tone light and her attention focused on the contents of the filing cabinet. 'Did you manage to talk to him?'

'Up to a point.' He's non-committal.

'But you went to his house?'

'His flat, yes. It's in Islington. He's a bit of a hipster, young Ben.'

'How young?' Pippa demands.

'Well, nearer your age than mine.'

'So does he know where his brother is?'

'He says not, no.'

'I sense a "but".'

'The guy was perfectly pleasant– charming, even. Told me a bit about their upbringing, how they both inherited money when their mum died, and Daniel used his share to go back-packing round Australia, then put what was left into Roseland Investments. Ben, meanwhile, has set up a very successful design business.'

'Married?' Pippa keeps her tone casual.

Cardle shakes his head. 'Nope. Not as far as I could tell. He may have a girlfriend but from appearances he lives alone.'

'So you're saying he wasn't very helpful?'

'He was friendly enough, made all the right noises, but I got the impression he was holding back.' Cardle rubs his chin. 'He knows more than he's letting on. I'm sure of it.'

'Will you talk to him again?'

'Not sure there's much point. I left him a card and he said he'd call if he heard from his brother, but honestly it feels like a dead end... anyway' – Cardle reaches for a file on his desk – 'I'll have to update Lindgren before much longer; tell him for now we've drawn a blank. Meanwhile, it's back to the day job.'

A few minutes later, Pippa overhears him on the phone through his open office door, and he's definitely not talking to Lindgren. There's a softer tone to his voice that she's never heard before.

'That would be great,' he's saying. 'If you're still up for it?'

There's a silence and then: 'So where shall we meet...? D'you fancy dinner?'

Jim's got a date, Pippa thinks. She feels vaguely perturbed, though she'd be at pains to explain why. Why shouldn't he be dating? He's single after all, and not unattractive. Plenty of women would probably be happy to go out with him.

'Great... I'll see you tonight.'

He glances in Pippa's direction as he hangs up the call, and she busies herself with sorting through invoices. 'Everything okay?' he asks, and there's a slightly cool edge to his voice.

'Yes, fine,' Pippa lies. 'Everything's fine.'

CHAPTER TWENTY-NINE

PIPPA

As soon as Cardle has left the office and gone to tail yet another unfaithful husband, Pippa takes the Halligan file from his desk and reads through the notes he has written.

Then she returns to her own desk and the laptop she has been bringing in from home, and looks up Keystone, Ben Halligan's design business. It's in Leonard Street, at the Old Street end of Shoreditch. *Of course,* thinks Pippa, smiling to herself as she remembers Cardle's description of Ben as 'a bit of a hipster'. *It would be Shoreditch.*

It's also no more than a twenty-five-minute walk from Greatorex Street. Pippa exchanges the shapeless cardigan she's been wearing all day for a linen jacket, then goes into the tiny bathroom on the communal landing and spends a few minutes arranging her hair. She shampooed it in the shower that morning so it's clean at least. She pins it at the side with a sparkly clip she finds at the bottom of her bag and adds some bright orangey-red lipstick.

'You look okay,' she says, smiling at her reflection with a touch of self-consciousness. 'Now go and get your hipster.'

At five forty-five, Pippa is positioned outside Keystone, which is housed in a converted four-storey yellow-brick warehouse. It's a pleasant early June evening, and drinkers in the surrounding pubs are spilling out onto the pavement, the babble of their chatter filling the narrow streets like the sound of excitable birds.

Workers are starting to emerge, sometimes alone, sometimes in twos and threes. Eventually, Ben Halligan comes out, with two colleagues. She recognises him from the photo on the website, but even without that she would have been able to pick him out as Daniel Halligan's brother. He's not as classically handsome; his face narrower and features less regular, but he still strongly resembles his brother, dressed in a washed-out blue chambray shirt and khaki combats. His hair is the same light chestnut colour, but cut into a fade at the sides, and there's a suggestion of facial hair: not five-day shadow like Cardle's, but a cultivated semi-beard.

Strolling casually and looking down at her phone screen to make herself blend in, Pippa follows him and his companions across the intersection with the Great Eastern Street to the Reliance. The cosy interior features bleached wood floors, and the folding doors of the ground floor bar have been opened up completely to allow the drinkers to spill out onto the pavement.

Ben goes straight to the bar and buys a round of drinks for the two men he's with. Pippa buys herself a mineral water and positions herself at one of the small round tables and watches him, thinking. This isn't going to be a quick job, she realises. Nobody is going to spill family secrets to a stranger after a brief exchange at a bar. She's going to have to get him alone, and get him relaxed. And short of going to bed with the man, the only way she can think of to achieve that is to get him drunk.

One of his friends is now looking at his watch and holding up his hand to refuse the offer of a second beer. He leaves, so Ben is down to just one drinking buddy. Now is probably the time, Pippa decides, because when the second friend leaves, Ben will probably just head home. She remembers a tactic that her university friend Ellie once used to get a man she fancied to speak to her. Approaching the bar, she squeezes into a tiny gap between Ben and the drinker to his right, and signals for the barman to pour her a gin and tonic, with plenty of ice. She places it on the bar a few inches from Ben's right forearm and makes a great play of rummaging in her bag to find her purse. Her left elbow shoots up and knocks the glass, splashing the drink over the sleeve of Ben's shirt.

'Oh, my God, I'm *so* sorry.' Her hands go to her face and she turns around so that they have eye contact when the icy liquid makes him automatically twist in her direction. His right arm flies up and – even better, thinks Pippa, with the thrill of kismet – he knocks her glass clean over.

'Oh, Christ, *I'm* sorry!' Ben gives her a rueful smile, covering his eyes with his hand momentarily. 'Let me get you another one?'

'No, honestly, there's no need, it was all my fault. I should be buying *you* a drink.'

Ben indicates his pint of real ale. 'As you can see, I'm okay. But thanks.'

'How about a chaser?' Pippa suggests.

He takes in her appearance, as though seeing her properly for the first time and liking what he sees. 'Go on, then… I'll have a single malt.' He grins, and Pippa can't help noticing how attractive he is. 'This is Gianpaolo,' he adds, introducing the smaller, darker man to his left. 'One of my colleagues.'

'What do you do?' Pippa asks, disingenuously, and Ben explains that he owns a digital design agency and talks to her about their client base. At some point during his exposition, Gianpaolo lifts his hand in a wave and leaves.

Great. I've successfully separated my prey from the herd.

'How about you, Pippa?' Ben is asking. 'What do you do for a living?'

She is about to tell him she works for a private detective, but catches herself in time.

'I do market analysis for an insurance firm. Very boring…'

Ben is twisting his empty glass of whisky to and fro. 'I'd still like to hear.'

'Let me get you another one. Trust me, you'll need it.'

She buys Ben another short and outlines briefly the sort of work she used to do at Portman Willis. Keen to change the subject she asks about where he lives, and they quickly get onto a good-natured dispute about the merits of residing north of the river versus south. Without asking him, Pippa nods at the barman and gets Ben another single malt. He drinks it.

'Tell you what, pretty Pippa,' he says, sounding a little tipsy. 'Why don't you and I go on somewhere else. Somewhere quieter?'

'Got somewhere in mind?'

'I have. I know just the place.'

They head to a place that calls itself a 'cocktail club', with dark painted walls and vintage velvet furniture, dimly lit by candles in wine bottles. Ben orders a Manhattan and Pippa sticks to a single gin and tonic. She needs to keep a clear head.

'So you live alone?' Ben is asking. They're on a small two-seater velvet sofa, and his thigh is pressed against hers. 'In this place in Clapham?'

Pippa nods. 'I've not lived there very long. I used to live in Ally Pally, in my fiancé's flat. Ex-fiancé. We split up.'

'Sorry to hear that,' Ben says, not entirely sincerely. 'So how close were you to actually getting married? Had you set a date?'

'Actually…' Pippa takes a mouthful of her drink through a straw before setting the glass down. 'It was on our wedding day. The break-up.'

'Oh… wow!' Ben's eyes widen. 'That's really hard core. D'you mind me asking… was it you who pulled the plug or him?'

'It was me,' admits Pippa. 'We'd been together a long time – since just after I left uni – but it didn't feel right. And later…'

She was about to say 'after the honeymoon', but doesn't want to reveal that she was at the exact same Mauritius resort as his own honeymooning brother. '…a week later, I discovered that he was seeing the girlfriend of one of his colleagues. I had a lucky escape, really.'

'What a douchebag,' mutters Ben. 'I'm sorry. Mind you, marriage is definitely not all it's cracked up to be. Not. At. All.' He's slurring slightly now, waving a hand to try and attract the drinks server.

'You've experienced it?' asks Pippa.

He shakes his head. 'No, God no. But my older brother got married recently. Lives in Australia. Swore he'd never do it, but he went back on his word and it's been a total fucking disaster.'

'Why, what happened?' Pippa's heart is pounding. They're finally getting to the information she needs.

'Oh, Christ, what didn't happen? He's screwing this mad Instagram model on and off, but the last thing his wants is to marry her. Then his business hits the skids and he's in all sorts of financial trouble, and she says she'll settle his debts but only if he marries her.'

Ben takes a slug of his second cocktail, running his hand through his hair so it stands up at an odd angle at the front. 'Anyway. Anyway… where was I?'

'Your brother's business,' prompts Pippa.

'Yes… he's quite a catch, is Danny. I mean he's very good-looking. Anyway, he still says no to the woman. But then, one night, he's visited by the man he did the original deal with – bought some land to build a retirement community, only it's dud – and they're arguing about this guy refusing to repay him. They get in a bit of a fight. And Dan gives the guy a shove, and he keels over and dies. Has a heart attack.'

'Bloody hell,' says Pippa, her eyes widening. A shiver goes through her as she remembers driving down the track to the Kellys' farm.

'I know,' slurs Ben. 'He's got a dead body in his hotel room…'

A dead body in his hotel room. Now all Pippa can see in her mind's eye is the inert figure of Nikki Lindgren.

'…total nightmare,' Ben is saying, 'And then this girl, Tansy' – he almost spits her name – 'this absolute piece of work, she gets her hired muscle to get rid of the body. Take it back to his farm and dump it there, making sure no questions get asked. And the price of her doing that for him is that he has to marry her. So he does. He doesn't want to, but he has to, to buy her silence.'

'So… what you're saying is, she's blackmailing him.'

''Zactly,' mumbles Ben. 'You've hit the nail on the head. And, of course, once she's got him, got what she wants, she instantly gets bored with him. Has no time for him. Can't be arsed any more. 'S fucked up.'

'And they're still together?' Pippa presses.

'What?' Ben's focus is wandering.

'Your brother – are he and his wife still together? In Australia.'

'That's the thing.' Ben's shaking his head. 'Nobody knows. He's not using his mobile number. Sent me an email a few weeks ago saying he was going travelling for a bit and not to worry.'

'Does his wife know where he is?' Pippa thinks back to the hours of surveillance outside the Belmont building.

Ben shrugs. 'I really don't know. She doesn't talk to me. But I doubt it, given he told me he'd left her…' He drains his second Manhattan. 'Anyway, 'nough about my brother, let's get back to talking about you.'

'Sorry, but I'm going to have to get going.' Pippa slides off the sofa and straightens her jacket.

'Still early.' Ben looks disappointed.

'I know, but I'm meeting someone,' she lies. 'Another time, maybe?'

They exchange phone numbers and Pippa slips out to her imaginary meeting, hurrying to Old Street station to catch the Northern line back to Clapham.

As she sits on the rattling tube, she can't quell her excitement at the prospect of revealing to Cardle what she's managed to find out. An image of him out on his date comes unbidden into her mind, but she pushes it away again.

CHAPTER THIRTY

PIPPA

Cardle arrives at the office late the next morning, and it's immediately obvious that he's in a bad mood.

'Shall I make coffee?' Pippa asks him, letting her voice trail off when he thrusts the takeaway cup he's holding into her line of vision.

'Got one,' he says, gruffly, and slams the door of the inner office.

Pippa pictures contrasting scenarios. Perhaps the date went badly, and that's the cause of his irritability. Or perhaps it went so well that he's been up all night and it's sleep deprivation that's making him bad-tempered. Either way, she can't help but feel deflated. She had been so eager to tell him what happened the evening before; to prove how useful she can be.

He stays in his office for at least two hours. When he emerges, Pippa holds up a hand to indicate she needs to talk to him, but he walks right past her. 'Going for a fag,' he grunts.

He returns, smelling of smoke, to find Pippa blocking his path. 'I need to talk to you. About last night.'

'Last night?' He looks confused. 'I was out last night.'

'Have a good time?' Pippa can't prevent herself from asking, but instantly regrets it, when he scowls back at her.

'Not particularly, as it goes. But I want to know what *you* were doing last night.'

'Well...' Pippa sits down on the sofa, hoping he'll join her, but he remains standing, looming over her. 'I did a bit of reconnaissance work of my own. I followed Ben Halligan from his offices to a pub. And I got talking to him. And the thing is, he told me—'

'You did what?' Cardle glowers. 'You went after a lead without consulting me?'

'Yes, I did. But I figured that as a girl... and as someone around the same age as Ben... I had a better chance of getting him to talk.'

'Oh, I see. You think you can do a better job than I can. You think that you know all about the PI game now, do you?'

'No, it's not that—'

'See my earlier point about not consulting me.' Cardle's Yorkshire accent becomes more pronounced when he's worked up. 'You went behind my back.'

'I was going to tell you, obviously,' Pippa says, weakly.

'Did it not occur to you what a risk you were taking, not telling me what you were doing? A woman on her own, without proper surveillance training, following a man. A man who could have dragged you off anywhere and done God knows what?'

'I wasn't alone with him. I would never have done that. We were in a pub first, and then in a bar. Then I went home. Anyway, it's not like I was tailing a known criminal. You said yourself that Ben Halligan was a pleasant, helpful guy.'

'That means nothing. I'm a man, and nearly twice his size. Men behave differently when women are around, especially young, good-looking women.'

Pippa flushes and looks down at her hands.

'If anything had happened to you, that would have rebounded on me. And hardly looked good for the agency. I'm trying to run a professional operation here, you know.' He rakes his hand angrily over his stubble. 'Honestly, I should never—'

Pippa presses the heels of her hands against her cheeks. 'If you're going to say that you should never have taken me on, and you want me to leave, then I'll save you the trouble.' She stands up and pushes past the coffee table. 'I'm going.'

'For fuck's sake… Pippa…!'

But she's already grabbed her laptop and her bag and walked out of the office, letting the door slam behind her.

The most hurtful thing, she decides later, and the thing that keeps her lying awake that night in her chintzy bedroom, is that Cardle didn't even ask her what it was she had found out. It didn't seem to have occurred to him that she might have done something important, even if he hadn't sanctioned it himself.

She gets up late the next morning, feeling as though she has a hangover. After dressing in workout gear, she goes to the main house and asks Rosemary if she can take Gus for a walk. Rosemary takes in her puffy eyes and ashen skin and agrees, but insists she goes into the kitchen first and have some of Marysia's coffee.

It's a beautiful midsummer morning, and after running for half an hour with Gus scampering at her heels, Pippa feels a little better. The job with Cardle wasn't a real job anyway, she reminds herself. For a start, she wasn't being paid a salary. It was only ever meant to be temporary. She needs to stop putting off the inevitable and find herself something permanent.

After showering, she makes more coffee and sits down at her laptop. She updates her LinkedIn profile and starts scrolling through job websites. It's not long before she's found an advertisement for the Metropolitan Police Graduate Scheme, which offers a chance to join CID and promises exceptional training and the opportunity for leadership.

I could do that, Pippa tells herself. In her own mind at least, she's proven she has an aptitude for investigative work. That would be one in the eye for Cardle too, if she became a police detective. That would show him. Quite what it would show him, an ex-police officer himself, she can't define, but the idea intrigues her and she downloads the very lengthy application form.

Over the next couple of days, her mood continues to stabilise. During the day she spends plenty of time outside, enjoying the lush green promise of full summer. At the weekend she meets Lauren for drinks in Covent Garden; the following Monday, she has supper with Robyn and Harry, a couple she met through Alastair, and who live in nearby Wandsworth. She was worried that dinner *à trois* would be awkward in the aftermath of her broken engagement, but Robyn asks over another single friend and they all sit outside and eat in the garden and it's fine. Being single in your early thirties, it turns out, is fine. Having always been part of a couple herself, this is something of a revelation to Pippa. On her way back from Wandsworth she receives a text from Ben Halligan asking her if she wants to meet for another drink sometime. She sends a non-committal reply, stalling him.

Word that she is back in circulation after the cancelled wedding seems to have got around. Another friend, Olivia, asks if she wants to go and see a movie the following night, but Pippa puts her off, deciding instead to spend the evening tidying the flat and painting her nails.

She's surprised, therefore, when at 8 p.m., just as she's changed into a vest top and pyjama shorts and selected a bottle of nail polish, her front doorbell rings.

She opens it to find Jim Cardle standing there. He's dressed in aviator shades, a white T-shirt and faded jeans, and holding a bottle of wine still wrapped in the tissue from the off-licence.

'Sorry to come round unannounced,' he says, holding out the bottle. 'But I thought if I asked first you'd have told me to bugger off. And you'd have been within your rights.'

Pippa feels acutely conscious of her skimpy clothing. *Don't be stupid*, she reminds herself. *He's already seen you in a bikini.* Nevertheless, she grabs a sweatshirt from the back of the sofa and tugs it on, minimising the amount of flesh on display.

'Come in,' she says, unsmiling. Taking the wine from him, she fetches corkscrew and glasses. The bottle must have been in the chiller at the off-licence because it's still acceptably cold. She pours two glasses and hands him one, but still says nothing.

Cardle is taking in the cosy, chintzy interior of the carriage house. 'Nice place,' he says, as Pippa hands him wine. They sit down, him filling an armchair, her on the sofa with her bare legs tucked underneath her.

'Look, it's obvious I've come round here to apologise to you. I shouldn't have spoken to you the way I did. It's no excuse, but I wasn't in the best of moods.'

'I noticed,' says Pippa, drily, sipping her wine. 'Bad date the night before, was it?'

He has the grace to look embarrassed. 'Something like that. That and a row with my ex about seeing the kids.'

'So you're seeing someone?' If they were in the office, she probably wouldn't ask, but he's in her personal space now, so she feels entitled.

'I have been… on and off. She… she's got a child herself, so it's a bit complicated.'

Pippa gives him a sharp look. 'This wouldn't be the same woman who once asked you if she could go with you to Australia?'

He nods ruefully. 'But it's off now. I finished it. That night. It was a bit messy, hence my not being in the most receptive frame of mind.'

'Understatement,' Pippa observes, coolly.

'But I had no right to take it out on you. It was unprofessional, and there I was banging on about being professional.' He sets down his wine and holds up his hands in a gesture of surrender. 'If you want to accuse me of hypocrisy, you've got me bang to rights.'

Pippa sighs. 'Well, I'm sorry too. I should have told you what I was planning to do.'

'Obviously, that would have been preferable.' Cardle gives a half-smile. 'If you're going to do something that relates to a case I'm contractually engaged on, it's best if I know about it. Even though I do admire your initiative.'

'Fine,' says Pippa, equably. 'Let's just put it behind us, shall we?' She crosses to the kitchen area, empties a bag of tortilla chips into a bowl and places it on the table between them, before topping up their glasses.

'Obviously, the other reason I'm here' – Cardle crams a fistful of chips into his mouth and crunches them noisily – 'is to find out what Ben Halligan told you. As my client, I have a duty to Arne Lindgren to know. I wouldn't be doing my job properly, otherwise.'

Pippa looks at him for a few seconds, twirling the end of a lock of hair. Then she sighs, sets her glass down and tells him everything that Ben revealed about his brother: that he was at the very least circumstantially involved in Martin Kelly's death, that both he and Tansy were responsible for covering up that fact, and that Tansy was effectively blackmailing him into playing the role of her husband, by threatening to expose what she knew.

'Bloody hell.' Cardle shakes his head slowly. 'Good work, Pippa. Bloody good.'

'Ben says he can't get hold of Daniel, either. All he's been told is that he's gone off travelling. He thinks Tansy's claim not to know where he's gone is genuine. And presumably she'd be able to force him back to heel if she did know.'

'And there, right there, is a bloody great motive for Daniel Halligan to bump off Tansy. Or someone he wrongly believes to be Tansy. She's forced him into a marriage he never wanted, effectively holding him hostage. People have killed for far less.'

Cardle pours himself another glass of wine and knocks it back. As he puts the empty glass back on the table he says, 'I'd better not have any more. I'm driving.'

He stands up, and Pippa looks up at him, her expression questioning.

'So are you prepared to un-resign?' he says, bluntly. 'Will you come back to work?'

'Do you want me to?'

'I do. At least until we've put this case to bed, anyway. I'm not sure how things will look after that. Is that okay with you?' He reaches in his pocket for his shades and props them on the top of his head.

Pippa nods.

'Tell you what, take the rest of the week off. Lindgren's back in Sweden for the summer, at his beach house, and he's flying me out there so I can brief him on where we are. You okay to head back into the office on Monday? I should be back by then.'

His eyes stray to the door of her bedroom. Seeing Cardle staring directly at her bed makes Pippa feel strange. She gets up, blocking his view.

'Of course,' she says, simply. 'I'll see you there.'

But when Monday arrives, Pippa does not return to the office in Greatorex Street.

Instead, at 8.30, as she is putting the finishing touches to her make-up, Cardle phones her.

'Don't come in,' he says, without preamble.

'Oh.' Slightly stunned, Pippa sits down hard on the dressing table stool.

'It won't be worth it.'

Surely the bloody man hasn't changed his mind again, and decided to get rid of me?

'I need you to meet me at Gatwick instead. With a case. Containing your hot weather stuff. And your passport, obviously.'

'What—'

'Look, I don't have time to chat now; I need to get on with sorting arrangements. But when I met with Lindgren over the weekend and told him what we'd found out, he's become even more convinced that it was Halligan who killed his wife, mistaking her for Tansy. But we need some hard evidence relating to what actually happened that night.'

'Oh…' Pippa realises what Cardle is leading up to and her heart rate quickens. 'So…'

'Yeah. You and I are heading back there. Back to Mauritius.'

CHAPTER THIRTY-ONE

PIPPA

'Hasn't changed a bit, has it?'

Pippa looks out of the window of the taxi at the sweep of Turtle Bay, with its coconut palms and mangroves fringing the inviting azure water.

'You'd hardly expect it to, in a matter of two months,' Cardle replies, acerbic as ever. 'Only difference is, it's their winter now.'

The air does indeed feel a little cooler and fresher than on their previous visit, but the atmosphere of tropical paradise pervades. This time, their glass of the welcome punch at the Excelsior reception desk is served by the manager himself, Ashvin Babajee.

Cardle must remember the conversation where Pippa confided to him that the man made her uncomfortable, because he positions himself close to her, in an overtly protective gesture.

'Welcome back, Miss Bryant,' Babajee says, grasping her hand and taking her in through the tinted fish-bowl lenses of his glasses. 'And so soon. What a pleasure.'

He smiles at Cardle too, but there is no warmth in it. 'Separate rooms, yes?' he confirms with the check-in clerk. 'One for Miss Bryant, one for Mr Cardle?'

'That's right,' says Pippa smiling, holding out her hand for the keys.

'Not a honeymoon this time?'

'No,' says Cardle, firmly. 'Not a honeymoon.'

There are, however, several honeymoon couples in the restaurant that evening, and when Pippa and Cardle meet there for dinner, they have to take their place among them.

He orders a cold beer and looks around at the connubial hand-holding and coy whispering at the other tables. 'We fit right in,' he observes, sarcastically.

'Don't worry, I don't think anyone would mistake us for a couple.' Pippa picks up the menu, which hasn't changed since her last visit. She already knows she's going to order the grilled coconut prawns.

Cardle leans back in his chair and crosses his arms across his broad chest. 'I don't see why not,' he says, feigning huffiness. 'Strapping Yorkshire lad like me.'

Pippa decides not to mention the thirteen-year age gap between them. 'You don't talk about your private life very much,' she observes, as the waiter brings her a mai tai and asks what they'd like to eat.

After they've ordered their food, Cardle replies, 'That's because I don't have much of one. The old cliché about being married to the job applies.'

'But you were dating someone recently. You told me that much last week.'

'Yes. Alice.' He lets out a sigh, staring gloomily into his half-empty beer glass. 'I know I've talked about not dating colleagues, but this was worse. She was a client. Or a former client, at least. For a while, it was... nice. She's... nice. It was good having someone to hang around with.'

'So what went wrong?'

He shrugs. 'It had been gradually fizzling out. We'd barely seen each other over the past few months. I'm just not very good at relationships. Bit of a lone wolf. I find it hard to let people in. "Trust issues" apparently, probably stemming from the fact that my dad walked out and left us when I was a kid.'

'I think I'm going to be developing trust issues too, I'm afraid.' Pippa twirls her glass. 'I mean, I knew there were things that Alastair and I were burying, but it never occurred to me that one of them was another woman. Which sounds stupid now, I know.'

Their food arrives: prawns for Pippa and swordfish steak for Cardle. In an attempt to lighten the mood, she tells him that Ben Halligan has been in touch, seeking another date.

'You've pulled!' Cardle laughs, loading fish onto his fork.

Pippa grimaces.

'What's wrong with that? Nice-looking lad, and seemed decent enough.'

'Not my type. Even if we can overlook him being the brother of a potential killer.' Pippa delicately removes the tail of a prawn and dips her fingertips in the bowl of lemon water provided. 'Speaking of which, how did things go in Sweden, with Arne Lindgren? How is he?'

'Doing a bit better, I think. I hope so, anyway. It's a lovely summer place he's got on the west coast, and he had family and old friends around him. He was happy with how far we'd managed to progress things, and feels the Tansy blackmail angle is a strong one. But most of all, he doesn't want us to give up now. And he feels the answers… some of them, at least… are right here. Hence this all-expenses paid "honeymoon" for the two of us.'

Pippa grimaces, looking around again at the intimate tables for two.

'There will be people who were here that week when the Halligans and the Lindgrens were. People who would have seen things, noticed things. We need to start talking to them.'

Pippa is thinking, remembering. 'That day you and I first spoke,' she says, suddenly animated. 'I wound up at the pool, but what

I'd hoped to do that day was take a catamaran trip from the dock. Do some snorkelling, eat lunch on the boat. It sounded fun, but I got there just too late. The Halligans and the Lindgrens did go on the trip, though, because I saw it leaving. They were all on the catamaran together.'

Cardle's expression brightens. 'Well, there we are then. First thing tomorrow, get your swimmers on. We're heading down to the dock.'

'Wow, you weren't kidding, were you?'

The next morning, Pippa takes in the sight of Cardle strolling towards her down the dock, dressed in pink flowered shorts from an expensive French swimwear brand. He has surprisingly good legs. She's wearing a bikini with a gauzy kaftan on top, and carrying a bag that contains, among other things, a bottle of strong sun block.

'There's a cat heading out to the coral reef in ten minutes,' she tells him. 'Fancy it? Apparently, we might spot some turtles if we're lucky.'

Cardle shrugs. 'Why not? We may as well, while we're here and Lindgren's willing to foot the bill.'

The morning air has a cool edge to it and there's a strong breeze. Apart from Pippa and Cardle, there are only two other customers wanting to take the trip. They give their personal details to the steward and seat themselves under flapping canvas awnings designed to mitigate the rays of the tropical sun that will be high in the sky in a couple of hours, and still fierce despite it being winter in the southern hemisphere.

'Look,' one of the crew says, pointing over the side of the boat as it navigates the turquoise water. Pippa peers over and sees a group of large turtles drifting dreamily just below the surface, their flippers barely moving.

'That's the green turtle,' the steward says, proudly. 'Our largest turtle.'

'Wow!' Pippa is lost in awe for a few moments, unable to tear her gaze away. 'Look, Jim!'

'Great,' he says, bending his head to light a cigarette. He glances over the side into the water, then gives her a look that reminds her not to lose sight of why they're on the catamaran in the first place. She turns back to face the hull of the boat and reaches for her sunscreen, starting to apply it to the parts of her body not covered by the kaftan.

'What's your name?' Pippa asks the crew member who'd pointed out the turtles and is now giving orders to the boat's chef, who is preparing lunch. He's handsome in his white uniform, with an open, smiling face and even, white teeth.

'I am Imraan, madam.'

'Were you here back in April? When the guest at the hotel died? Mrs Lindgren. They were on their honeymoon.'

Imraan looks briefly taken aback. His face falls. 'Ah, yes,' he says. 'That was very sad. Very terrible indeed.'

'Nikki Lindgren took this trip, didn't she?' Cardle interjects, exhaling smoke from the corner of his mouth. 'I believe it might even have been the same day she died. Were you here then?'

Imraan nods. 'Yes. I was on the boat. With her and her husband. Very nice people. Very happy and in love.' He makes a heart shape with his fingers, a gesture that Pippa finds endearing.

'And there was another couple on the boat that day, I think?' Pippa goes on. 'Mr and Mrs Halligan?'

Imraan shakes his head. 'Just Mr Halligan. He is very handsome. I hear she is very pretty also, but she was not on the trip. Another honeymoon couple,' he adds, but this time he does not, Pippa notes, make a sign of a heart indicating a couple in love.

'Whatever we're having for lunch, it smells great,' Cardle says, as the smell of frying garlic and spices floats up from the galley. Imraan is becoming uncomfortable and Pippa can tell that Cardle's trying to keep things light, stubbing out his cigarette and making a show of reaching into the cooler and helping himself to a beer. 'The three of them were friendly… was that the impression you got? Halligan and the Lindgrens.'

Imraan shrugs. 'The two men talked about their work, their jobs. The wife, Mrs Lindgren…' He stops dead, as if only just remembering what had happened to her. 'She was snorkelling.'

'She and Tansy Halligan had become friendly too,' Pippa says. 'In fact, so much so that she borrowed clothes from Tansy.'

'Ah, yes,' says Imraan. 'I do remember this. I heard him… Mr Halligan… tell Mrs Lindgren that his wife had arranged for a special dress to be cleaned and sent over to her room. For her to wear that evening.' He shakes his head, looking troubled. 'I believe she wore it…'

When she died.

The thought hangs there between them, unsaid.

'Hang on.' Cardle sets down his beer abruptly and runs his hand over his chin. 'Let me get this straight… Daniel Halligan told Nikki Lindgren that the purple dress she admired would be on its way over to her. For her to wear.'

'Yes.' Imraan's discomfort is even more evident, and Pippa shoots Cardle a warning look. 'Excuse me, I must go and see if lunch is nearly ready.' He hurries down the steep steps to the hold.

Cardle takes Pippa by the hand and leads her to the edge of the craft, out of earshot of the other couple. He points to the water as if showing her more turtles.

'You got that, did you?' he growls under his breath. 'Bloody hell.'

Pippa nods, wordlessly, watching the undulating shapes of the reef slide by.

'If he passed on that message to Nikki Lindgren, then he knew,' Cardle mutters. 'Daniel Halligan knew that Nikki would be wearing that particular dress on that particular evening. And it was very distinctive, wasn't it? I'm not wrong about that?'

Pippa shakes her head.

'It had all those different coloured fabric butterflies stuck all over it. A one-off… I doubt Tansy had more than one like it, or she wouldn't have needed to get it cleaned specially.' He turns his head sideways in Pippa's direction and looks her directly in the eye. 'So there's no way that Halligan would have seen the dress and thought it was his wife. Whatever he felt about Tansy… and we know he had good reason to despise her… he knew that the woman wearing that dress wasn't her. He knew it was Nikki Lindgren.'

CHAPTER THIRTY-TWO

PIPPA

'So now we've either got Daniel Halligan attacking Nikki Lindgren, an apparent stranger, for reasons unknown, or we're completely wrong about this and the killer is someone else.'

Cardle and Pippa are sitting on the terrace of her pavilion that evening. He's smoking. The evening air is cool, but Pippa's skin is smarting underneath her cotton shirt. She caught too much sun on the boat trip.

'Okay, let's go back over it and break this thing down, using everything we can recall from that night. Here's what I remember,' Cardle starts. 'You came over just after eight thirty. We were sitting outside my room, and I'd only just poured us a drink when we heard the scream.'

'Two screams,' interjects Pippa.

'That's right. Two screams.' Cardle taps off a column of ash into the ashtray. 'Then several members of staff run past us. And Daniel Halligan appears on the path outside my pavilion and says something about the maid having found "her", and wanting us to go in there with him. And we follow him and see Nikki on the floor. But by then, obviously, it's all too late.' Cardle takes a deep drag on his cigarette. 'We need to try and form a picture of what happened earlier. Before the screams.'

'Did you talk to Arne Lindgren about it?' Pippa opens a packet of nuts from the minibar and starts picking at them.

'I asked him what he could remember, yes. He says they were getting ready to go to dinner. He watched Nikki doing her make-up and changing into Tansy's dress, which had – as we know – been dropped off earlier by someone from housekeeping. She was delighted with it. The colour suited her, apparently. Lindgren said she looked beautiful in it.' He sighs heavily, breathing out a little cloud of smoke that hangs in the beam of light from an ornamental outdoor lantern. 'Then he took his turn in the shower, and when he came out of the bathroom to get dressed, Nikki wasn't there. She wasn't on the terrace either, but he wasn't particularly worried. She had some insect bites and had said something earlier about going to reception to ask if they had something in their first aid kit she could use to help with the itching. Arne just assumed she'd walked up to the main building. So he dressed at his leisure, and when she didn't reappear, he decided he'd stroll up and meet her and they could go straight to the restaurant. Then he heard all the commotion, and one of the security guards appeared and told him what had happened.'

He puffs more smoke. 'Your turn. What do you remember?'

Pippa finishes the nut she's chewing and licks the salt from her fingers. 'The same, really. I talked to my cousin on the phone, and told her I was thinking of asking you if you wanted a drink.'

She's glad it's dark and that Cardle can't see her colouring slightly. It feels strange confessing this, now that he's effectively her boss.

'I set off in the direction of your place, then decided I shouldn't go empty-handed and went back in and grabbed the minibar champagne….' She half closes her eyes, trying to sharpen the memory. 'That's right… as I came out again, I saw the manager, Babajee, lurking on the path outside my room.' She shudders. 'Creepy little man.'

'What was he doing there? Did he say?'

She shakes her head. 'I don't think so. He wished me good evening, but not before he'd looked me up and down. It wasn't the first time I'd seen him hanging around, either. There was that other time I caught him, and got this weird gut feeling he'd been snooping.'

'Interesting… got any beer?'

Pippa fetches a Budweiser from her fridge and Cardle drinks straight from the bottle, then tips a fresh cigarette from the pack and lights it. He catches Pippa's expression. 'Last one, I promise… So Babajee is hanging around in the dark outside guests' rooms, at the exact time that one of those guests is killed. That can't be insignificant, surely? If nothing else, he was positioned to see or hear something.'

'But then presumably the police spoke to him when they were interviewing everyone.'

'I expect they did. But there are no guarantees what he told them was the truth.' Cardle helps himself to some of the nuts, and washes them down with a mouthful of beer. 'I want you to go and talk to him. See what you can get out of him.'

'Me?' Pippa shudders.

'Clearly he has a thing for you. Which is grim, I know, but we may as well capitalise on it. He'd be intimidated by me, but if you turn on the charm, flatter him a bit, he may open up. I have a feeling he'll know something. Something that will turn out to be important.'

After breakfast the next morning, Pippa heads to the main reception desk in the lobby.

'Can I speak to Mr Babajee?' she asks the receptionist on duty. 'The general manager.'

The girl looks flustered. 'Is there something wrong? Do you have a complaint? I can call our duty manager.'

Pippa smiles reassuringly, shaking her head. 'No, nothing's wrong. I just need to speak to him about something, that's all.'

'One moment.' The girl places a call, speaking in Mauritian Creole, with the occasional glance in Pippa's direction. She hangs up and points behind her, to the corridor leading to a rear lobby.

'The office is down there. Last on the right.'

As promised, there is a veneered wooden door with 'Mr A. Babajee, General Manager' picked out in brass letters on a black sign. Pippa knocks.

'Come in.' The voice is female.

Pippa sticks her head round the door. The carpeted office is air-conditioned to a chilly temperature. The walls are covered with posters of Mauritius – the sort usually seen in travel agencies – and there are fussy arrangements of artificial flowers on every spare surface. Two desks face one another, the larger one with a nameplate that reads 'A. Babajee'. A woman of Indo-Mauritian descent is sitting at the other, typing at a computer terminal.

'Can I help you?'

'I'm looking for Mr Babajee.'

'He's not here right now, I'm afraid. I'm expecting him back later.'

'How much later?'

His assistant seems reluctant to be drawn. 'This morning. Yes, later this morning, I think.'

Pippa wrinkles her nose. There's an extra chair, she notices, but she doesn't want to wait for hours in this fridge of an office. 'Have you any idea where I might find him? It's really very important.'

The woman hesitates, as though weighing in the balance the consequences of revealing her boss's whereabouts against turning away a guest with a serious concern. 'He's in the other office,' she says.

'The other office?'

'This is the general management office… he has another office. A private office.' She points down at the floor. 'On lower ground floor.'

Pippa takes the fire stairs down one level. It's mostly taken up with the area for housekeeping's operations, and storage of catering supplies, so it doesn't take her long to identify the 'private' office. This time there's no name plaque on the door.

Some instinct tells her not to knock. She opens the door quietly and is admitted to a windowless basement room.

Babajee is seated in front of a huge computer monitor, broken up into a flickering black and white patchwork of at least twelve other screens. The bank of images comes and goes, cuts and re-sets. Images of people. Staff. Other guests, going about their business.

As soon as he realises that he has been disturbed, Babajee hits a key on the keyboard and the camera feeds disappear.

'Wait,' says Pippa, pointing. 'Was that CCTV footage?'

He gives a dry cough and a barely perceptible nod, before gathering himself and turning around in his chair to face her, extending a hand. In the dim light the tint in his lenses is pale, revealing his eyes: disturbing. 'Miss Bryant, it is a pleasure to see you. How may I be of assistance?'

Pippa ignores the hand. 'I thought you told the police that the CCTV cameras were all dummies. During the investigation. When Nikki Lindgren died.'

'Ah, yes, that was indeed the case. But given that unfortunate incident, and to calm the nervousness of our clients, we have recently installed a new security system. I was checking it, as I do daily, to make sure that all is well. That it is working as it should.'

'And is it?' asks Pippa.

'Yes, all is well. No need for you or the other ladies to be worrying. And now' – he stands up and gives an obsequious half-bow – 'if you wish to speak to me, may I suggest we go up to the general office. It's more comfortable, I think, and Miss Jadu can fetch you coffee.'

'No, it's okay.' He's trying to edge his way to the door, but Pippa is blocking him. 'It's probably better if we speak alone.'

'Of course. If I can help, I will.'

'It's about the night that Nikki Lindgren died. I—'

'You are with Mr James Cardle, I think. And he is an investigator.' Babajee cuts in, and there's a less friendly tone to his voice now: almost – but not quite – menacing.

Better if u don't talk about Mauritius…

'I am.' Pippa smiles blandly, standing her ground. 'We're acting on behalf of Mrs Lindgren's widower. And we wondered what you could recall about that night.'

'Very little, as I told the police. I was in the main building, in my office, and security alerted me that one of the chambermaids had found Mrs Lindgren's body. I summoned the police myself.'

'But you were there,' Pippa says, calmly. 'I remember seeing you on the pathway outside my pavilion. You even spoke to me.'

Babajee is standing very close to her now, close enough for her to smell the sourness of his breath and catch the glint from his gold tooth. He reaches past her and yanks the door open, making a small bowing movement to indicate that she should leave.

'I can assure you that was not the case, Miss Bryant. It was after sunset and the paths on that part of the property are not brightly lit. I think you are mistaken.'

CHAPTER THIRTY-THREE

PIPPA

Pippa heads straight back to Cardle's pavilion, but halfway there she is intercepted by a text from him.

At the beach bar. J

'I thought I might as well use the facilities,' he says wryly, when she finds him. He holds up his bottle of beer. 'And keep an eye on those idiots.'

He's back in his bright swim shorts and aviators, lounging in an Adirondack chair with his toes buried into the sugary white sand, watching some of their fellow hotel guests who are roaring up and down on jet skis. 'So – what d'you find out?'

Pippa recounts the visit to the secondary office, and the discovery of a fully functioning security system.

'Surely it's suspicious that he denies seeing me that night,' she says. She waves over the barman and orders a non-alcoholic punch. 'Especially given I saw him walk off in the direction of the Halligans' villa.'

'No doubt about that.' Cardle reaches for his cigarettes then, glancing in Pippa's direction, stops. He knows she doesn't like him smoking, even if they're outside. 'He's firmly in the persons-of-interest column now.' He gazes out to sea again, where one jet ski has ploughed into another one, tossing its rider into the water. 'But most of all I need to take a look at that CCTV set-up.'

'Will you ask him to show it to you?'

Cardle shakes his head. 'Now, what would be the bloody point of that? Even if he agreed, he'd only show me what he wanted me to see. No,' he says in a low growl, tapping his fingers on his cigarette carton, 'we're going to go and look for ourselves.'

They meet at eleven thirty that evening, in the main building. Late enough for the restaurant to have closed and guest numbers to be thinning out, but not so late that their presence looks suspicious.

Cardle follows Pippa down to the lower ground level and they wait, concealed in a doorway, until a gaggle of housekeeping staff have loaded up their trolleys and moved away to the lifts. She leads him to the door of Babajee's second office. It's locked.

'Time to learn a spot of breaking and entering,' he tells Pippa, cheerfully. 'An essential skill in this job.'

He reaches into the pocket of his bomber jacket and pulls out a small set of metal tools, which look to Pippa like something a dental hygienist would use. Then he lowers his large frame into a crouch and examines the lock more closely.

'Just a double-sided wafer,' he grunts. 'Nothing too fancy.' He selects a pick with two prongs that looks like a miniature wrench, inserts it into the keyhole, and manipulates it from side to side. The mechanism gives with a satisfying clunk.

'Easy peasy.' Cardle smiles up at Pippa. 'Remind me to give you a lock pick set for Christmas.'

Once they've closed the door behind them, he switches on the lights. 'No windows, so no one will notice,' he says. He nods to the panel of switches on the wall. 'Turn that lot on and let's see what we've got.'

The huge computer screen flickers into life, displaying a grid of twenty-four smaller screens. All of them are live, and relaying feed from different locations on the property.

Cardle watches for a while. 'So it's monitoring live, twenty-four hours a day…' He squints more closely at the images, then starts hitting keys on the keyboard. 'What we need to work out is how all this is being recorded.'

Pippa shrugs, feeling helpless. 'Not my area of expertise, I'm afraid.'

'Just as well I had some training in this when I was with the Met then, isn't it…?' He sits down in the desk chair, minimising the feed from the remote cameras and navigating his way around the hard drive. 'Well, for starters, this is not a brand-new system. This was operational when we were here back in April.'

He looks up at Pippa and she shakes her head slowly. 'So… so why would Babajee claim back then that it was just a dummy system?'

'That's what we're here to find out.' Cardle turns back to the monitor and starts opening files on the desk top, examining their contents. 'Hmm… this all looks legit enough.'

Then he opens the directory for the hard drive and examines the contents.

'What's this?'

Pippa peers over his shoulder. He's pointing to a folder named simply 'AB'. 'A. B. Ashvin Babajee?'

Cardle opens the folder. Inside it are dozens of file icons, labelled with dates.

'They're AVI files…' Cardle muses. 'These are taken from the camera feeds.'

He goes into the Tools menu and selects File Playback. Footage begins to play, the lighting poor but the images still clear enough to discern. The camera is covering the living area of one of the pavilions. A young woman in a bikini, with a towel wrapped round her, has clearly just come in from the beach or pool. She drops the towel to the ground and peels off her wet bikini, tossing this to the floor too, and standing completely naked at the centre of the room. She shakes her wet hair down her back, which makes her breasts jiggle, then turns and saunters in the direction of the bathroom. It's clear from her body language that she believes herself to be unobserved.

'Oh, Jesus,' mutters Cardle.

Pippa is staring at the screen, unable to tear her gaze away. 'Check the others,' she urges.

Cardle clicks through another half-dozen of the files. They are all of the hotel interiors and all feature women dressing, undressing and showering, completely or partially naked. One shows a couple having sex on top of their bed.

'Well, well, well.' He opens another file, and there in all her glory is Tansy Dimaano, strutting around in the skimpiest of underwear. 'He wasn't going to pass up the chance to perv at *her*.'

'This can't be right, surely,' Pippa whispers. 'The hotel's not allowed to film its guests in private.'

'It won't be the hotel.' Cardle's tone is grim. 'It'll be our pal Babajee who's doing it on the sly. Inserting his own spy cams into the rooms and then linking them up to the existing surveillance system. With wireless units it's easy enough to do, but it's certainly not cheap. Each camera unit costs at least six hundred quid.' He leans back in the chair. 'Apart from anything else, I'd like to know where he's getting the cash from.'

'He always gave me a bad vibe,' says Pippa, with a shudder. 'Hanging around outside my room…' She and Cardle look at one another. 'Oh God, you don't think—?'

'That he's recorded you?' he asks, bluntly. 'Want me to check through the files?'

'No.' Pippa shakes her head firmly. 'I do not. If he has, I'd really rather not know.'

He clicks through a few more of the settings, then shuts down the computer and stands back.

'Well, if nothing else, we've answered our own question. About why he lied and said the CCTV system was a deterrent only and not recording. He didn't want anyone checking up and finding he was using it as his own private porn channel.'

'Let's go,' says Pippa, heading to the door. 'This place freaks me out.'

As they hurry back down the corridor, she catches sight of Cardle's expression and slows her pace. 'What?' she demands. He's humming under his breath, quite relaxed. 'What on earth have you got to be so cheerful about? That was awful.'

'Because I checked before I powered down, and the security system is backed up to the cloud. That means they've got access to all of it: all their footage. And we've just seen from the video of Tansy that Babajee had one of his non-kosher cameras in the Halligans' villa. Put those two things together, and we can find out exactly what happened the night Nikki Lindgren was killed.'

CHAPTER THIRTY-FOUR

PIPPA

'He's not going to want to talk to us,' Pippa says to Cardle the next morning, as they head to the manager's office.

'Course he's not.' He shrugs. 'But one way or another, he's going to have to.'

They find Miss Jadu alone in the office, typing rapidly at her terminal. Pippa, prepared this time, pulls down the sleeves of her sweater at the icy blast from the air-conditioning.

'Babajee in?' Cardle growls, without preamble.

Miss Jadu looks startled, taking off the large glasses which hang round her neck on a chain. 'No, sir, I'm afraid he is not. May I assist you? Or I can call our duty manager, Mr Pierre?'

'No.' Pippa looks askance at him and he adds, 'Thank you. It has to be Ashvin Babajee himself. Any idea when he'll be back?'

'I'm afraid Mr Babajee is sick. He's taken leave.'

'Sick, my arse,' Cardle mutters, as they leave the office.

'I suppose we could try and find a home address for him,' Pippa suggests. 'Someone who works here must know where he lives.'

'No need.' He smiles slightly, striding out of the reception lobby and onto the circular entrance drive, where he lights a cigarette. 'Two words: private office.'

'You mean—'

Cardle blows out several, short rhythmic gusts of smoke. 'Now he knows we're on to him, what's the first thing he's going to do?'

'Delete the dodgy footage.'

'Exactly.'

Pippa sidesteps the puffs of smoke. 'But I don't get why he hasn't done that already. Surely after I went and confronted him down there, it would be the first thing he'd do after I left. Start deleting all his peeping Tom stuff.'

'Ah, but think about it, young Pip. He's been hoarding those clips for months; a couple of years, in some cases. He's very attached to them. They give him a thrill, get him going.'

Pippa grimaces.

'He's not going to just wipe them outright. He's going to copy them, download them so he can hang on to them and view them somewhere else. My guess is he's spending his sick day down in Port Louis buying a USB stick and a remote hard drive. As soon as he's got those he'll be back to collect the evidence. All we need to do is wait.'

Folding up her sweater and using it as a makeshift cushion doesn't make the waiting any easier. After two hours of sitting on the hard stone floor on the lower ground level of the hotel building, Pippa is stiff and sore.

Cardle was convinced that Babajee wouldn't return until after dark, so after a lazy afternoon spent swimming and sunbathing by the pool, they took up their posts at dusk.

'What if he doesn't come?' Pippa whispers. 'I don't know how much longer I can sit here.'

In response, he merely taps his watch then lifts a finger to his lips.

And, sure enough, thirty minutes later the lift doors ping and Babajee exits with his odd crab-like gait. He glances around briefly before unlocking the door to his second office.

'Quick,' Cardle whispers. 'Before he's had time to delete anything.'

He flings the door of the office open, making Babajee jump visibly. 'Evening.'

The large screen with its patchwork of camera feeds is on, the images shifting like a huge square kaleidoscope.

'Mr Cardle.'

It takes him a split second but Babajee quickly shifts into professional obsequiousness. He smiles, revealing the gold tooth. 'And Miss Bryant. There is a problem?'

'Oh, you know there is.' Cardle glowers, his tall frame dwarfing the other man. 'When there was a suspicious death on this property two months ago, you told law enforcement that the security cameras were not recording. That they were dummies. And the good folk of the Mauritius Police Force took your word for it. God knows they're far from perfect, but the Metropolitan Police back in London would have checked the equipment for themselves, see if it was true.' He grimaces slightly. 'At least, I bloody hope they would have done.'

Babajee is backing away from Cardle, shaking his head, his eyes fish-like behind his glasses.

'But you had a very good reason for keeping them away from the CCTV input, didn't you? Because you'd taken the liberty of installing a few cameras of your own. Cameras that allowed you to watch female guests during their private moments.'

'I don't know what you want—'

'I'll tell you what we want,' Cardle says, repressively. 'We want you to go to the video files backed up in the cloud, and we want you to find the feed for the camera you installed in the villa that Daniel and Tansy Halligan were staying in. For the night of the twenty-first of April.'

Babajee is shaking his head, looking terrified. 'I can't—'

'Do it,' Cardle tells him. 'Or I can call Inspector Ramsamy right now and ask him to come and help you.' He pulls his mobile from his jeans pocket and waggles it, to reinforce his point.

His hands trembling, Babajee sits down, minimises the camera feed and starts accessing the remote file directory. After a few clicks, he selects a video file and opens it.

'This is it.'

'Go on. Press play.'

Pippa and Cardle position themselves at either shoulder, watching the screen. Pippa has her fist pressed against her mouth.

Babajee hesitates for a second, then clicks the 'Play' arrow.

The digital time display says 20.42. The living room of the villa is empty, the draught from the overhead fan gently lifting muslin drapes and making the candle flames flicker. Then Tansy appears in shot, her long hair wet, staring distractedly at her phone. She shouts something over her shoulder in the direction of the bedroom, then disappears.

'She was going to get her hair done by her stylist, in his room,' Pippa says. 'That's where she was when… when it happened.'

Now Daniel appears in shot. He too looks as though he has just emerged from the shower. His hair is slicked back damply from his forehead and he's threading a belt through the loops in his linen trousers.

He looks up suddenly, as though he's heard something, then heads in the direction of the door.

Babajee is becoming agitated. His hands hover over the keyboard. 'I really don't think—'

'Leave it,' snarls Cardle.

On screen, the time stamp is now 20.46. Pippa takes in a breath sharply as Nikki Lindgren enters the shot, wearing the butterfly-embellished kaftan that Tansy lent her. Daniel is smiling politely, points to the drinks tray on the coffee table. Nikki shakes her head. Then she begins to speak. She talks for several minutes, gesticulating effusively with her hands. Daniel's expression moves through polite interest, to surprise, then shock and then something altogether darker. He begins to wave his own hands, and although there is no audio, it's clear from his movements that he's shouting.

'Bloody hell…' murmurs Pippa. 'What on earth did the two of them have to argue about like that? I thought they didn't know one another.'

Babajee's hand once again reaches to the 'Stop' button on the feed.

'Don't you dare.' Cardle holds up a warning hand.

Nikki Lindgren is only visible from the rear, but it's clearly her turn to be shocked now. She raises her hands in a gesture of surrender, then presses them against the sides of her head as she shakes it.

No, no, no. Pippa can feel the word, even though she can't hear it.

Daniel's body language is menacing now, and Nikki Lindgren shrinks away from him. He's still shouting, and she's still shaking her head. He lunges at her, grabbing her by her shoulders and shaking her hard. They grapple, and their bodies twist round so that now the camera is showing the back of Daniel's head. Nikki's face is just visible, and she looks horrified. Daniel's hands go up to her neck and he shakes her so hard her feet almost leave the ground. Rage ripples through his body. Nikki's arms flail.

Then, abruptly, as if he's thinking better of it, Daniel releases her with a rough push. She stumbles backwards, her calf catching against the coffee table, and she falls, her head smacking down so hard on the glass surface that it almost bounces off. Her eyes close and she slithers to the floor, blood oozing from her forehead and left ear.

Daniel stands over her, panting, but seemingly unable to move. His hands fly up to his temples and now it's his turn to shake his head.

No, no, no.

Taking care to avoid the pooling blood, he reaches forward and touches his fingers to Nikki's pulse. He looks around wildly, the camera catching his features now frozen in disbelief. Then he grabs his mobile from the other end of the coffee table and heads out of shot. The time stamp reads 20.57.

'Fucking hell,' exhales Cardle, as Pippa turns instinctively to look in his direction.

For another seven minutes there is no movement save the flickering of candle flames. Nikki Lindgren lies inert. Then a uniformed chambermaid enters the shot with a pile of towels, drops them as she clamps her hands to her mouth, and just as abruptly exits.

'Okay, you can stop it now,' Cardle tells Babajee. He does so, and turns his chair around, away from the terminal.

'I take it you've seen this before?'

Babajee nods silently.

'And you didn't think to share it with the police who were conducting the investigation?'

'I wanted to, but I was afraid.'

'Afraid they'd discover your stash of historic amateur porn videos, eh? Covering your own back. No thought for the relatives of the deceased woman? Jesus!'

Babajee makes a strangled, whimpering sound.

'Okay, I'll tell you what's going to happen. Right now, you're going to send a copy of this video file to this email address.' He hands over one of his business cards.

Babajee hesitates.

'Now!' Cardle demands. 'So I can see you do it.' He leans over Babajee, making sure he is complying. 'And tomorrow morning, you're going to share this with Inspector Ramsamy. You're going to tell him exactly why you failed to disclose it before this point.

And you're going to take down every single one of the "extra" cameras you've installed. Do you hear me?'

Babajee nods.

'And don't think I won't be checking that you've done it. Because I will. Come on, Pippa.'

He turns on his heel in disgust.

They head up the stairs and out into the warm, scented air without speaking. Cardle reflexively lights a cigarette.

'So, what's your theory?' Pippa asks him. 'Was Nikki Lindgren an ex? A slighted lover?'

'Maybe.'

'It surely couldn't have anything to do with the Horizon Lakes development… maybe it had something to do with Tansy? Maybe Nikki got herself tied up in the Hiraya scam.'

'Maybe,' repeats Cardle, thoughtfully. 'We've covered the who, now we need to work on the why.' He grinds out his cigarette under the heel of his shoe. 'Let's go back to mine, I need a bloody drink.'

He holds out his hand as though to take hers, and Pippa feels herself reaching for him instinctively. Just as their fingertips touch, he pulls back with a rueful smile. 'On second thoughts, it's been a long day. I'll see you in the morning. We'll work out our next move then.'

PART FOUR

CHAPTER THIRTY-FIVE

DANIEL

'I need you,' Tansy says to her husband.

They're back in the Belmont penthouse after their hurried departure from Mauritius. Tansy wasted no time, and is in her workout gear, having just filmed an Instagram Live from her static bike, flask of Hiraya Green in one hand ('Hi, guys, I'm back from honeymoon and straight back at it…').

Daniel glances up from the screen of his tablet, where he is scrolling through the financial news.

'Tonight, seven forty-five,' Tansy says, impatiently. 'I've got a red-carpet thing, step and repeat, and I need you there to be photographed with me.'

Daniel rolls his eyes. 'Really?'

'Yes, really!' Tansy flicks her hair over her shoulder and cycles harder. 'The fucking disaster of a dead girl being found in our honeymoon suite is already in the news. Have you any idea how terrible it could be for my brand? I need to do some damage limitation. And the fact that she was wearing an Iluka dress that *I'd* lent her… well, that's my sponsorship deal with them over.'

Daniel winces. The image of the coloured silk butterflies spattered with blood, so much blood, is fixed in his brain. He closes his eyes, opens them, tries to focus on his wife's lovely, ill-tempered face but he can't shake it. Can't rid himself of that mental picture.

Tansy is saying something.

'What?' he mumbles.

'Aren't you listening? I said it's vital that we're seen out and about as a couple. So I want you on the red carpet with me, looking your handsome British self in a tux.' She smirks. 'My own personal James Bond. In fact…' Her eyes gleam and she snatches up her phone to make herself a note. 'That would make a great hashtag. I'll use it on the pics I post.'

Daniel puts down his tablet, walks over to the floor-to-ceiling window and stands with his hands in his pockets, looking out over the view of Sydney Harbour. A five-million-dollar view, he'd told Tansy when he sold her this place. And now it's his five-million-dollar prison.

'Tell you what.' He swivels on his heel to face her. 'I'll do you a deal. I'll come with you tonight, all dressed up like your pet Action Man, and smile for the cameras – if you'll give me the rest of the money I owe. I need to pay back the rest of my investors.'

Tansy scowls. 'We already have a deal. I said I'd let you have half the money when we got engaged, and the rest on our first anniversary.'

'Does it matter, if you're going to pay it anyway?'

'Of course it does.' Tansy hops off the bike and throws a towel round her neck. 'I need you to have an incentive to stick around. I need to post content about what a great wifey I am. My followers love that shit. And after… that dead girl…' She pulls a face as though she's just tasted something unpleasant. 'All the more reason we need to put on a united front, for the sake of the brand.'

Daniel opens his mouth to speak but she cuts across him. 'I know, I know, it was an accident – those over-polished marble floors were a bloody nightmare. No wonder someone ended up slipping and hitting their head. But still, it doesn't look good. Being mentioned in the same news reports.'

'Okay,' Daniel says, flatly. 'I'll come. But if I do, can we at least talk about settling those debts? I don't want the financial watchdogs breathing down my neck, or a load of lawsuits. That's not good for our brand, either.'

Tansy gives him a shrewd look. 'Is your tux back from the cleaners? The Tom Ford one I bought you?'

Daniel nods.

'Good. If you gussy up and smile nicely, we'll talk about it.'

They return from the event just after midnight. Daniel was standing on the red carpet for what felt like hours, with his arm circling Tansy's waist, smiling as flashbulbs popped around them.

'Well, goodnight then,' he says, tugging off his black tie and retreating in the direction of the spare room, where he has been sleeping since the honeymoon.

'Oh, no, you don't.' Tansy flicks her tongue provocatively over her top lip, a gesture he remembers well from their apartment-hunting days. Her pupils grow dark in the tawny irises. 'You're not finished yet.'

She grabs him by the wrist and pulls him into the master bedroom, then shrugs out of her shell-pink Dolce and Gabbana silk gown, revealing a strapless bra and thong. She tugs his dress shirt over his head, and before he can even summon the breath to protest, her fingers are fumbling at the waistband of his trousers.

Her bra is unhooked and tossed aside and she wriggles out of the thong, arranging her body on the bed like an appetiser, her olive skin gleaming in the dim glow of the bedside lamp.

'You want me to service you, as if I'm a farm animal?' Daniel scoffs. He stands there looking down at her. Tansy, who is so beautiful and alluring. Tansy, who he doesn't love at all, doesn't even like.

'If you want to have a discussion about money, then yes,' says Tansy, her clipped tone at odds with the pornographic posing.

Daniel has sex with his wife. He's not in the least aroused, so it's not easy. He has to close his eyes and let his mind drift somewhere else entirely, to a former, happier time and another dark-haired beauty. The mental image consumes him like a dream, until he's brought back to reality by the little grunt that lets him know Tansy's satisfied, and his task is complete. He gathers his clothes and heads back to the spare bedroom, and she doesn't try to stop him.

The next morning, over coffee on the terrace, he brings up Roseland's outstanding debts again.

Tansy, who is having her make-up done by Ljubica for yet another Instagram post, wrinkles her nose.

'You know what, I've thought about it, and I'm not going to do it. Not now. I think we should stick to our original agreement. You'll get the rest of the money next January.'

'Christ, Tansy…' Daniel feels an ice-cold block of rage under his sternum. He clenches his fists, just about resisting the urge to slap her. Adrenaline surges through him, with an accompanying wave of nausea. 'You said—'

'Here's the thing.' She bats away the powder brush Ljubica is dragging over her cheekbones with an impatient movement. 'If I let you have the cash now and you settle your debts, you'll leave.'

He opens his mouth to protest, but she holds up a hand. 'Don't deny it, you will. And I need you to stick around until at least next year. After that you can do what you like; I don't care. But for now, you stay.'

CHAPTER THIRTY-SIX

DANIEL

Three days later, Daniel receives a call from an unknown number.

He ignores it, but the same number appears again and again, until eventually he answers it.

'Is that Daniel Halligan?'

'Yes.'

'This is Evelyn Howell. I'm a Senior Executive in the Misconduct and Breach Team at ASIC.'

'ASIC?'

Daniel is pretty sure he knows what this means, but is playing for time.

'The Australian Securities and Investments Commission. I need to talk to you about your company, Roseland Investments.'

'Ah. Actually, that's not possible. Roseland doesn't exist anymore. You can check on your own paperwork.'

'I'm aware of that, Mr Halligan, but we still need to talk to you. I'd be grateful if you'd come into our Sydney office, on Market Street, for a chat. I'll transfer you to my assistant, and she'll make an appointment for you. Oh, and if you want to bring legal representation, that would be perfectly in order.'

*

The following Monday morning, Daniel finds himself dressed in a suit, standing outside the huge granite and glass edifice of 100 Market Street.

He tried to engage the services of Nadya Melzer, the specialist environmental lawyer he'd previously consulted, but she was unavailable. He didn't feel able to approach Warren Bishop after the catastrophic end to his relationship with Maxine, so he heads to the fifth floor alone.

Evelyn Howell is heavy-jawed woman with short grey hair, wearing the sort of boxy suit favoured by female politicians. She's completely unmoved by Daniel's flagrant good looks, barely glancing at him before motioning him to sit down.

She begins by quoting various Commission regulations pertaining to the running of investment funds. Daniel nods along, trying not to glaze over.

'…which brings us to the obvious breach concerning Roseland Investments.'

'Which is?'

'I believe you used the professional services of Tucker Harvey, at GHC Surveying?'

'Yes,' Daniel nods.

'That was' – Howell consults her notes – 'in October? And he reported back to you that the land you proposed to build on had been contaminated by a substance called PFOA?'

'That's right.' Daniel tries smiling at her, but she ignores him.

'And yet, subsequent to that, in early December, you held a pitch meeting in Canberra to attract further investment.'

'I did.'

She stares at him coldly over the rim of her reading glasses. 'Are you aware, Mr Halligan, of the term "Ponzi scheme"?'

'Yes, of course I am.' He's equally cold now.

'It's defined as a fraud in which returns to primary investors in a non-existent enterprise are paid with money from later investors.

Isn't that what you did, Mr Halligan? You repaid your short-term investors by getting more people to invest.'

'No.' Daniel shakes his head firmly. 'By the time I held the event in Canberra, I'd already engaged the services of a water engineering company called Eauzone, to sort out the problem with the PFOA. We were in the process of providing a clean water supply. You can check the dates with my contact, a guy called Ravi.'

Howell makes a note.

'So' – Daniel exhales slowly, trying to keep his temper under check – 'it wasn't a non-existent enterprise. As far as I was concerned, the issues were going to be dealt with and the homes were still going to be built. That's the honest truth.'

She looks at him for a long beat. 'But you're not building the homes any longer. You wound up the development and closed the company.'

'Yes, but only because the story was leaked to the press…'

By my own fucking wife.

'…and the buyers all lost confidence and wanted their money back. So I had to refund them. I had no choice.'

'But according to our enquiries, you haven't repaid all your investors. I am aware of some outstanding cases that have been raised to that effect.'

'I know. But I will. I will repay them. I can promise you, that is my intention.'

Howell sighs and lays down her pen. 'I'll make a note of our conversation today, and pass my findings on to our Enforcement department. You can expect them to contact you about a hearing soon. And when you attend, I advise you to take a lawyer.'

Daniel makes an appointment for a follow-up meeting at the Commission, but he has no intention of attending.

He goes straight back to the penthouse, practically running across the lobby, checking his watch as he gets into the elevator. It's twelve twenty. Tansy, he knows, is attending one of her 'seminars'; the gatherings where she gives an inspirational speech about her lupus battle, and a new cohort of believers is recruited to spend their own money on her products and try to sell them on. She was due to leave around eleven, make her personal appearance at midday, and then return, probably between one and two. He has enough time. Just.

Back in the apartment, he finds a weekend holdall in the dressing room and throws a few changes of clothes into it, along with his passport and the personal effects he has pushed to the back of a drawer in the spare room. Then he takes Tansy's iPad from her bedside drawer and unlocks it. He knows the passcode off by heart: she made him memorise it so that he could prompt her when she couldn't remember it herself.

Daniel opens the banking app. Her account is password protected, but the password is stored in a keychain and automatically entered by simply answering 'yes' to a prompt. Her personal account has a balance of $30,000. There's another $75,000 in a high interest account. Not enough.

He opens the Hiraya business account, the one from which an allowance is transferred monthly to his own account. The balance stands at $11.75 million.

At the foot of the page is a button. 'Send money'. He clicks on it. A box opens for payee. He's already on the list of saved payees because of the monthly payment she makes to his account. He looks at the saved name for these transactions. 'Pocket Money'. Jesus.

Seeing those two words crystallises things in his mind. 'Pocket money'. He's her husband, for God's sake. Her money is *their* money. How dare she withhold funds to keep him around for as long as he's useful?

He still owes around one-and-half-million dollars to Roseland investors. In the 'Amount to transfer' box, he types in '2,000,000'. Frankly, he tells himself, he's entitled to more. He presses 'Make transfer'.

His phone pings with a text. It's from Tansy.

In car on way back. Where are you?

She'll probably get an automatic notification from her bank of the transfer that's just been made. Or possibly a phone call to ask if she authorised it herself, given the size of the sum. There's no time to waste. He switches off his mobile. Then, grabbing his bag, he leaves the apartment, pausing just long enough for one last look at that view.

The departure board at Sydney International offers plenty of options.

Unable to make a decision, Daniel climbs onto a bar stool at one of the food outlets and orders a burger and a beer. What will Tansy be expecting him to do? he wonders. Return to the Gold Coast, perhaps? Go to Melbourne? She's always been dismissive of the city, just as he's always insisted it's a great place and confessed a desire to spend more time there.

So not Melbourne, then. Too obvious. There's a flight leaving for Perth in forty-five minutes. Perth, a place he has absolutely no interest in, but which is the jumping-off point for all of South East Asia. Only a few hours by plane to Bali, Malaysia, Thailand. He finishes his meal, withdraws the maximum amount of cash from an ATM and goes to the Qantas sales desk, handing over a wad of twenty-dollar notes.

'If you've got a seat in first, that would be great.'

'Certainly, Mr Halligan, let's see what we can do for you,' the clerk says, with a bright smile. 'And will this be a return ticket?'

'No,' says Daniel, not returning her smile. 'One way.'

CHAPTER THIRTY-SEVEN

DANIEL

Perth is a pretty city, Daniel acknowledges, after spending the afternoon and evening wandering around Elizabeth Quay. He admires the sunset, gold and blue, against the arched silhouette of the bridge. It feels remote here, far away from anywhere else. He likes that.

He has checked into the Ritz Carlton for two nights, insisting on paying with cash, which the management initially resisted. Back in his hotel room, he logs on to his own bank account, making transfers to the accounts of all his outstanding creditors. He emails Ben, telling him that he's left Tansy and gone travelling for a while, and not to worry about the lack of phone contact. Then he falls asleep watching the television news, and enjoys the best sleep he has had for weeks – months, even.

Eventually, after a leisurely room service breakfast and a lot of coffee, he switches on his mobile. There are two voicemails from Tansy. In the first, she screeches at him about stealing her money, threatens to have him arrested, says she will tell the police that he killed Martin Kelly. She won't, he knows that now. She was too closely involved in moving the body, too reluctant to have scandal taint her precious brand.

Her second voicemail, a decibel or two quieter, informs him that two people have been to the apartment looking for him.

'That big guy, Cardle, and the pretty brown-haired girl who was always hanging around him. They were in Mauritius at the same time we were, sticking their beaks in. I know you spoke to them. Anyway, he's a private detective, British, and he's in Australia looking for you. Fuck knows what they want, but it must be serious. Thought you ought to know. Fuck you, anyway.'

Daniel can guess what they want. He closes his eyes and sees it again. Nikki Lindgren's body oozing blood, the silk butterflies fanned by the breeze. What was that quote about the law of unintended consequences? He tries to remember it now. Because he didn't mean for her to die. Not really. He just wanted her to feel pain. To feel hurt, just as he'd been hurt terribly by her.

He switches the phone off and heads out of the hotel, walking aimlessly around the shopping malls in the city centre. He waits for a plan to form in his mind, but nothing comes, only a blank numbness.

*

Several weeks pass in this way, with Daniel doing little more than eating and walking around the city. He moves from the Ritz Carlton to a serviced apartment, and enjoys the rudimentary pleasure of shopping at the various growers' markets for fruit and vegetables. Apart from overseeing the barbecue when he lived with Maxine, he hasn't really cooked before, and he finds that he enjoys it. Preparing meals for himself becomes a distraction, a way of using some of the empty time that weighs heavily. He needs to make a decision, but feels paralysed by some form of post-traumatic shock.

Eventually, in the third week of June, he switches on his mobile again. There are various threatening messages from Tansy and a voicemail from the Securities and Investments Commission asking why he's missed his appointment with the representative from their Enforcement department. He deletes them all.

There's also a missed call and voicemail from an overseas number. He plays it.

'*This is a message for Mr Daniel Halligan… Mr Halligan, my name is Kishan Ramsamy. I'm with the Mauritius Police Force. I spoke with you in April at the Excelsior hotel, regarding the death of Mrs Nicole Lindgren, and in the light of new evidence we have received, it's extremely important that I speak with you again regarding this matter. Please call back on this number as a matter of the utmost urgency.*'

Daniel plays the message back once, then again. Several times.

'*In the light of new evidence…*'

So they know something about what happened in that villa, something significant. Something damning. It has to be, or why would they contact him? The evidence can only point to him, because he is the one to blame.

He knows there isn't a whole lot a small organisation like the Mauritius Police Force can do to pursue him. They have no idea where he is, and lack the manpower to find him. But from his time in the army, he also knows a little about international cooperation between security agencies, and he has no doubt that it's only a matter of time before there's an Interpol red notice in his name, flagging up his travel across borders. He'll soon be on a flight watchlist, a database for passport screening. Perhaps he already is.

The decision has been made for him, and it comes as a relief. Wearing a baseball cap and shades, he goes to the nearest ATM and withdraws as much cash as he can. Then he packs up his modest bag of belongings and heads straight to Perth Airport.

The first thing that strikes Daniel when he lands is how hot it is.

It's several years since he has visited London, and the last handful of trips have all been for Christmas. He has completely forgotten how stifling the heat of a midsummer heatwave can be in this city. Mid-winter Perth was still sunny, but cool. It's only

6.30 a.m., but already the twenty-eight degrees and high humidity knock him sideways as he walks out of Terminal 3 at Heathrow. The black cab he is allocated has no air-conditioning, and he has to plead with the driver to open the windows.

The driver deposits him on Upper Street an hour later, just as the local Starbucks is opening. Daniel orders an iced coffee and sits outside under the awning, waiting. Ben won't have left for work yet. He'll be in his flat, getting ready to leave. Because he always phoned him from Sydney first thing UK time, he knows Ben's routine well. He'll set off to his office in Old Street at around eight forty. And only then will Daniel go to the flat, once Ben has left. He desperately wants to see his younger brother, but he can't. Not now.

He heads to the industrial conversion on the banks of the Grand Union Canal at nine thirty, after the presence of morning commuters on the street has died down. The heat from the baking pavements is already building, making his shirt stick to his back with sweat.

His brother gave him a set of keys during a previous overnight stay, to allow him to come and go freely, and he never returned them. This key fob was one of the things he packed in his holdall when he left Tansy's apartment. He worries, briefly, that an attempted break-in or romantic break-up might have led to Ben changing the locks, but the key to the street door of the building still works. He waits until the porter has stepped away from his desk to deal with a delivery before letting himself in, and takes the lift up to the fourth floor. The front door key still works too.

The place is a mess. Of the two of them, Ben had always been the sloppy, untidy one. Daniel is tempted to collect the crusty mugs, make the bed and wash the heap of dirty dishes in the sink, but he has to resist the temptation. Ben mustn't know he's been here. He feels the same temptation over the framed family photos on the bookshelf in the living room. There's one in particular he'd like to sneak into his bag, but its absence might be noticed.

The problem with untidy people, Daniel reflects, as he pokes through overflowing drawers, is trying to work out where they keep things. The disorder means that nothing is stored anywhere obvious. The drawers in the bedroom dresser yield nothing but a jumble of underwear, T-shirts and sweatshirts. The wardrobe is a little more orderly, with dress shirts and jackets on hangers and shoes in serried rows on the wardrobe floor. He checks jacket pockets – nothing. He even looks inside the shoes.

Ben's home workstation is no more than a Scandinavian trestle-style table, with no drawers. Underneath it is a shoe box, from which pieces of paper protrude: receipts and bills. Daniel kneels down, tips out all the contents and trawls through an ill-assorted pile that even contains foil-wrapped condoms. Eventually, near the bottom of the box, he finds what he's looking for.

'Bloody hell, Ben,' he says out loud, making a mental note to buy him some proper storage for Christmas. Except that they won't be together at Christmas. This one, or any other Christmas.

He opens Ben's passport and looks at the photo. The hair is different, and Ben has a short beard, but facially the two brothers are very alike. He strokes his own three-day stubble, grateful that he hasn't bothered to shave. It would need to grow for several weeks more before it resembled Ben's facial hair, and that's time he doesn't have. Not with his own passport having just been scanned at Heathrow. But he won't shave again.

A crushing heaviness settles in his chest as he looks around the flat before leaving.

'I'm sorry, bro,' he whispers, his voice cracking on the words. 'Love you.'

*

Daniel walks back to Upper Street in the thick, fume-heavy air and finds a barber's shop, where he gets them to cut his hair in a facsimile of Ben's: long on top, shaved at the sides. Then he checks into a three-star chain hotel on City Road, paying with cash and using Ben's passport for ID.

He will have to withdraw more cash from his own bank account. The transaction will leave a digital footprint, but there's no way around this problem: he has no other source of funds. But when he leaves London – which will have to be soon – he will be travelling as Ben Halligan, not Daniel. Not a perfect solution, but one which will buy him some valuable time. And the upside of Ben's untidiness is that he's unlikely to notice that his passport has gone missing. Not until he needs it to travel himself, which Daniel knows will be his brother's annual trip to Ibiza in August.

The next morning, after only a few hours' restless, sweaty sleep in the under-ventilated hotel room, he makes a trip to a City branch of his bank and withdraws the maximum amount of cash. He does the same the next day, at a West End branch; all the time forcing himself not to weaken, not to phone his brother and tell him he's in London. Ben doesn't currently know his geographic location, just that he's left Tansy, and he needs things to stay that way. He keeps his phone switched off, buying a basic burner phone for day-to-day tasks.

On the third day, unable to stand the choking London heat any longer, and with his stubble growth almost beardlike, he heads back to Heathrow and once again purchases a one-way ticket for cash. Only this time there's no need to scan the flight departure boards for inspiration. He knows exactly where he's going. There's only one place he *can* go.

CHAPTER THIRTY-EIGHT

DANIEL

26TH DECEMBER 2004

KHAO LAK RESORT, THAILAND

It started like all the other mornings on their honeymoon.

They rose at around eight, dressed in their swimwear and had breakfast on the veranda of their private villa, served by one of the ever-smiling hotel staff. Papaya with fresh lime, soft white rolls with butter and local honey, coffee. At nine, they grabbed towels, sunscreen and woven beach mats and walked the few yards to the beach, leaving the villa to be cleaned by the housekeepers.

Rosie noticed it first.

She looked up from rubbing sunscreen into her left forearm and pointed. 'Oh my goodness: look at that! How bizarre. Wow.'

That was typical of Rosie. She was intrigued rather than alarmed. She stood up, shading her eyes with her hand, and took a few steps closer. It was still early for the holidaymakers, but there were a few other people on the beach. Several of them stood staring too.

'It's going backwards,' Rosie said, laughing. She turned to him and grinned. 'How weird is that?'

It was weird. It was fucking weird. Instead of rolling in towards the beach, the sea was receding. Disappearing. He discovered later that this was what's known as 'drawback', caused by a change of pressure at the site of an earthquake. It's the warning sign that a deadly wave is on its way. But at the time they didn't know any of that.

Rosie, along with a few other tourists, started out across the sand towards the sea. Behind them, in the resort, people were shouting to them to come back, but they couldn't hear.

'Rosie!' he called. 'Ro, come back. It might not be safe.'

In response she just turned and waved, her neon-yellow bikini a bright dot on the horizon. He knew Rosie. She would keep on going until she caught up with the sea again. From a distance she looked ridiculously young – childlike, even. But then she was only twenty-one. Barely more than a girl. Everyone had said they were too young to get married, but they did it anyway. He wanted to be with her forever and she wanted to be with him forever. It was that simple. She was the only woman he had ever loved. The only woman he *would* ever love.

When the water changed direction and started rolling in again, he was relieved at first. The wave looked small, innocuous. But this was a tsunami. The waves don't stop or break when they reach the shore. They keep on going, with a relentless power that can tear up trees and toss ships around as though they're toy boats.

Rosie and the others were trying to swim, but it became horribly clear that they couldn't. The currents were so strong that it wasn't possible. By now some of the hotel staff had run down to the beach and were screaming at all of them who were still there.

'Get back! Get back!'

And most of them did. Those that could grabbed their belongings and ran up the path to the resort without looking back. But he didn't. He couldn't.

Someone grabbed his arm and tried to pull him away, shouting at him angrily.

'My wife!' he shouted back. 'My wife is in the water! We have to try and help her.'

He plunged into the churning surf, trying to find her. Immediately he was sucked under, his ears, eyes and lungs all filling with filthy water. Somehow, he righted himself, broke to the surface. He knew he didn't have long. Probably only seconds. If he was to save her, he had to act fast.

And then he spotted her. He caught a flash of bright yellow a few feet away from him. Rosie's bikini.

'Oh, thank God!' he gasped, though there was no one to hear him. He just had to reach her somehow. If he could just reach her and grab her, they could still make their way to dry land. His limbs flailed. Time and time again he was sucked under, tossed about like a doll. Eventually he righted himself and saw that she was right next to him, her hair streaming over her face. He grabbed the yellow straps of her bikini and kicked onto his back, hauling her against his chest and cradling her under his chin as he'd been taught in lifesaving lessons in the school pool. In that moment, he thanked the powers-that-be for those lessons.

After what seemed like an age they reached what had once been the tree-lined pathway to the beach. He managed to grab the trunk of a palm tree and, as he did so, felt hands reach out to help them. They were lifted clear and carried up to the nearest patch of dry land. He curled onto his side, coughing up the brackish water. A few feet away someone was trying to revive Rosie. Her body twitched and water and vomit gushed out of her mouth and nose.

'She's alive!' someone said.

'Thank Christ…' He slumped forward, weak with relief, as a towel was draped around his shoulders. After a few seconds he managed to lift his head and look over in Rosie's direction.

And then he froze.

It wasn't Rosie. This was some other young, slim, European holidaymaker wearing a yellow bikini. Someone he had pulled from the waves while his beautiful wife of just one week had been left to drown mere feet away.

He had rescued the wrong woman.

PART FIVE

CHAPTER THIRTY-NINE

PIPPA

When Pippa arrives in the Greatorex Street office she realises instantly that Cardle has something on his mind. Something that's gnawing at him.

She has learned to read him thoroughly: his body language, his facial expressions. He doesn't need to speak for her to know what sort of mood he's in.

It's the Monday morning following their return from Mauritius. Pippa slept all weekend but still feels unsteady and spaced out from jet lag. And it's hot, too, with temperatures higher than they've just experienced in the Indian Ocean. She's dressed in sandals and a strappy sundress but still feels stale and sticky after a fetid commute on a Northern line train.

Cardle has faint sweat patches under the sleeves of his linen shirt and a morose expression. He's dressed more formally than usual because they're expecting a visit from Arne Lindgren for a final debrief.

'Come on then, let's have it.' Pippa has also learned that it's pointless tiptoeing around her boss when he's in one of his darker moods. 'What's bothering you?' She stands in the doorway of his office, sucking up the remainder of an iced latte through a straw.

'Pippa…' His tone is heavy, but he looks up and manages a smile. 'The thing is… now we're winding up the Lindgren case, I can't justify employing you any longer.'

'You're not employing me,' she returns calmly, though her stomach sinks. 'You're not paying me a wage. My travel expenses have all been covered by Arne Lindgren, otherwise I've been living off my savings.'

Cardle is shaking his head slowly. 'My point exactly. You can't go on doing that. You need a job.'

'I'm fine, honestly. I've got plenty of money in my account, and I live virtually for nothing in Rosemary's flat.'

'Yes, but you won't have plenty of money for ever. At some point it will run out and you'll need a proper salary. And I can't afford to pay you one. I barely have enough work to pay myself.'

'So, what are you saying?' Pippa's mouth is dry, despite the watery dregs of coffee she has just swallowed.

'I'm saying…' He sighs, and she is gratified to see that he seems genuinely sorry. 'That you need to spend your time investigating career options, not investigating stuff for me.'

'Actually, I was thinking about applying to the Met. To their fast-track CID intake.'

'Well, there you are then. You'd be an ideal candidate: they'd be lucky to get you.' He scrapes his palm across his stubble. 'And it goes without saying that I'll be happy to provide a reference.'

Pippa looks down at her bare toes. They're tanned from Mauritius, but the polish on the nails is chipped, needs replacing. Still, it looks as though she'll have plenty of time for such frivolous pursuits now.

She looks up again. 'Can I just do one more thing?'

'What's that?'

'Can I sit in on the debrief with Lindgren?'

'Sure.' Cardle smiles. 'Only fair since you did most of the work busting Babajee. But I think given our air-conditioning set-up' – he indicates the one creaky desk fan which is the only cooling they have – 'instead of him coming here, we'd better go to him.'

*

Lindgren is staying at what used to be the Great Eastern Hotel, in Liverpool Street.

They meet him in the elegant Art Deco bar, with its carved marble friezes. The air-conditioning there is so fierce that Pippa feels positively chilly in her sleeveless dress. A waiter brings them a cocktail menu, but Lindgren asks for a tray of coffee and pastries instead. He looks better and seems more relaxed than the last time Pippa saw him. His lean face is tanned again, and he's gained a little weight.

'So,' he says, in his immaculate English. 'Tell me about Mauritius.' He pours them all coffee from a French press.

Cardle relays, in detail, but without any undue dramatic flourish, everything they discovered when they returned to the Excelsior Resort.

Lindgren lets his eyes close, and takes a few deep breaths. 'I knew it,' he says, quietly. 'I knew it wasn't an accident. That Halligan had something to do with it. I was right.'

'I have a copy of the video file we saw,' Cardle says, carefully, glancing at Pippa. 'I will, of course, make it available to you should you wish but… well, to put it bluntly, the contents are distressing. I'm not sure I'd recommend you watch it.'

Lindgren nods. 'Keep it for now. Let me think about that.'

'Obviously this is now a criminal matter and it's in the hands of the Mauritian police. They don't deal with a lot of serious crime, and I get the impression they have almost no cross-border experience, but they will liaise with Interpol who will help them track down Halligan.'

'And you don't have any theories about where he could be now?'

Cardle shakes his head. 'Your guess is as good as mine.' He catches sight of Pippa frowning slightly and adds, 'As ours. We were fairly confident before that he was no longer in Sydney, and probably no longer in Australia. Other than that, he could be anywhere.'

Lindgren presses his long, elegant fingers to his forehead. 'And we're still no clearer on why? On why Halligan did this.'

'We can speculate, but that's all it is, speculation.'

'There's no audio on the footage,' Pippa begins carefully. 'But from the visuals, it almost looks like a row between two lovers. It's very heated, very impassioned. Is it possible they were once in a relationship? They're around the same age.'

Lindgren frowns, perplexed. 'I don't think so, no. She's never mentioned his name previously. Nikki was a very open person; she would have mentioned it if we'd bumped into an ex… I mean, we socialised with them, had dinner, took the catamaran trip. There was no spark, no atmosphere between the two of them. I'm sure I would have picked up… you know, the vibe' – the word sounds more like 'wibe' in his Swedish accent – 'if there had been a previous love affair. When you were investigating him, you didn't come across anything in Halligan's own relationship history that would fit this theory?'

'No,' says Pippa. 'We didn't.'

'I'm sorry,' Cardle says. 'But at least we do have some answers. We know exactly what happened that night.' He swallows the last mouthful of his pain au chocolat and extends a hand to Lindgren. 'I'll make up my final invoice and send it to you.'

But Lindgren doesn't shake it. 'No,' he says, polite but firm. 'I want to retain you a little longer. Both of you, since you make such an effective team. I want you to go on investigating until you've found out why. Why did Daniel Halligan want to kill my wife?'

CHAPTER FORTY

PIPPA

'So, thanks to Lindgren, you've had a reprieve,' Cardle says drily, as a taxi whisks them back to Greatorex Street. 'Looks like I'm stuck with you for a while longer.'

The taxi driver has the vehicle's ventilation system cranked up to full power, but it's merely recycling warm, humid air. Pippa can feel the backs of her thighs sticking to the seat. On a mild day it would be less than a fifteen-minute walk from Liverpool Street; the taxi is a concession to the extreme heat.

'You never know,' she says, with a half-smile. 'Maybe more jobs like this will come in. Ones that involve using two people. Maybe it could lead to something permanent.'

Cardle looks out of the window. 'Unfortunately, not all my clients are like Lindgren. He's a wealthy man. He can afford to chuck as much money as he likes at the problem, for as long as he likes. Your run-of-the-mill cuckolded husband doesn't have those kinds of resources.'

'But if—'

'I'm not going to discuss this now, Pippa,' he says, firmly. 'Let's concentrate on the job in hand. We've got work to do.'

Once they're back in the office, Pippa offers to make an emergency cold drinks run to the local corner shop. The truth is that she needs a few minutes to herself, to process the flip-flopping from her job being over, to being temporarily rehired, to Cardle's renewed determination to end the arrangement.

You made him give you the work in the first place, she chides herself. *And you knew full well it was only a short-term thing. So stop acting like…*

She catches herself mid-thought, but the voice in her head persists anyway.

… like a rejected girlfriend.

When Pippa gets back to the office with a carrier bag containing ice lollies and cold cans of Coke, Cardle has his eyes locked on his computer screen.

'I'm trying to find out if Halligan has any previous convictions for assault,' he tells Pippa, accepting the can with a grunt of thanks. 'I need you to find out more about his time in the army. See if you can find a contact we can talk to.'

They research in silence for a while, Pippa fielding phone enquiries as she does so, with melting orange lolly juice running down her wrist. She keeps her phone manner professional, but inwardly she's scowling.

He doesn't deserve me. He doesn't appreciate all the stuff I do.

She goes to wash the sticky remains of the ice lolly from her hands, and when she returns Cardle is standing by her desk, his notebook in his hand.

'So… I've accessed police records—'

'Your secret databases access again,' says Pippa, acerbically.

Cardle chooses to ignore this. 'Halligan doesn't have any sort of criminal conviction. Just a caution for a breach of the peace when he was a teenager. He and a mate chucking mud at passing cars. Boys acting like dickheads kind of stuff, but not what you would call violence.'

Pippa nods, and takes a gulp from her Coke can.

'How d'you get on?'

'He joined the Second Battalion Grenadier Guards when he was twenty-five. Based mostly at the barracks in Aldershot, did a brief tour in Iraq. Released from his commission three years later, which was the earliest opportunity he could leave, suggesting the life of a soldier was not for him.'

'Good,' says Cardle, shortly. 'Find anyone we can talk to?'

'There's another officer called Hugo Manners. Ex public school, usual profile. He joined the battalion at the same time as Daniel and left a year later. They're next to one another in their cadets' passing-out parade at Sandhurst. I found an old photo on the Grenadiers' website.'

'Any chance of finding him?'

Pippa nods. 'I think so. Works at a bond trading place in the City. Luckily he seems to be fairly active on social media. Or at least his wife is. She's called Posy.'

Cardle snorts. 'Of course she is. Posy by name, probably Posy by nature.'

Pippa grins, despite herself. 'So… do you want to reach out to him, or shall I?'

'You do it. I suspect it will be better received coming from a good-looking girl his own age than a middle-aged Yorkshire copper.'

The compliment, Pippa knows, is his way of trying to mollify her. She remains outwardly unmoved, however. 'Woman,' she reproves him, coolly. 'Not girl.'

*

The following evening, Pippa is seated across from Hugo Manners at a wine bar in Fenchurch Street.

'Gosh,' he says, sweeping his gelled hair back from his forehead, a signet ring flashing on his little finger. 'An undercover investigation. Exciting.' He has a square, slightly florid face and his hair, underneath the product, is a sandy blond colour.

'Thanks very much for meeting me,' Pippa begins formally, sipping the Château Pape Clément that she invited him to choose. He seems like the sort of man who expects to choose the wine. 'So did you know Daniel Halligan well?'

'Yah, knew him pretty well. We were quite good mates when we were in the Guards, and we saw each other socially when we'd both left. That said, I haven't seen him in years. He buggered off abroad, I think, and we pretty much lost touch. He didn't really do Facebook, all that stuff.'

Pippa swills the dark wine around her balloon-sized glass, while Manners pours himself a generous top up. 'Did you ever meet his girlfriend?'

He gives a braying laugh. 'Which one? I mean, there were so bloody many. He was a real player, our Hally. I mean, have you ever met him?'

Pippa nods. 'I have.'

'Dishy bastard, isn't he? Bit of a moody sod too, mind you, but he could be charming if he wanted to. Certainly charmed a string of women into his bed. A player. Or what I believe the kids these days call a "fuck boy".'

He grins at his own wit.

'Was there anyone serious?'

Manners smoothes his hair back again. 'Not that I remember. He was dead against settling down. Said he'd never marry, I do remember that. Very sceptical if ever one of our mates got hitched.'

'Do you remember him ever going out with a girl called Nikki? Slim build, dark hair, pretty but not stunning. May have been known as Nicola or Nicole.'

'Nikki...' Manners sloshes yet more wine into his glass. 'I don't remember a Nikki, no, but I can't honestly say I kept track of who he was seeing. Revolving door to the bedroom, that kind of thing. They rarely lasted more than a few weeks.'

'Is there anyone else who might know?'

'I'll ask Posy if you like. My wife. We were dating at the time, and she paid much more attention than I did to what Hally was up to. She had a bit of a crush on him, truth be told, so she tended to keep track of him pretty closely. Annoyed me a bit at the time, if I'm honest.'

The hearty manner slips, and there's a slight turning down of his mouth as he remembers this.

Pippa empties her glass, scribbling her contact details onto one of Cardle's business cards, before handing it to Manners.

'I'd be really grateful if you could ask Posy what she remembers, and get back to me. Or she can call me herself. Either is fine.'

In the end, it's Posy Manners who phones, the next afternoon.

'Hiiiiii.' She draws out the syllable. Her voice is high, girlish. 'Is that Pippa Bryant?'

'It is. Hi.'

'Hugo told me you were asking about Daniel. About whether he ever dated a girl called Nikki. Is that right?'

'Yes, that's right.'

'Only I've thought about it and… trust me, I remember everything Daniel got up to…' She gives a breathy little giggle. 'And there was definitely never anyone called Nikki, or Nicola. Unless it was someone he met in Australia, obviously. I don't know what happened out there; we lost touch.'

Pippa thanks her and relays this information to Cardle.

'Nikki Lindgren never lived in Australia,' he says. 'I'm sure Lindgren would have mentioned it. But I'll double check with him, of course.'

'So, what now?'

Cardle leans back in his desk chair, his hands behind his head. 'I've been in touch with a mate of mine at the National Crime Agency. He's got access to Interpol databases.'

'Handy,' says Pippa. 'And?'

'A red notice was issued for Halligan after he failed to respond to requests for further interview with the Mauritian police. His passport was flagged in use three days ago.'

Pippa's eyes widen. 'Where?'

Cardle can't resist a smile of satisfaction. 'Flying into Heathrow.'

'He's here?'

'Looks like it. At least, he's not been picked up leaving.'

'What do we do now?' Pippa's heart rate quickens. 'D'you think we have any chance of finding him?'

Cardle tips back in his chair again and rests his forearms on the desk. 'It's a long shot. But I'll tell you what our best lead is…'

Pippa shoots him a questioning look, but she's already pretty sure what he's about to say.

'…you need to go back to Ben Halligan.'

For a week or so after they met in the Reliance, Ben texted Pippa at regular intervals. But when she failed to engage beyond the polite minimum, and resisted suggestions to meet up, the messages dwindled to nothing.

Now she has to try and rekindle his interest and resurrect some sort of relationship.

'I'm really not very good at this,' she tells Cardle. 'I mean, I've only ever really been in a relationship with Alastair. I've never used a dating app. I don't know what to say.'

'Well, he obviously liked you. Just be yourself.'

Pippa spends several minutes composing and editing a text.

Hi Ben, how's it going?

No, that sounds too cheesy.

Hi, been meaning to get in touch, but I've been busy.

Too apologetic.
In the end she simply writes: *Hi, it's Pippa.*
Ten minutes later, she receives a response.

Well, well, well. I was wondering what happened to you.

I've been away for work, she types. This is true, after all. *But now I'm back in London I'd love to have that drink.*

Sounds good.

When are you free?

She hears nothing for an hour, then receives:

How about this… I've got a couple of tickets for Lovebox Festival in Vicky Park on Saturday. Fancy coming with me?

Saturday is three days away. Ideally, she needs to probe Ben sooner.

How about a drink tomorrow?

Sorry, got to work late tomorrow, and have a dinner on Fri. Saturday's the earliest. Glad you're keen tho! So… see you then?

He adds a winky face emoji.

Shit, thinks Pippa. *Now I'm coming off as keen, when I'm not really interested at all.* It feels dishonest. But then she reminds herself that she does actually like Ben Halligan. She finds him attractive. And it's just a date, not a long-term commitment.

Yes, she replies. *See you on Saturday.*

CHAPTER FORTY-ONE

PIPPA

'No,' says Cardle immediately, when she tells him the plan. 'Saturday's too late; it has to be sooner. Who knows where Daniel might be in three days' time.'

Pippa shrugs helplessly. 'What can I do; he's not free until then.'

'You contrived a meeting with him before, you can do it again. Do it tonight. Go round to his flat.'

'I don't officially know where he lives, remember? You do, but he doesn't know I'm your colleague. I could go to his office again and "bump into him".' She makes air quotes.

But Cardle's shaking his head. 'It has to be his flat, because if Daniel's still in London, that's where he's likely to be. And you have to arrive unannounced so there's no chance to hide evidence of his brother being there… you sure he didn't tell you where he lived?'

Pippa thinks for a moment. 'When we were talking about whether it was better to live north or south of the river, I think he did mention the building he'd bought a flat in. It's a converted print works, I think?'

'That's right: the Royle Building. It's quite well known, so it wouldn't be strange for you to remember it.'

'And…' Pippa warms to the narrative. 'While we were on the subject, I mentioned to him that Alastair and I had friends who live in Islington. So if I were visiting them…'

'…and you remembered where he lives, it wouldn't be all that strange if you dropped round to see him.'

'Especially if I had to tell him that I couldn't make Saturday after all.'

They grin at each other, pleased with their logic. Cardle checks his watch. 'It's three o'clock now… go home and change, get yourself looking irresistible.'

'This isn't a honey trap,' Pippa says, hotly. 'I'm not going to dress up.'

'No, I know, I'm sorry. Don't do – or wear – anything that makes you feel uncomfortable. But, let's face it, in this weather a shower and a change of clothes are not going to be a hardship.'

Pippa can't deny that she's happy to get home to her flat and take a long, cool shower. In the end she settles on a pair of ripped white jeans and a silky grey halter neck top that exposes her tanned shoulders. Comfortable and – if not irresistible – then at least stylish. Tying up her hair into a ponytail to keep her neck from sweating, she slips on jewelled flip-flops and catches the Northern line to Angel.

It's only when she approaches the Royle Building that it occurs to Pippa that Ben might not be in. The haze of midsummer heat is still in the air, evening sun bouncing off window panes. He's surely more likely to be outside somewhere, in a beer garden.

She's surprised, and relieved, when his disembodied voice crackles over the intercom.

'Hello?'

'Ben, it's Pippa. Can I come up?'

'Pippa.' There's a pause, then a confused: 'But it's Wednesday.'

'I know, but could you—'

The entry lock buzzes loudly.

Inside, the lobby has the original terrazzo tiled floor, leading onto a wide, tiled staircase. A porter sits at a desk in the corner. 'Can I help you, miss?'

'Halligan?'

'Fourth floor.'

She's greeted at the door by Ben, wearing a white T-shirt and cargo shorts. His feet are bare, and he's brandishing a half-drunk bottle of craft beer. 'This is a bit of a surprise.'

Pippa repeats the story about visiting her friends in the area and remembering which building he lived in. '…so I thought I'd call round because I've realised I can't make the festival on Saturday. We've got a family do. Wedding anniversary.'

As she talks she's looking past Ben's shoulder and into the flat, scanning the room for evidence of a second occupant. There are engineered wood floors, brick walls and the original metal-framed windows leading onto a small balcony. The place is untidy in a uniquely male way: sports kit lying on the floor exactly where it was dropped, empty wine and beer bottles in random places, odd socks under the sofa. There is, however, no sign of Daniel Halligan.

'You are on your own?' she confirms. 'Only if it's not convenient, I'll…'

'Yes, on my own.' Ben is drinking her in, taking in her glossy ponytail, and the shiny fabric cutaway to reveal her naked back and shoulders. 'Come in, come in – don't stand in the doorway.' Pippa smiles and walks into the apartment. 'I must say, it's very nice to see you. And you look great… been somewhere hot?'

'Yes,' says Pippa. She can't say it was Mauritius, because Ben will know about Daniel honeymooning there. And the trip was supposed to have been for work. 'The States,' she lies. 'California.'

'Nice,' Ben nods slowly. 'Bloody nice work if you can get it. Beer?'

'Ummm…'

'Hold on, let me see if I've got wine.' He opens the door of the large American fridge in the open-plan kitchen and scans the shelves. 'Nope, sorry. Just beer. Obviously if I'd known you were coming, I'd have got some in.'

'Fine. I'll have beer,' Pippa says, holding out her hand for the proffered bottle. It's well chilled at least. Ben helps himself to another bottle. From the number of empties on the draining board, he's well ahead of her.

'Come and sit down.' He clears some magazines off the sofa and pats the space next to him. 'It's nice to see you, it really is. I was hoping you'd get in touch.'

'So, what have you been up to?' Pippa asks, perching as far from him as she can. 'Have you heard from your brother? Last time we met, you said he'd lost contact.'

She may as well ask him, she decides, before the beer has too much of an effect.

Ben exhales hard, shaking his head. 'No, I haven't. Not since he emailed me. And d'you know what's freaking me out? I had a visit from some cops the other day. London office of Interpol. Wanting to know if I'd seen Dan.'

'Oh, my God.' Pippa feigns surprise that she doesn't feel. 'Shit, that's worrying.'

'I know.' Ben necks half the bottle of beer in one go. 'In my opinion, *she* must have something to do with it. The wife. She must have shopped him about the guy who died in his hotel room, like she was threatening him to. Anyway…' He smiles at her. 'Let's not talk about that now. How are you enjoying this weather? Nightmare, isn't it?'

They compare heatwave war stories for a while, then Ben stands up. 'Scuse me a sec, need a pee.'

He disappears into the bathroom. Pippa starts scouring the room for something, anything, that might be linked to Dan.

Despite the generalised mess, there's very little of a personal nature, apart from a group of framed photographs on the bookshelves that take up one wall. One in particular draws her attention, but there's no time to examine it close up. She pulls out her phone and takes screenshots of each of them in turn, quickly moving to the window as Ben returns, pretending to admire the view of the canal.

He stands behind her, resting a hand lightly on her naked back.

'Lovely place,' she says, turning to smile at him. 'Is it just a one-bedroom?'

'Yes.' He gives her a slightly suggestive look. 'Want to see it?'

'Ummm…' Pippa hesitates. If she says yes, it will sound as if she wants to go to bed with him. On the other hand, there may be something in there that could be useful. 'Okay, then. But just the lightning tour… I really need to get going.'

Ben's disappointment is obvious, but he ushers her into the bedroom anyway. It's a typical bachelor set-up: just a double bed with rumpled sheets, a dresser and built-in wardrobes.

'Bed's really comfy.' He demonstrates by sprawling over it. 'Try it.'

'Ben…'

He reaches up and grabs her by the wrist, pulling her down onto the bed with him. He smells of beer and some sort of woody aftershave. She's pinioned at an awkward angle, and he starts kissing her before she has the chance to wriggle free.

And it's a good kiss, the kiss of someone who has had many years of practice. Pippa is not repulsed: far from it. She quite enjoys it. But with a prickle of guilt she acknowledges that this is not the kiss she really wants. The thought stirs up some dark, uncomfortable feelings that she's not willing to address. She extricates herself from the embrace after several seconds and stands up.

'Sorry, Ben, it's been lovely but I really have to go.'

'Really?' he wheedles. 'It was just getting fun.'

'Yes, really.'

'When will I see you again?'

'I don't know,' Pippa says, then adds in a softer tone. 'Soon, I hope. I'll text you.'

The sun has set, but it's still very warm as she walks back along the bank of the canal, thinking about kissing somebody else.

CHAPTER FORTY-TWO

PIPPA

Go okay? Cardle texts her as she's walking back across Clapham Common.

Yes fine.

She doesn't plan on divulging that she let Ben Halligan kiss her. It would make her sound unprofessional, she decides. Either that, or Cardle would start worrying about her personal safety being at risk. But he will be wanting to know more, so she sends a second text as she's unlocking the door to the annexe flat.

D definitely not there. Will tell you what I found out tomorrow.

A few minutes later she receives a single word text.

Night.

The following morning, she transfers the images from her phone to her laptop and prints off copies so that she and Cardle can examine them.

'This is the one that caught my eye,' she says, after she has spread them out on the coffee table. It's still hot, and the rattly desk fan is lurching noisily from side to side.

Cardle takes the photo and examines it, close up to his face. Pippa suspects he needs reading glasses but is too vain, or too macho, to wear them.

'This is Daniel,' he says, pointing to a much younger and even more good-looking incarnation of Ben's older brother. 'Wonder who this is?'

The photo is taken in a wintry English garden, with hoar frost dusting the branches. Daniel is wearing a smart suit and tie, and has his arm around a slim, pretty girl with long brown hair, wearing a bright red coat and a white fur scarf. She has her face turned towards him, laughing. It's a laugh that conveys total adoration.

'Handsome couple,' Cardle observes, gruffly.

'It's this that caught my eye.' Pippa points to the girl's left hand. She's wearing both a diamond solitaire and a gold wedding band on her third finger. 'She's married.'

Cardle scrapes his stubble with the tips of his fingers. 'Halligan is either messing around very blatantly with somebody else's missus, or…'

'…or he was married to her.'

'Bloody hell.' Cardle jabs two fingers into his forehead. 'Why the fuck didn't I think to check? To see if he'd been married before.'

'Because everybody we spoke to said he was anti-marriage. That until Tansy came along, he'd vowed never to do it.' Pippa's tone is soothing. 'It was an understandable oversight.'

'No, it wasn't,' Cardle growls. 'It's the most basic mistake. First thing we should have looked up.'

'We still don't know that it *is* his wife,' Pippa offers reasonably. 'It could be a family friend. Or a cousin.' But she knows as she says this that the girl has to be married to Daniel. Only a woman in love would look at him like that. 'I'll check the General Register Office records.'

Cardle stumps off back to his office and Pippa gets to work. An hour later, she knocks on his door. 'Jim…I've found it.'

He turns his gaze from his computer and swivels his chair from side to side. 'Go on.'

She reads from her notebook. 'On the nineteenth of December 2004, at St Nicholas Church, Arundel, Sussex. Daniel Joseph Halligan and Rosanna Isobel Keeling.'

'I see.' Cardle taps his pen on the desk. 'I reckon that photo must have been taken at the reception. Or soon afterwards.'

Pippa shrugs. 'I suppose it could have been. Or at Christmas, with their families… I'll see if I can find their decree absolute if you like, only you have to know which county court dealt with it before you can get very far.' She turns to go.

'No, hold on a minute… wait there.' Cardle returns to his screen and starts clicking away. 'His wife's date of birth?'

Pippa looks at her notes again. 'July the third, 1983. She was twenty-one, he was twenty-two.'

'I thought so,' Cardle says, grimly, after a few minutes. 'Jesus.'

Pippa walks around the desk and stands behind him so she can see what he's looking at.

It's a death certificate for Rosanna Halligan, dated 26th December 2004.

'Oh, my God…' Pippa breathes. Her body is quivering with the shock and she grips the back of Cardle's chair. 'Oh, no. *'Cause of death…drowning'*. And they'd been married exactly a week.'

'Look at the place of death.'

'Khao Lak, Thailand… so they must have been on their honeymoon. Oh, God, poor Daniel… what a terrible tragedy.'

'It was a tragedy, all right,' Cardle states grimly, twisting in his chair to look at her. 'Date not ring any bells with you? I suppose you're a bit young to remember.'

Pippa is shaking her head.

'One of the deadliest disasters in history, killed a quarter of a million people.'

'Oh, God, you mean—?'

'Rosanna Halligan died in the 2004 tsunami.'

'You okay?'

Cardle comes out of his office a few minutes later, after Pippa has sat down at her desk again. She's staring at her screen, her hands in her lap.

'Yes, I'm fine.' She manages a brief smile. 'It's a lot to take in, that's all.'

'Certainly explains why Halligan went about saying he'd never marry. What he meant was he'd never marry again. Not after losing his first wife on his honeymoon.'

Pippa nods slowly. 'And the trip to a Mauritius beach resort must have been hellish for him. The last thing he would have wanted to do. And maybe…' She looks up. 'Maybe he called his company Roseland Investments because of her.'

'Look,' says Cardle. 'I'd like you to do some more research into Rosanna Halligan, but why don't you go and do it at home?' He nods in the direction of the ineffectual fan. 'You'll probably find it easier to concentrate there.'

Rosemary Vesey has given Pippa open access to her large garden, so once she gets back to Clapham, she changes into shorts and T-shirt and takes her laptop outside, sitting on the shaded terrace at the back of the house. Gus follows her outside and lies at her feet, panting.

After a few minutes of trawling the internet, she finds a link to an article in the *Arundel Argus*.

Local tsunami victim laid to rest

Bride buried in church where she was married three weeks ago.

The family and friends of Rosanna Halligan, 21, gathered at St Nicholas Church, Arundel on Friday for her funeral. Local girl Rosanna, who was known as Rosie, was swept to her death when the tsunami hit the Shangri La Hotel at the Thai resort of Khao Lak where she was on her honeymoon. Leading the mourners was her devastated husband, Daniel, aged 22, who survived the disaster.

There is a grainy, passport-sized photo of Rosie, and a larger photo of a coffin heaped with flowers being carried into the church, followed by a cohort of black-clad mourners. The lead pall bearer is Daniel Halligan, his face stricken and twisted by grief. Alongside him, the coffin on his right shoulder, is a pale, stunned young man whom Pippa realises is a teenage Ben Halligan.

She stares at the image for a few seconds, her heart thudding. Then she ploughs on, reading first-hand accounts of the tsunami hitting the west coast of Thailand. Of people sunbathing and snorkelling one minute, and the next running for their lives. Of a seething, broiling mass of water that seemed to appear from nowhere, and then receded as fast as it had appeared. Of sun loungers, boats and hotel structures being washed away. So many stories; some horrifying, some uplifting. She reads for what feels like hours, reaching down occasionally to pet Gus, accepting a glass of iced tea from Marysia.

Then she finds a news article that makes her stop her scrolling and stare long and hard, reading and re-reading. It's from the *Guildford Times*, dated the same week as Rosanna Halligan's funeral. A cold chill runs down her spine, despite the hot June sun.

She snatches up her phone and texts Cardle.

Can you ask Arne Lindgren his wife's maiden name?

He doesn't reply for forty minutes. Pippa is about to phone him and ask whether he got her message, when he replies simply *Simmons*

Pippa copies the link to the article and emails it to him with the subject line: 'I think you need to read this. Look at the photo.'

Local girl rescued from horror tsunami

The family of a local girl, Nicole Simmons, today spoke of their relief at her surviving the tsunami as it hit their holiday resort in Thailand. The Simmons family were spending Christmas at the Shangri La Resort in Khao Lak when the tsunami devastated the hotel and killed several holidaymakers. Mr and Mrs Simmons were eating in the restaurant when the deadly wave hit, but Nicole, 19, a sociology student at Goldsmiths College, London was on the beach with friends. She was pulled from the water by rescuers.

'It's a miracle,' said Malcolm Simmons, 51. 'When the water began rushing in, we had to evacuate the hotel, but Nikki wasn't with us. When we realised that she'd been on the beach, my wife and I honestly feared the worst. The hotel building was destroyed and we had to go to a local shelter. One of the other guests, who spoke Thai, offered to come with us to the local hospital, and we found Nikki there, battered and bruised but alive.'

'It was like a miracle,' adds Gwen Simmons, 48. 'We never thought we'd see our daughter again. There are no words for how grateful we are to the people who helped her.'

Five minutes after she has pressed 'Send' on the email, her phone rings. She answers it, turning her face to enjoy the gentle breeze blowing onto the terrace.

'Well done,' Cardle says, slightly less gruff than usual. 'May be an old photo but you can definitely tell it's her. I knew there had to be a link and you found it.' He pauses for a beat. 'Same place, same day. Only Nikki Lindgren survived, and Rosie Halligan died.'

CHAPTER FORTY-THREE

PIPPA

'How many now?' Pippa asks Cardle.

'How many what?'

'How many air miles have we travelled together?'

'I don't know.' He sighs, pulling out his lighter and flicking the wheel impatiently. 'A fair few thousand. Tens of thousands, possibly.'

The two of them are at Terminal 2 at Heathrow, waiting for a Thai Airways flight to Bangkok. Arne Lindgren confirmed that his late wife had indeed mentioned being in Thailand when the 2004 tsunami hit, but that she found it too traumatic to talk about. When he heard that Daniel Halligan and his new wife were there in the same resort, his response was immediate and unequivocal.

'You must go out there,' he told Cardle. 'Go to Khao Lak and talk to people. See if anyone remembers what happened. I don't care what it costs; that's where we're going to find answers. There has to be a link between the Halligans and Nikki.'

'You think this is a waste of time, don't you?' Pippa asks, as they watch the departures board, waiting for their gate to be announced.

Cardle shrugs. 'Honestly, I have no idea.'

'But you don't want to go?'

He rounds on her, unable to suppress his bad temper. 'Well, do you? Another twelve hours on a bloody plane. Another time zone. More jet lag, when we've only just got over the last lot. And the rainy season's about to start out there: it's going to be wet and humid as hell.'

Pippa raises her eyebrows but does not comment. She's not looking forward to the flying or the jet lag either, but she's certainly not about to tell Cardle that she enjoys the experience of spending uninterrupted time with him, relishes the enforced proximity so much that she doesn't mind how much they have to travel.

After Pippa and Cardle have landed in Bangkok, disorientated by the time difference, they catch an internal flight to Phuket, then take an hour's taxi ride up the coast to Khao Lak. As Cardle predicted, the heat and humidity are overwhelming, and the sky is obscured with a blanket of grey-white cloud.

'Rain coming,' the taxi driver observes. 'Rainy season start early, I think.'

'Great,' mutters Cardle, turning his head to stare morosely out of the car window. 'All we need.'

Their rooms are individual beach huts with bamboo thatch, with the ocean in front of them and dense banks of casuarinas and coconut palms behind. After declining the management's offer of a couples' massage, they agree to meet and explore the beach together once they've freshened up.

'Hard to imagine all this being completely destroyed,' Pippa observes, as they walk along the endless stretch of golden sand.

'Oh, I don't know…' Cardle points up at the bank of dark cloud lowering above, turning the water from turquoise to greyish-green. 'I can imagine it all too well.' He fumbles in his shirt pocket for his packet of cigarettes and lights one.

'So, how are we going to go about this?' Pippa asks. 'We can't ask staff at the hotel where the Halligans and the Simmons were staying in 2004, because it was completely destroyed.'

Cardle puffs out a stream of smoke. 'To be honest, I'm not entirely sure. We'll just have to question as many people as we can until we find someone who remembers them. There must have been some interaction between Daniel Halligan and Nikki Simmons. Or perhaps between Rosie Halligan and Nikki Simmons. They were a similar age; maybe they became friendly.'

'Or maybe Nikki and Daniel became friendly. Too friendly.'

Cardle looks askance at Pippa. 'On their honeymoon?'

'Why not? Strange things can happen on a honeymoon. I should know.'

The next morning, armed with photographs of Daniel and Rosie Halligan, and the picture of the young Nicole Simmons that appeared in the *Guildford Times*, they set about questioning as many of the hotel staff that will speak to them. In response to mention of the former Shangri La Hotel, the younger ones look confused and the older ones shake their heads.

'All gone. Tsunami.'

'No more Shangri La. Tsunami.'

Pippa eventually finds a middle-aged kitchen porter who admits to knowing staff previously employed at the Shangri La, but explains sadly that they were both killed when the water hit. He looks blank when shown the photographs.

'This is impossible,' she says gloomily, when they convene for lunch. 'According to Google maps, there are at least twenty hotels on this stretch of coast, and people who remember the Halligans and the Simmons could be in any one of them. Even if we could question every potential employee between us, it's going to take us far too long.'

Cardle looks up from shovelling rice into his mouth. 'There is one good piece of news, though.'

'What's that?'

'According to this morning's *Sydney Herald*, Hiraya has been ordered by the Therapeutic Goods Administration to suspend trading, pending an investigation into false medical claims for their products.'

'Well, that's something,' Pippa admits grudgingly, sipping on her iced barley tea. 'I hope it gives the Webbers some comfort, now that we're finished on Meredith's case.' She pauses to see if he'll challenge the 'we'. 'So, the plan for this afternoon—?'

'We keep going, for as long as the weather holds,' Cardle says, flatly. 'We tackle the next hotel along the beach and then the next one, and so on.'

'People here don't like talking about the tsunami.' Pippa sighs, scratching at her arm where she has been bitten by mosquitoes in the night. 'That's the impression I get.'

'Can you blame them?'

She doesn't even try to look enthusiastic as they set off again after lunch, splitting up to cover more ground. But at the third hotel she goes to that afternoon, the Ocean Sands Resort, one of the delightfully pretty reception staff, resplendent in a traditional Thai dress, with orchids in her hair, tells her that her uncle used to be a manager at the defunct Shangri La.

'He speak very good English,' says the girl, whose name badge says 'Anong'. 'He know many English people at that hotel.'

'And he was there, when… when the wave hit?' Pippa asks.

Anong nods sombrely. 'Yes. He help the people. He help the people to run.'

'And where is your uncle now?' Pippa asks. 'Can I speak to him? Does he still work in the tourist business?'

Anong shakes her head sadly. 'No. No more hotels now. He works in town, in Khuekkhak, at Pak Pran supermarket.' She takes a complement slip from her desk and carefully writes down 'Mr Sanoh Cherinsuk', followed by an address.

'Can I talk to him today?'

'Not there today. Try tomorrow.' The girl points out of the window of the hotel lobby. 'Storm coming, I think.'

A steady stream of rain is already falling, rattling on the leaves of the dense tropical undergrowth, bouncing up off the ground with a heady, earthy scent. As Pippa leaves the hotel building, the stream has turned into a deluge. The storm drains are swirling with muddy brown water, and her clothes are sticking to her skin, her hair plastered to her head.

Her phone buzzes with a text and she shelters under an umbrella on the hotel terrace to read it.

Heading back, Cardle has written. *Think you should too.*

The relentless onslaught of the rain continues into the evening, resulting in several inches of standing water. After she's taken a hot shower, Pippa notices a text on her phone.

How was the family reunion? B x

Ben. She stares at it for a while, wondering what he means. Then it comes back with a rush that she cancelled their prospective date, for a wedding anniversary celebration that was supposed to have happened twenty-four hours ago.

Fine she types, then deletes this and replaces it with *Great, thanks x*

How about meeting for a drink or dinner this week? x

Sorry, I can't. Away on business again x

Ben sends a shocked face emoji. *Where this time?*

Pippa hesitates for a few seconds.

Far East.

You get around a hell of a lot for someone who works in insurance! He adds a sceptical face emoji with hand on chin.

Shit, is he getting suspicious about my back story? Has Daniel been in touch, and her name mentioned to him by Ben, only for his older brother to tell him that the woman he believes he's dating works as a private investigator?

Pippa tells herself that she's being paranoid, but nevertheless types nothing more revealing than a smiley face, and does not respond to Ben's next message. She and Cardle have mutually agreed that they will not attempt to wade to the restaurant, but instead order room service and let the staff worry about the logistics of getting it to their respective rooms. He phones her after they've both eaten, and she tells him about her breakthrough in finding someone who probably met the Halligans on their honeymoon.

'Good going,' he says, and she can hear the inhalation of cigarette smoke against the backdrop of the incessant downpour. 'Bloody good going, in the circumstances.'

'And I was also thinking, perhaps we could try talking to the staff at the local hospitals?'

'No,' says Cardle, flatly. 'I think if this hotel guy doesn't come up trumps then we should fly back to London. Tell Lindgren that a combination of collective amnesia and the rainy season made it impossible to progress our enquiries further. He'll just have to wait until Interpol tracks down Daniel Halligan to find out what happened.'

'But Jim—'

'That's the decision.' Cardle is firm. 'And I'm the one who makes them, remember? But you never know, this contact might work out. Now, get some sleep and I'll see you in the morning.'

Before she can object further, he hangs up.

CHAPTER FORTY-FOUR

PIPPA

After the phone call, Pippa lies back on her bed, feeling disgruntled.

The rain is clattering loudly on the bamboo thatch above her, but she's exhausted by both the time difference and the day's physical exertion. Despite the noise she's quickly asleep, the bedside lamp still on.

An hour and a half later, she's woken by the shocking onslaught of someone tipping a bucket of cold water over her head. Sitting bolt upright, spluttering, she looks around the room to see who would have done this to her. She's alone. More water pours over her shoulders and she realises it's coming from above her. Looking up at the ceiling she can see a chasm in the roof where the bamboo has given way under the weight of the torrent. Even if she manages to dry herself off, the sheet and the mattress are now drenched. She can't stay there.

Picking up the handset on the nightstand, Pippa tries to phone reception, but the line is dead. She uses her mobile to call Cardle. At the third attempt he picks up, with a sleepy, 'Hello?'

'I'm coming over to your room,' she says. 'My roof's leaking and I can't get hold of the hotel staff; the phone line's down.'

He mumbles something incoherent and cuts the call.

Pippa towels herself off, changes into dry pyjama shorts and vest and sets off to wade the 200 yards between her beach hut and

Cardle's; dirty water swirling round her calves. The dry pyjamas are quickly as wet as the ones she has just changed out of. She finds him sitting on the edge of his bed wearing only boxer shorts, and acknowledges privately – not for the first time – that he has a good body for his age.

'What a fucking carry on,' is all he says.

'At least your room's dry.' Pippa feels suddenly acutely awkward.

Cardle stands up, and points to the bed, shrouded in a white mosquito net. 'You can have this,' he says. 'And I'll take the sofa.' But they realise as he speaks just how absurd this suggestion is. The 'sofa' is a small bamboo love seat no more than four feet long. Even if he curled into a foetal position, Cardle would not be able to fit his huge frame onto it. Even Pippa, considerably smaller, would struggle.

'No, I'll take the sofa,' she says.

'Don't be bloody ridiculous. I'm not going to let you do that.'

'I can spread the cushions on the floor and lie on them.' Pippa tries to sound upbeat even though the floor is tiled, the cushions thin and insubstantial and her nightwear wet. 'It'll be fine.'

'No.'

They exchange a long look. Cardle's eyes sweep the length of Pippa's body. She can smell him; a now-familiar scent mixing shaving soap and sandalwood and nicotine. A prickle of electricity surges through her and despite herself, despite every rational instinct, she reaches for him. And suddenly they are kissing, with a fierce intensity that feels adversarial, almost angry.

'Jim, we can't,' Pippa gasps, breaking off. But she does not move away from him. Instead she presses closer, giving in to the kiss again. His hand is now behind her neck, pulling her towards him so that the length of her torso is pressed against his.

'Christ…' he mutters. 'If you knew how much I've wanted to…'

His voice tails off and he kisses her for a few seconds longer, then lifts her so that her feet leave the floor. He twists his body so that his centre of gravity is shifted and they both tumble sideways onto the bed, pulling the mosquito net down from the ceiling and over their outstretched legs.

We mustn't, Pippa tells herself. *We absolutely must not do this.* But her thoughts are drowned out by the relentless ferocity of the rain, lashing the roof above them.

At some point, just before dawn, they sleep.

When Pippa opens her eyes, it's still raining, but quietly, the force of the storm now spent. Cardle is already out of bed and must have showered, because he now has a towel wrapped around his waist. He hands her a glass of papaya juice.

'Can't do coffee, I'm afraid,' he says, gruffly, not making eye contact. 'Bloody power's out.'

He regrets it, she thinks instantly. She wants to come right out and say as much but instead sips the juice wordlessly. He sits down on the edge of the bed.

'Pippa…' He lets her name hang there in the air. 'Pippa, last night was amazing, and we were both equally… well, let's just say it was nobody's fault. But I think you know what this means.'

She looks over at him questioningly, daring him to say it.

'You realise we can't work together anymore. You know I have a hard and fast rule about not… not getting involved with people I work with.'

He reaches for her hand but she pulls it away. 'I know we're not going to be working together when we get back, anyway,' she says, her eyes trying to make contact with his. 'We went over this. I'm only here because Arne Lindgren wanted us to come here together. It's just until we're finished with this case.'

'No, what I'm saying is…' He falters.

'Go on.' Her tone is waspish, masking a deep sense of disappointment, and she turns her face away. 'Spit it out.'

'I think we need to stop working together as of right now. You should fly back to London tonight. I'll stay here a couple of days longer and follow up on that lead you were given.'

Pippa throws him a look of disgust and gets out of the bed, retrieving the damp pyjamas she was wearing when she arrived and putting them back on. Her hair is tangled and she urgently needs to brush her teeth.

'Go back and start packing your stuff, and I'll arrange with the concierge for a car to take you back to Pattaya.' Cardle looks out of the window. 'The water level's going down, so the roads should be okay.'

Pippa strides to the door and yanks it open. 'So that's it then? Now you've had me, you just want to get rid of me?'

'Pip, you know bloody well it's not like that…'

'What is it like then? Explain it to me.'

'There's an attraction between us. On my part, it's been there from the start, and I'm pretty sure it has been for you too—?'

She doesn't reply.

'Well, hasn't it?' he demands.

'I suppose so. Yes, okay, it has. But we work well together. I don't see why it has to stop now.'

'Because it does. Because when sex gets involved…' He catches sight of her expression and corrects himself. 'When emotions get involved, that's when your judgement gets clouded. And when your judgement's clouded, mistakes get made. It can compromise a case.'

'And, of course, that's all that matters, isn't it, Jim? The sodding case!'

He reaches for her hand, but she yanks her arm away, turns on her heel and leaves, squelching down the muddy path and back to her own hut.

*

The roof is still leaking, though the flow has dwindled to a few drips. Pippa does indeed pack her suitcase and wheel it to the hotel lobby, but she leaves it with the bellhop and asks him to get her a taxi. She's not just going to turn tail and be despatched back to London, surplus to requirements. It was she who found the lead, she reasons, it should be she who follows it.

The piece of paper that Anong gave her is sodden from being caught in the deluge, and the writing is almost illegible.

'I need to go to a supermarket in Khuekkhak,' she tells the driver. 'It begins with a P… two words…'

'Pak Pran?' the driver suggests.

'That sounds right. Do you know it?'

'Pak Pran,' says the driver, nodding happily. 'Petchkasem Road.'

It turns out to be the only supermarket and the largest shop in the low-rise, built-up area that passes as a town. It has a tiled hip and gable roof that makes it look like a temple, which seems fitting given the bustle of commercial activity inside. The aisles are full with yet to be unpacked boxes of bottles and cans, and there are rows of exotic fruits sealed in cellophane wrapping, next to a huge refreshment counter with soft drinks in every colour of the rainbow. The heady smell, which mingles the sweet and the savoury, is overwhelming.

Pippa approaches a woman who is stacking a pile of bagged peanuts. 'I'm looking for the manager. Mr Cheri…' She squints at the smudged paper again. 'Cherisok?'

The woman looks blank for a moment. 'Ah… Cherinsuk,' she says, and beckons for Pippa to follow her. They go to the back of the store, and the woman points to a door near the exit, then bustles away.

Pippa knocks. A short man in his late forties or early fifties answers, wearing a short-sleeved dress shirt. His black hair is slicked back from his forehead and he has a pleasant open face.

'Mr Cherinsuk?'

He nods and points proudly to the badge that says 'Sanoh Cherinsuk, Store Manager'.

'My name's Pippa Bryant. Can I please speak to you about something?'

He waves her into the room and points to the chair facing the desk. 'Of course. You're welcome. Would you like a drink?' He points to a tray of soft drinks, but Pippa shakes her head.

'I'm here from London, making enquiries into something that happened during the tsunami in 2004. I'm... an investigator,' she adds, redundantly. 'I spoke to your niece, Anong, and she told me that you worked at the Shangri La Hotel then?'

Cherinsuk nods gravely. 'Yes. That's true.'

'I wonder, do you remember there being a British guest there, who drowned? She was called Rosanna... Rosie... Halligan.' Pippa takes out her phone and opens the camera roll, which includes the photos from her research. 'This is her.'

'May I?' He takes the phone from her and examines the grainy black and white photo. 'Yes,' he sighs. 'I do remember her. She was on her honeymoon.'

'So you remember her husband? Daniel Halligan?' She scrolls through the photos, past a current image of him, until she comes to the picture of him that was in Ben's flat. 'This is how he looked then.'

Cherinsuk's eyes widen. 'I know him, yes. He's here.'

'Here? You mean—?'

The phone is taken from her hand again and Cherinsuk flicks back to the photo of the thirty-eight-year-old Halligan that was used to illustrate the article about his failed Horizon Lakes development. 'This is him now, yes?'

'Yes, but—'

'He is here in Khao Lak. I saw him. I recognised him.'

Pippa takes her phone back, staring at him. 'Are you sure? The same man?'

'Yes, I am sure. He has a beard now, but he has not changed much, I think.'

Of course, Pippa thinks, with a rush of dawning realisation. *Of course he's come here. It makes perfect sense. He's run away from his life with Tansy, from the police; where else would he go? It's the place where he was last with the wife he loved.*

'You want to see this man?' Cherinsuk asks.

'You mean you know where he is now?'

'Yes.' He nods. 'I know exactly where he is.'

CHAPTER FORTY-FIVE

PIPPA

Sanoh Cherinsuk is insistent that Pippa will not be able to locate Daniel Halligan's rental property unaided, so she is forced to wait another hour and a half until he can take a break from the store.

She wanders down the main road, past brightly painted buildings that contain a pharmacy, a beauty salon, several back-packing hostels and a scuba diving centre, until she reaches a coffee shop that doubles as an art gallery. She orders an iced coffee and a piece of cake, and takes out her phone to check it.

Three missed calls and a text from Cardle.

> *Front desk said you took off in a taxi? Have you already gone to the airport?*

Her phone buzzes again while it's in her hand, and she switches it off. She doesn't want to talk to Cardle. Not now, at least. If Cherinsuk is right about Daniel, then she will have to report back to him at some point. But for now, he can stew.

Her mind is assaulted by the image of his large, strong body over hers. She pushes it firmly away.

*

After finishing her coffee and whiling away another thirty minutes in souvenir shops crammed with bales of silk, ceramics and coconut oil, Pippa makes her way back to the Pak Pran supermarket. Cherinsuk is standing outside waiting for her. He leads her away from the main street and down a warren of unmetalled side roads. After they've walked for ten minutes, the landscape becomes more rural, with thick stands of palms and glimpses of distant mountains. Scrawny chickens scratch at the side of the road.

'How do you know where Mr Halligan is staying?' Pippa asks her guide. 'Did you speak to him?'

'No,' says Cherinsuk. 'I saw him in Khuekkhak, buying food, but I did not speak with him. I don't know if he recognised me, but I don't think he wished to talk.'

'So, someone else told you?'

Cherinsuk smiles. 'This is a small place. My cousin is a friend of the owner of this vacation rental. That is how I know.'

They've reached a traditional Thai timber house, raised on stilts, with a steep gabled roof. The gable edge trim, the panel above the front door and the balustrade on the front steps are all made from ornate fretwork.

'It's just a single apartment.' Cherinsuk points up at the small veranda that spans the width of the house. 'Would you like me to come in?'

'No, thank you,' Pippa tells him. 'I'll be fine on my own. Thank you very much for bringing me.'

She reaches into her bag for a five hundred baht note, but he pushes it away, bringing his hands together in prayer position and giving a small bow before turning and walking back up the overgrown path. Pippa takes a deep breath, then walks up the wooden steps and knocks on the front door.

There's no reply. She knocks again.

Through the fretwork screen that covers the window, she becomes aware of movement. There are no lights on and the screens admit very little daylight, but she can make out a shadowy figure in the middle of the room. Through the gaps in the carved wood she can make out that it's someone tall, male. He moves and the light catches his face. It's Daniel Halligan. He may have grown a beard, but it doesn't quite hide those handsome, regular features.

'Daniel.' She knocks again. 'Daniel, it's Pippa Bryant. I need to talk to you.'

Realising that she's not going to go away, he flings open the door. He's wearing a faded green T-shirt and black shorts, his feet bare. The floor of the apartment is dark, polished teak and the walls are wood panelled. There's no kitchen, just a dresser with a kettle and some rudimentary cooking equipment. Through an archway is a small bedroom, with a pedestal electric fan next to the bed and a half-packed holdall on the floor. A sliding door is half open, revealing a basic bathroom.

Daniel frowns at her. 'You're that girl from the Excelsior… what the fuck are you doing here?'

'I need to talk to you,' she says, trying to remain calm in the face of his overt hostility. 'About Rosie.'

She has his attention now. He steps aside to let her in, closing the door behind her. A simple wood table is at one side of the room, flanked with two chairs, a vase of orchids the only decorative touch. He indicates that she can sit there, but does not join her, remaining on his feet.

'What can you possibly have to say about my wife?' His tone is flat, distant. 'You do realise she's dead? She died over sixteen years ago.'

'Yes, I know that.'

'And you work with that private eye, don't you? What's his name, Carter?'

'Cardle.'

'Whatever. I know the pair of you came to Sydney, trying to find me.'

A thought occurs to Pippa. 'Was it you who texted me?'

He frowns. 'Texted you?'

'After we were in Mauritius… I received a couple of threatening texts. Warning me to keep my mouth shut.'

'Not me.' He shakes his head. 'Sounds more Tansy's style.'

'But how would she get my number?'

Daniel gives a bitter little laugh. 'Trust me, my lovely second wife has ways of finding information she needs. And plenty of dodgy people willing to help her. But never mind Tansy, can we get back to what the fuck you're doing here?' His eyes narrow slightly. 'How did you know where to find me? Please don't tell me you're working with the police.'

Pippa shakes her head. 'A local source knows where you're staying. For now, no one else apart from me knows where you are.' She struggles to mask her nerves beneath the neutral tone.

'Not even Cardle?'

'Not even him.'

He would never have let me come and see a known killer alone. He'd have said it was sheer lunacy.

Daniel still does not sit down. 'Go on, then. You may as well say what you came here to say. But then I'd like you to leave.'

'I'm aware,' Pippa chooses her words carefully, 'that Nikki Lindgren – Nikki Simmons as she was then – was staying at the same hotel as you and Rosie back in 2004. Then the two of you are also in the same hotel in Mauritius, and she winds up dead.'

'It was an accident,' Daniel says, flatly. 'She tripped and fell. That was what the investigation concluded.'

Pippa shakes her head slowly, looking straight at him in an attempt to disguise her fear. 'Except that CCTV footage has come to light that shows the two of you together in your villa. You were having a pretty heated argument that turned into a physical fight. You pushed her onto that glass table.'

'It's not true,' he says, but there's no conviction in his voice.

'So… why?' Pippa asks. 'What happened between you here, all those years ago?'

'Why on earth would I tell you?' Daniel sneers bitterly. 'What would that achieve, for fuck's sake? You're nothing more than a paid busybody.'

Not even that, not now. All of a sudden, Cardle's voice comes back to her: '*You realise we can't work together any longer.*'

Pippa shoulders her bag and stands up. 'Okay, then. But you're going to have to talk about it at some point. And I'd say that was pretty soon.'

She turns towards the door but Daniel is too quick for her, darting across the room and locking it. He snatches a knife from the dresser, the sort used for preparing meat. Its eight-inch blade glints menacingly as he points it towards her.

'Oh, no, no, no… you're going nowhere. D'you think I'm stupid? Obviously once you leave here, you're going to go straight to the police and tell them where I am.'

Pippa stares at the knife, her heart pounding. 'No. I wouldn't.'

He laughs. 'Oh, come off it. We both know that's bullshit.' With the blade held up to her neck he manoeuvres her into the bedroom. 'Sit down,' he says, indicating the bed with a jerk of his head. He's sweating, and the hand holding the knife is shaking. 'Don't move.'

The fan is connected to the mains by a long reel of extension cable. Daniel pulls the cable free from its socket, then severs it to make two equal lengths. 'Put your arms behind you,' he orders Pippa, grabbing her wrists and binding them tightly with the cable. It cuts into her flesh.

'What on earth will this achieve?' she demands, her eyes on the knife, which is lying a couple of feet away from her on the bed. 'You can't keep me here for ever. The contact who gave me this address knows I'm here. People will start looking.'

'Maybe,' he says coldly. 'But who knows how long that will take. And I'm not going to let anyone find *me* here, obviously. By the time they find you… or what's left of you… I'll be long gone.'

Pippa starts trying to edge her way off the bed, but he catches sight of her out of the corner of his eye and snatches up the knife again, placing it next to him on the floor. He starts throwing items of clothing and shaving kit into the holdall.

Then Pippa remembers, with a sickening lurch of her stomach, that Cardle thinks she has left Khao Lak in a fit of anger and is already on her way back to London. After all his lectures on personal safety, why didn't she swallow her pride and text him back? And Cherinsuk knows where she is, but how long will it be before he or anyone else finds out that she's missing? Days, probably, if not longer.

'Please,' she says, forcing her voice not to break. 'Look, I know I can't stop you leaving. But before you go, please at least tell me what happened. When you were here on your honeymoon… did you meet Nikki?'

He pauses, sitting back on his haunches. 'Not exactly.'

'What does that mean?'

'Okay, then…' He lets out a long sigh, turning to face her. 'Since it makes fuck-all difference at this point, I'll tell you exactly what happened.'

CHAPTER FORTY-SIX

PIPPA

'She… Nikki… was on holiday with her parents. Apparently they were in the same hotel as us but I honestly have no recollection of seeing her there. Rosie and I were on honeymoon, and completely wrapped up in each other.'

He gives another long, shuddering sigh.

'We were on the beach the morning the tsunami hit. Boxing Day, it was. It was so bizarre, at first we thought… well, I suppose we thought it was exciting. Intriguing. We were young and carefree. Especially Rosie. She viewed everything as an adventure. When the tide disappeared, like it was rolling backwards, Ro went after it. I called to her to come back, but she didn't. And then it all happened so quickly. This surge of water hurtling towards the land. She disappeared under the surface. I was quite a strong swimmer, so I went in after her. I remember the sand was so churned up that it was really difficult to see. She was wearing a bright yellow bikini and it was that that I spotted. And I was just so bloody relieved.

'Somehow I made my way towards her and grabbed her. Grabbed the straps of her bikini and managed to drag her… drag both of us… back up onto what was left of the beach. Well, there was no beach, really. The water was in the building by then. But somehow we both got onto dry land, with me not even knowing if she was alive. She looked as though she was dead. But then someone started CPR and she spluttered and came round.'

Pippa is staring straight at him, her expression confused. 'But I thought—'

He gives her a look of furious disdain. 'It wasn't fucking well her, was it? It was another young European woman wearing a yellow bikini.'

'Nikki Simmons.'

He nods slowly, his expression tortured. 'Yes. I'd pulled the wrong woman from the sea. While I was saving this… this stranger… my wife, my Rosie, was drowning.'

Unable to move her hands, Pippa merely shakes her head from side to side. 'Oh, my God. How totally fucking awful.'

'We found her body five days later. Christ, at least we found her; a lot of victims were never recovered. Oh, and the Simmons family were so bloody grateful to me. They told the hospital and hotel staff that they wanted to thank me in person for saving their daughter. But that was the last thing I wanted. I refused to meet with them, and made it clear I didn't want them to speak to the press about what I'd done. I didn't want to be labelled as Nikki Simmons' saviour for the rest of my life, not when Rosie was gone.'

He hangs his head, and his shoulders heave with the effort of suppressing sobs. 'She was everything to me,' he croaks. 'Everything. And I didn't save her.'

'But it wasn't your fault,' Pippa speaks gently. 'You couldn't possibly have known. And maybe… maybe your wife was beyond rescue, anyway. Maybe she'd been swept too far away. Surely it's better that you saved someone, rather than no one.'

Daniel's eyes are still wet, but he manages a grim smile. 'Oh, yes, sure. That's what I tried to tell myself. And I did a fairly good job of rationalising it that way. Most of the time. And for a long time. Until…'

'Until you met Nikki Lindgren,' says Pippa, quietly.

'Exactly. When we were on the boat trip, I saw her passport and her name rang a bell. But to start with I couldn't quite place it. It nagged away at me subconsciously. It was her who made the connection in the end. As a teenager she'd been told the name of the man who saved her life, but never expected to meet him. And then she was introduced to me on her honeymoon. On my second honeymoon: the fucking irony. It had been sixteen years, so just like for me, the penny didn't drop straight away. But as soon as she realised who I was, she couldn't wait to speak to me. That's why she came to the villa that night. And I…'

He reaches in his pocket for a handkerchief and wipes the sweat from his forehead. His voice cracks again. 'The truth is, I just couldn't handle it. There she was, grown up and happy, living a wonderful life. In love with her husband. And there *I* was, married to a woman I despised, still missing Rosie every single day of my life. And all I could think was, it should have been Rosie who survived, not *her*. Not this woman telling me how great it was to meet me, how grateful she was because if I hadn't saved her she'd never have got to meet Arne and be this happy. She went on and on. And I just…'

He breaks off for a few seconds, shaking his head vigorously as if to rid himself of the memory. 'People talk about seeing a red mist, and I never knew what they meant. But that was what it was like. Every single cell in my body was overtaken by this rage, an irresistible force just like the bloody wave that came up that beach on Boxing Day. I never intended to but I just' – his voice is so quiet that Pippa can barely hear him – 'I just went for her.'

He begins to weep in earnest. Pippa, sitting helplessly on the bed with her wrists smarting with pain, closes her eyes.

'You should come forward and tell people this,' she says, eventually. 'You didn't mean her to die. You'll be charged with manslaughter rather than murder. You'll probably only serve a few years. Then you can start again. Start a new life.'

'No,' says Daniel, bitterly. 'There'll never be a new life. Because whatever happens, I will always have saved Nikki while Rosie drowned.'

He zips up the holdall and stands up, hooking the straps over his shoulder and picking up the knife.

'Daniel, please, wait!'

'Sorry. It's good to talk and all that, but I'm going to have to leave you here anyway.' A thought seems to occur to him and he sets down the bag, taking the second length of cable and using it to tie Pippa's ankles. She squirms, trying to resist, but with her arms already tied and his superior strength, her efforts are futile.

Just as he's finished trussing her, there's the sound of a car engine growing closer. Footsteps bang up the steps of the house and someone hammers on the door. Daniel snatches up the knife and raises a finger to his lips to indicate that Pippa should stay silent. Someone is now kicking or shouldering the door, hard. The old, weathered wood splinters and the lock gives way after the third blow. Two police officers in grey uniform come through the broken door, drawing handguns from their belts as soon as they see Daniel and Pippa. He pulls her to her feet with one hand and holds the knife blade pressed hard against her throat with the other, to keep them back.

'Don't think I won't do it,' he hisses at them. She feels a sharp stinging as the metal scores her skin, wetness as blood starts to ooze. 'I've not got much to lose at this point, have I?'

'You get your fucking hands off her, Halligan!'

There are more footsteps, heavier this time, and Cardle bursts into the room, sweeping past the policemen and lurching straight at Daniel's lower torso in a move akin to a rugby tackle. Caught completely off guard, Daniel loses his footing, dropping the knife. Cardle snatches it up. Then his huge arms are around Pippa, pulling her free and untying the cables, pressing a handkerchief against the cut on her neck. The policemen restrain and handcuff Daniel, and one of them reads him his rights in halting English.

'Daniel Halligan, you are under arrest for the unlawful homicide of Nicole Lindgren. You are entitled to remain silent. Your statement may be used as evidence at trial. You are entitled to take advice from counsel…'

'Wait!' Pippa's voice comes out as a croak. She tries to catch Daniel's eye as he's led away, feeling a strange need to comfort or reassure him in some way. But he keeps his face averted from her, eyes towards the ceiling. Her legs feel as though they will no longer hold her weight, and she sinks down onto the edge of the bed, shivering with shock.

Cardle places a large hand on her shoulder. 'Are you okay?'

She shrugs. 'Not really. But I will be.' She twists to face him. 'How did you find me?'

'I'm a detective, remember; it's what I do.' Seeing that she's not in the mood for humour, he goes on. 'Always check your facts, right? When you didn't reply to my text, I asked the hotel if they'd arranged transport to take you to the airport and they said they hadn't. That you'd requested a taxi for a local trip. I figured you had to be ignoring my instructions and checking your lead, so I legged it straight to the Ocean Sands and spoke to the girl who gave you the Shangri La contact. That led me to the supermarket where the delightful Mr Cherinsuk works, and thankfully he'd just returned to his office after bringing you here. If I'd missed him, then Christ knows…'

He breaks off, staring into space for a beat. 'Did you get to talk to Halligan?'

Pippa nods, dabbing the blood from her neck. 'I did. And I understand now. I know exactly why he killed Nikki Lindgren.' She shakes her head slowly. 'Honestly, I don't know who I feel more sorry for. For Nikki, for her husband, or… for Daniel.'

'We ought to get you looked at by a medic.' Cardle holds out a large hand and she allows herself to be pulled to her feet. 'Look, I know I said we can't work together, but will you at least remain part of J. Cardle Investigations long enough to speak to Arne Lindgren? To explain it all to him, so he can have some peace of mind. Please, for me.'

She shakes her head. 'I won't do it for you. It will be for Lindgren's sake. But yes, I will do it.'

EPILOGUE

PIPPA

LONDON, TWO MONTHS LATER

Pippa takes a discreet look in her handbag mirror while she's waiting.

Her hair is freshly washed and styled, her make-up on point. She wants to be looking her best; it's important to her.

Cardle arrives at the coffee shop in Spitalfields fifteen minutes late. She's at an outside table and spots him before he sees her, striding through the crowds of tourists and teenagers enjoying the last few days of their school holidays. It's a dull, cloudy day at the start of September, the leaves fading and a sense of the changing season in the air.

'Hi,' he says when he sees her, appraising her appearance as he pulls out the chair opposite her, taking in her tight black trousers and cream blazer. 'You look well.'

'Thank you,' she says, adding, 'So do you,' although he's unshaven and dressed in his usual jeans and shirt combination.

'How have you been?' he asks, after he's ordered a black coffee. He lights a cigarette, instantly registering her look of distaste. 'I'm giving up,' he says, disingenuously.

'I can see that.'

'So… are you dating? How about Ben Halligan?'

'I've spoken to Ben, yes,' Pippa says carefully. 'But only to come clean about who I am, and to fill him in on Daniel. No dates. With him, or anyone else. Honestly, I don't have the time to think about that right now.'

And I'm not over you. Not yet.

'So, have you applied for the Met fast track?' He takes a drag, then holds the offending cigarette as far away from her as he can.

She shakes her head. 'I decided I wasn't sure about joining the police. Not yet, anyway. I may revisit the idea.'

'But you are working?'

'About to be. I'm starting a part-time job in intelligence research in a couple of weeks, so you'll be getting a reference request any day now. And from the beginning of next month I'll also be back at uni, doing a Criminology and Forensic Psychology course. Part time, obviously.'

Cardle widens his eyes. 'Wow. That's great. See? I always knew you were too good to work as my office assistant.'

She takes a sip of her cappuccino. 'That's not why I stopped working for you, and you know it.'

The memory of their night together is suddenly omnipresent, filling the space around them.

'It would have had to stop at some point.' Cardle maintains an even tone, but keeps his gaze focused on the fingers holding the cigarette. 'It's better this way.'

'You're referring to the work? Or us sleeping together?'

He has the grace to redden slightly. 'I was referring to work. And on that note, one reason I wanted to see you was to pass on some news. My contact at the Australian Federal Police told me that Tansy Halligan has been arrested and charged with perverting the course of justice with regards to the moving of Martin Kelly's body. Carries a potential life sentence, though I doubt she'll get more than a couple of years. But still.'

Pippa nods. 'And Daniel?'

'Charged with involuntary manslaughter of Martin Kelly, though I think they'll struggle with proving that one. Plus there are the charges of unlawfully imprisoning and wounding you; Christ knows what's going to happen with those. Since Mauritius is a member of the Commonwealth, the authorities have agreed for him to be tried for Nikki Lindgren's manslaughter back in Australia. He spent a couple of weeks in a Thai jail, then they extradited him. He's on remand in Sydney, pending a bail hearing.'

She grows quiet, unable to dispel the image of Daniel on the Thai beach, having pulled the wrong woman from the ocean, a woman who was not the young bride he loved so much. 'I hope it's not too late,' she says, quietly. 'I hope it's not too late for him to find happiness.'

Cardle reaches for her hand, and she allows him to entwine his fingers through hers. 'Even though you can't follow instructions, you did good,' he says. 'Bloody good.' He drains his coffee cup, then stands, raising her hand to his lips and kissing it.

The warmth of his lips lingers after he's walked away. 'I'll see you around, Pip.'

A LETTER FROM ALISON

Dear reader,

I want to say a huge thank you for choosing to read *The Guilty Wife*. If you did enjoy it, and want to keep up to date with all my latest releases, just sign up at the following link. Your email address will never be shared and you can unsubscribe at any time.

www.bookouture.com/alison-james

I was reading a real-life account of a tsunami survivor who rescued a stranger while his own fiancée drowned, and the scenario felt very much like the start of a thriller: one which ended up becoming *The Guilty Wife*. I really hope you've enjoyed it, and if you did I would be very grateful if you could write a review. I'd love to hear what you think, and it makes such a difference helping new readers to discover one of my books for the first time.

I love hearing from my readers – you can get in touch on my Facebook page, through Twitter, Goodreads or my website.

Thanks,
Alison James

17361567.Alison_James

@AlisonJbooks

Alison James books

Made in the USA
Middletown, DE
31 January 2024

48871571R00184